Whiskey & Wine

LULU HART

Contents

Whiskey & Wine

Copyright © 2025 by Lulu Hart

Cover Design by Premium Romance Book Covers

Editing by Sarah Hart

First Edition

 Created with Vellum

Content Warning

Graphic Sex
Double Vaginal Penetration

Potential Triggers
Gun Violence
Kidnapping
Mentions of Sex Trafficking
Murder
Vulgar Language

Playlist

"I'm Shipping up to Boston" by Dropkick Murphys
"Bad Decisions" by Bad Omens
"Brooklyn Baby" by Lana Del Rey
"Simple Man" (Rock Version) by Shinedown
"Break" by I See Stars
"Bang Bang Bang" by Big Bang
"Aqua Regia" by Sleep Token
"Tom's Diner" by AnnenMayKantereit and Giant Rooks
"Soap" by Melanie Martinez
"Let Her Go" by Passenger
"Repeated Apology" by Late 9
"Body Like a Back Road" by Sam Hunt
"Give" by Sleep Token
"Galway Girl" by Ed Sheeran
"Drunk in Love" by The Dan Band
"Live For What I'd Die For" by Jess Mills

Chapter One

CONNOR

With my business obligations concluded, I wander the bustling streets, eagerly hunting for a good pub to unwind in. Given that I'm in Boston, this quest shouldn't present much of a challenge. The city streets, with their charming cobblestone paths and historic brick buildings, bear a striking resemblance to those of Dublin—my hometown.

Perhaps I'll settle here once I leave Ireland for good. My half-brother, Ryan, is four hours away in New York City. Even though we don't currently have the best relationship, it would be nice to build one.

This early evening, the glow of downtown's city lights reflects off the glass skyscrapers as I stroll along the sidewalk. The hum of traffic and chatter of pedestrians create the very definition of urban life.

I pause, watching a group of young professionals laugh as they file out of a bar. Their carefree demeanor reminds me why I'm here—why I'm planning this escape.

A fresh start. That's what I need more than anything.

Dublin may be home, but it's become a prison of memories and constant reminders. My father's voice still echoes in my head sometimes—his constant criticism, mind games, and iron grip on every decision I've ever made.

First Ryan flees to America, now me. The Dublin syndicate will be left without its princes, and the king without his heirs. The thought brings a bitter smile to my face as I continue walking. How will it look to his enemies—to his allies—when both his sons choose exile over inheritance? The mighty Declan O'Brady, abandoned by his own blood.

Ryan had the courage to leave first, though we never discussed it openly. He simply disappeared when he turned eighteen, resurfacing in New York with the Fitzpatrick clan, an Irish syndicate. I envied him even as father raged for weeks, calling him every name for traitor in both English and Gaelic.

Now it's my turn. Father always pitted us against each other, and in the end, we've chosen the same path, just years apart.

Ryan's found peace here in America. More than that, he's found love.

I watch a couple across the street. They're holding hands, leaning into each other against the November chill. Something twists in my chest—envy? Longing? I'm not sure.

Could I have that someday—a real connection untainted by fear or obligation? The thought feels foreign, almost ridiculous. Father always says emotions are a weakness—love, especially—and he isn't wrong.

Which brings me to Isabelle. All these years should be enough to forget someone's smile. But not hers.

Even now, thousands of miles from where I last saw her, I

can still recall the soft curve of her lips when she spoke my name. It haunts me on repeat.

I want to forget her. God knows I've tried. Whiskey hasn't done it. Work hasn't done it. And marrying Camille hasn't done it. Perhaps that's my punishment—to remember everything about a woman I can never have again.

I've accepted it now, this constant ache. It's the tax I pay for having loved her at all, the price of admission for those few perfect years when she was mine. Sometimes I wonder if I'd choose differently if I could go back. Would I walk away before I fell? Or would I still dive headlong into that magnificent disaster, knowing the wreckage that awaited me?

Boston has no ghosts for me.

As I round a sharp corner, I bump into a woman, and soft gasps of surprise escape from both of us. When we collide, I feel the slight pressure of her body against mine even though her petite frame barely reaches my shoulder. Her hands briefly touch my chest before pushing herself back. In the moment of contact, I catch a whiff of her perfume, a delicate floral scent. She stumbles slightly, catching herself with a quick step backward. I instinctively reach out to steady her, but she must notice I'm about to touch her, because she pulls herself back, completely steadying herself on her own.

"Motherfucker!" she yells. "Watch where the fuck you're going, asshole."

Her hair is a rich chocolate brown, hanging down her back in a sleek ponytail with wispy bangs that fall across her forehead. She's dressed in flared jeans that hug her figure and a snug coat to ward off the chill. She wears fingerless gloves that add a touch of edginess to her look. Her eyes, a mesmerizing shade of green, capture my attention, drawing me in. It's then that I truly take in the rest of her face, noting the striking symmetry and delicate features that combine to make her undeniably beautiful.

"Such a dirty mouth for a pretty little thing," I state with a dry laugh.

She holds my stare, probably admiring my Irish accent as most women in North America do. But then she kneels and picks up papers that are scattered on the ground. She must have been carrying them, and they dropped in the collision.

I spot a piece of paper on the sidewalk and quickly hurry over to stomp on it, keeping it there so it won't fly away with the slight breeze. "Got one!" I announce, proud that I helped.

"Fuck!" she yells and crawls the short distance from where she is on the concrete sidewalk over to where I'm standing. She pushes my shoe aside to get it off her paper. When she picks it up, she waves it in the air. "Great, now there's a dirty shoe print on it, wonderful…"

Damn, there's no pleasing this woman, is there?

"Sorry for trying to help," I say and walk away.

"I need a fucking drink," she mutters to herself.

As soon as her words reach my ears, I halt mid-step, pivot on my heel, and face her with a grin. "Funny you mention that. I was heading to an Irish pub a few blocks away. How about I buy you a drink for all the trouble?"

She picks up the last of her papers, meticulously aligning the edges to straighten the stack in her hands before rolling them up and putting them in her inside coat pocket. Her eyes lift to meet mine. "You can buy me two or three. My troubles go beyond you," she mentions.

"All right, then," I reply, extending my hand in a gesture toward the path ahead.

4

A slight smile curves her lips. Her beauty intensifies, her features softening, transforming her from the captivating figure she is when annoyed into someone even more enchanting.

We walk in silence to the pub, a brick building that stands tall with large windows. A wooden sign hangs above the entrance, painted with Gaelic script. Green ivy creeps up the sides of the building, giving it a charming and cozy feel. The smell of fish and chips drifts from the door as patrons leave. I pull open the heavy wood door and gesture for her to enter first, embodying the gentlemanly demeanor I've always prided myself on. However, her expression remains unchanged, her eyes fixed forward as if the gesture was invisible.

Well, as I mentioned before, there is no pleasing this woman.

She leads the way to two open seats at the bar. It's surprisingly busy for a Thanksgiving night. The chatter of various conversations fills the room. Many are watching one of the multiple muted televisions playing Thanksgiving Day football while traditional Irish music plays on overhead speakers.

She shrugs off her coat. Fuck, she's attractive. She reveals a toned figure that seems sculpted to perfection with accentuating flared hips that her jeans sit low on, exposing a few inches of her taut stomach. Her smooth skin glows with pale gold undertones, and her black crop top clings to her petite frame with uplifted breasts that seem blessed for a woman of her size.

I too remove my coat, placing both on the hooks underneath the bar, and we settle onto the high stools. I raise my hand to catch the bartender's attention. A tall man with a neatly trimmed beard and rolled-up sleeves approaches us. He tosses a round cardboard coaster on the wooden bar in front of us and leans in slightly. "What can I get you?"

"Jameson, double, neat," I reply. "And whatever the lady wants."

She glances at the menu chalked up on a blackboard behind the bar on the wall. "I'll have the merlot you have on special, thank you," she decides.

"Wine?" I raise an eyebrow, my voice teasing. "You're at an Irish pub, and you order wine?"

She laughs. It's a cute sound that mingles with the low hum of conversation around us. "Hey! You said whatever the lady wants, and this lady," she says, pointing a finger at herself, "prefers wine."

I chuckle, lifting my hands in mock surrender. "Okay, fine," I concede, grinning.

She pulls out the small stack of rolled papers from her coat pocket, smooths them out, and looks at them. That's when I notice they're sketches. No wonder she's mad about the shoe print.

"Did I completely ruin it?" I ask, glancing at the sketch with the black shoe print stamping the page.

"No...." She turns the vertical page sideways. "If you look at it like this, it looks like a fairy with a turtle shell on her back." We share a smile as she delivers her sarcastic remark.

The bartender sets our drinks on the coasters. "Tab open or closed?" he asks, wiping his hands on a towel tucked into his waistband.

"Open," she replies with a playful grin, nudging me with her elbow. "This man owes me a few drinks." Her eyes sparkle with mischief as she tilts her glass toward me. She's cute when she's being passive-aggressive. And flirty? I think she's flirting with me.

The bartender nods, takes my credit card, and strides away to the register.

She takes a sip from her wine glass, her eyes momentarily closing as the rich liquid touches her lips. I find myself captivated by her beauty, particularly drawn to her full, kissable lips painted with red lipstick. I wonder what it would be like to have those lips, the same ones that swore at me not too long ago, on my lips—between my teeth—around my cock.

I snap out of my thoughts and chase them with whiskey. It's warm and smooth as it slides down my throat, leaving a taste of oak and caramel on my tongue. It brings a temporary numbness to my mind, helping to chase away the intrusive thoughts and desires.

"I'm Connor," I say, extending my hand.

Her eyes squint briefly before she shakes her head, a small, amused smile on her lips. "No, thank you."

Surprised, I raise an eyebrow. "No, thank you? You won't tell me your name?"

"No point," she replies with a shrug, her voice light and nonchalant.

I lean back on my stool, trying to play along with her mystery. "Okay, so what do I call you?"

Her gaze drops to her wine glass, and she twirls the stem slowly between her fingers, the deep red liquid swirling gently. It's as if she's contemplating something profound. "How about Merlot?" she suggests.

"Okay." I chuckle, nodding at her choice, "Well, at least that's easier to say than Sauvignon Blanc."

A soft laugh escapes her lips, a genuine sound that lifts the tension between us. Her eyes crinkle at the corners, and the worry that had settled there seems to lighten. As her expression softens, a warmth spreads through me, knowing that—if only for a moment—I helped ease the burden of her troubles.

Her shoulders relax, and she tucks a stray lock of hair behind her ear. She takes a sip of her wine, and I notice a dusting of freckles on the apples of her cheeks. She's not wearing a lot of makeup, if any at all, so the wine is causing her to blush naturally.

I shoot back the rest of my whiskey and signal to our bartender for another round.

"How's your merlot?"

"Delicious," she murmurs. She has no idea how sensuous her voice sounds. Her tongue slowly sweeps across her lips, leaving a glistening sheen. I watch, unsure if the playful look in her eyes is intentional or if I'm reading too much into the moment.

No—this woman wants me. It reminds me I haven't done this in a long time—simply have a drink or a conversation with a woman.

"Do you live around here?" Merlot asks.

"No, not close at all," I answer. "Ireland."

The bartender places the second round in front of us, and Merlot immediately straightens her back and reaches for the glass. She takes a couple large gulps—I watch as her throat works to take the wine.

"You have a hotel room, then?" she asks, not looking at me. She's turning the glass stem with her fingers, seemingly nervous.

"Zinfandel," I say, and she gives me a confused look but quickly realizes I'm mocking her game with the fake wine name. "Do you want to have a drink at my hotel?"

There is an undeniable pull between us, yet we both seem to be in a position hesitant to open up about our personal lives. I know it's not the right time to let anyone in—I'm figuring out my life and technically married. Still, part of me can't help but think about what one night with her might be like.

Chapter Two

KIMBERLY

I SHOULD SAY NO, but he's not from here, and the chances of seeing him again are highly unlikely. *So why not?* I've let my disaster of a life prioritize any joy that comes my way. I deserve this—one night with a gorgeous Irishman.

"Yes," I reply, lifting my eyes to meet his emerald-green ones. I take a moment to wander my gaze over his physique for what must be the eighth time this evening. He's dressed in a navy suit that exudes sophistication. He styled his short, dark brown hair with a subtle, artfully tousled spike. His smile is devastatingly handsome; his chiseled features resemble those of a male model.

Connor picks up his glass of whiskey with his hand—long-fingered and strong—downs the rest, then calls to the bartender, "We're ready to close out." God, the sound of his voice—the Irish accent—it's a definite turn-on. The bartender nods to him and goes to his computer at the end of the bar.

I pick up my wine glass, stare at the deep red liquid, then

take a breath and finish it, savoring the bittersweet blend of flavors that match my current emotional state. The alcohol courses through my body, adding to my already heightened emotions. It's excitement and anxiety mixed with a tangle of fear. Not a fear of Connor, but the repercussions of this one-night stand, should *he* find out.

The bartender brings over his receipt and credit card. Connor fills in a tip amount and scribbles his signature before standing up.

"My lady..." he says, reaching out his hand so I can take it and ease my short stature off the stool.

When I drop on my feet, I admire how tall he is—well over six feet. I'm only five-foot-four, but don't be fooled... Every bit of me is fierce—as my friends would say.

We walk in silence for a few blocks to a high-end hotel. It means nothing to me that this Irishman is probably wealthy. In fact, it deducts a few points from his tally I was mentally keeping. But I'm a hypocrite, because I am currently in a relationship with a man who has money. Money I need, and he's willing to give, just to make myself available to him.

Once inside the room, I shed my coat, gloves, and shoes.

He removes his jacket, rolls up his dress shirt sleeves, and heads to the wet bar off the sitting area.

"Rosé, can I get you a glass of rosé?" he asks, holding out a bottle by its neck to show me.

I giggle. He's really playing up this wine-name thing. "Sure."

He pops the cork and pours two glasses. "Two?" I ask.

"I'll have one with you."

I start to sit on the sofa as he walks over with our drinks

and hands one to me, our fingers briefly touching in the exchange, causing butterflies in my stomach to activate.

He holds out his glass and says, "Here's to those who wish us well; and those who don't can go to hell."

He's a stranger to me, but his toast captures exactly how I feel. It's reassuring to realize that someone I don't know is in a different circumstance but might be experiencing similar feelings.

I smile and clink my glass against his, and then we both take a sip.

I sink into the plush cushions of the sofa and, with a gentle tug, I slip the elastic band from my ponytail. My hair cascades, spreading over my shoulders and laying against my back.

Connor's watching me closely. His gaze follows a lock of hair that runs over the top of my breast, then drifts to the exposed skin of my midriff, a slight smile tugging at the corners of his lips.

He gives me a sexy smirk, his eyes glinting with mischief as he places his flute gently on the coffee table in front of us. He goes for my glass, setting it beside his before sliding closer to me. His hand reaches out and cradles one side of my face. His thumb rests just below my ear while his palm supports the back of my head. Leaning in, he closes the distance, capturing my lips with his. The kiss is slow and thoughtful at first, as if drugging me in doses. His tongue traces the seam of my lips, and I open for him, deepening the kiss.

His free hand wanders to my chest where he lightly palms a breast before trailing it down my stomach to my jeans. He works the button on the denim, then drags down the zipper. As his fingers reach for the silk of my thong underwear, he wastes no time moving it aside and pushing two fingers into my waiting pussy.

I gasp softly at his touch—his fingertips explore me in a deliberate and teasing rhythm while we make out. And with each stroke of his fingers, I can feel the wetness between my legs growing, aching for more. *Fingering is an art, and ladies, this man is an artist.* Most men I have been with cannot multitask fingering and kissing simultaneously. Usually, one or the other is lacking. But not Connor. He's good.

My hand feels for his crotch, and I find the hardness easily. I'm stunned by how long and thick he seems to be.

He adds another finger inside me while using his thumb to massage my clit, eliciting a moan from me.

Our tongues dance together as Connor devours my mouth. My body feels so connected and in-sync with him. I come hard. My juices feel as though they are pouring out of me and onto his hand. He continues to stroke my sensitive clit while I ride the orgasm with subtle twitches.

He pulls his lips away from mine, then brings the fingers that were inside me to his mouth, licking my cum off them one by one, not breaking eye contact with me.

I go for his pants, and my fingers slip the button free. I slide the zipper down smoothly before lowering myself to my knees, the soft carpet easing the move. He leans forward, his hands joining mine to tug the fabric over his hips. Together, we ease his pants and boxer briefs down until they're pooled around his ankles, then removed entirely.

My breath catches in my throat as I stare at his cock—thick and veined, with a swollen head— standing at attention.

"Jesus," I whisper. There's no way that's going to fit inside me.

The thought barely forms in my mind before I realize I've actually voiced it out loud.

Connor's lips curl into a knowing smile.

"I'll make it fit," he says firmly as he stares at me hungrily while unbuttoning his shirt, removing it and tossing it aside, revealing his trim waist and a six pack.

I lean down and lick his length from bottom to top before taking as much of him into my mouth as I can. He wraps a hand around my hair and holds it back so he can clearly see.

He leans back on the sofa, spreading his legs wider to give me better access. I use my tongue to lick around the head, savoring the taste of his precum while my hand grips the base firmly. His breathing becomes heavier, his fingers tangling deep in my hair as he guides my movements.

"That's it," he groans, his Irish accent thickening with pleasure. "Just like that."

I hollow my cheeks, creating suction as I take him deeper. His thigh tenses against my free hand as I hold onto him. I establish a rhythm—up and down, occasionally circling my tongue on the sensitive ridge beneath the head. When I glance up, I find his emerald eyes locked on mine.

"You're fucking gorgeous," he whispers, brushing a strand of hair from my face. "The sight of you like this..."

I moan around him; the vibration makes him buck his hips slightly. His hand tightens in my hair, not painfully, but enough to communicate his rising pleasure.

"You're incredible, Merlot."

The false name reminds me of our temporary arrangement and somehow makes me bolder—like I'm someone else. I increase the suction while making eye contact. His pupils dilate as he watches me, his abs tensing with each bob of my head.

"Fuck baby, this feels too good."

Knowing those words are a sign of a man who's about to explode, I ease off him with an audible wet 'pop'. I'm selfish. I don't want him to come too soon. I need him inside me.

As I rise from the floor, I grasp the hem of my top, peeling it over my head and letting it fall to the carpet. My breasts are perky and firm enough that I don't wear bras. Next, I hook my thumbs into the waistband of my jeans, shimmying them over my hips and down my legs, followed by my underwear.

Connor raises one finger and curls it in a slow, deliberate motion, beckoning me to come to him, with a sexy smirk on his face, and his lips curl into a teasing, confident grin.

I swing my leg over his lap, settling myself so that I'm facing him on the plush sofa. As our eyes lock, he leans forward and captures my lips with his once more, igniting a spark that tingles through my body.

He pulls away. "Fuck, I wasn't planning on this. I don't have a condom."

"I'm clean and on birth control—promise. Are you clean?" I ask.

"Yes, I swear it."

With that, I reach my hand between our bodies, wrap my fingers around his length, and guide him inside of me. We both moan as I sink down and seat myself, getting comfortable. *Fuck, he does fit--barely.*

His thickness stretches me deliciously as I rock my hips, finding a rhythm. His hands slide to my waist, his fingertips digging into my skin. I place my palms flat against his chest, feeling the hard planes of muscle.

"Fuck," I moan. "Your cock feels incredible."

I rise until he's almost completely withdrawn before sinking back down. The fullness is exquisite, hitting spots inside me that make my toes curl.

"Ride me, baby," he commands.

I increase my pace, rolling my hips in figure-eights. The sofa cushions shift beneath our weight, the fabric catching the sweat beginning to form on our bodies. He leans forward, capturing one of my sensitive swollen nipples in his mouth, his tongue circling the bud before sucking hard. The dual sensation of his cock inside me and his lips on my breast sends waves of pleasure coursing through me. I arch my back, changing the angle so he hits that perfect spot.

"Look at me," he says softly.

I open my eyes—I didn't realize they were closed—to find his intense green gaze locked on mine. Something passes between us—something more than just physical pleasure. For a moment, I forget this is a one-night stand, that he doesn't even know my real name.

He shifts beneath me, planting his feet firmly on the floor for leverage. He thrusts upward as I come down, creating a perfect counterpoint that drives him impossibly deeper. The sound of skin against skin fills the hotel suite, punctuated by our increasingly ragged breathing.

"Connor." I moan his name and immediately feel bad that I don't get to hear him say mine with his sexy Irish accent. I never will, either. But I push those feelings aside and ride this man as if he's the last I'll ever be with.

I'm so fucking close to ecstasy, I can feel it. He must be too, because he's taking more control. And thank God he does, because right now my entire body is tensing as the pressure builds low in my belly. The coil inside me winds tighter and tighter until suddenly—it snaps. My walls clench around him rhythmically as I shudder. He thrusts up once, twice, and then his body goes rigid beneath me. A guttural groan escapes his lips as he pulses inside me, the warm rush of his cum filling me. I feel every throb, every spurt, as he empties himself.

The intensity is overwhelming. It's unlike anything I've ever experienced—beyond physical, almost spiritual. My chest constricts, and before I can stop it, to my horror, tears fall from my eyes, sliding silently down my cheeks. I'm not sad—but this orgasm has opened something raw and vulnerable inside me.

He notices immediately, and concern flashes across his face.

"Hey, baby, are you okay?"

I've never cried after sex before.

I can't answer right away because my body continues to pulse around him as aftershocks mix with unexpected emotion.

I'm mortified. *Right after sex with a stranger, I burst into tears? What the fuck is wrong with me?*

"I'm fine," I finally manage to say, my voice barely above a whisper. "I'm sorry—that was just intense for me, you know?" And I say that like he'll understand what I mean, but I have no clue if men have the ability to cry after sex like women do.

"You don't have to apologize." His large hands cup my face, thumbs gently wiping away the tears that fell on my cheeks. There's understanding in his eyes, not judgement. "Jesus Christ," Connor breathes, his forehead pressed against mine. "That was... I've never..." He shakes his head slightly, still catching his breath. "Nothing in my life has ever felt like that. Not even close."

I feel a flutter in my chest at his words but quickly shut it down. This is still just a one-night stand.

"You're not just saying that?" I ask, trying to sound casual while I'm still straddling him, our bodies still connected.

His eyes lock with mine, serious now. "I don't say things I don't mean, Merlot. That was the most incredible experience of my life." His hands slide up my back, tracing my spine. "Something happened between us. I felt it."

I bite my lip, unsure how to respond. I'd felt it too—that inexplicable connection that transcended the physical.

His still-stiff cock twitches inside me. I make a move to get off him, but he holds me still and smiles. "I'm ready for round two, if you are, Chardonnay."

I laugh out loud and appreciate him for lightening the mood.

A lot of men can't go again so quickly. It seems like I've hit the jackpot with this one. Too bad I can't keep him.

Chapter Three

CONNOR

OUR BREATHING slowly returns to normal as we lie tangled in the sheets. Merlot and I collapsed on the bed after a second round of mind-blowing sex. I catch my breath, my heart still racing from the intensity of our connection, and prop myself up on one elbow to trace a path with my lips along her collarbone. Then I position myself over her so that I can kiss down the valley between her full breasts, across her ribs, and over the swell of her hips.

I'll fucking worship this woman all night if she'll let me.

As my lips brush against her navel, a loud rumble emanates from beneath my mouth. Her eyes widen before she bursts into laughter, and I can't help but join her.

"Was that...?" I pause, looking up at her with a grin.

"How embarrassing," she admits, covering her face with her hands.

I pull them away and kiss her palms. "Don't be

embarrassed. We've been burning a lot of calories. We should probably refuel."

"God, yes. I'm starving," she says and giggles, stretching her arms above her head. "How do you feel about pizza?"

"Pizza sounds perfect," I say, planting one more kiss on her stomach before reluctantly peeling myself away.

Ten minutes later, we're dressed and heading out the door. I reach for her hand, our fingers interlacing as if we've done it a thousand times before. There's no awkwardness, no hesitation—just her hand in mine.

The streets are quiet. Most people are home with their families for Thanksgiving.

We turn the corner, and the neon sign for Tony's Slice glows like a beacon, our greasy salvation, "OPEN 24 HRS" flickering in red beneath the logo of a smiling pizza chef. The warmth hits us as soon as we step inside, the scent of baking dough and melted cheese making my stomach growl in anticipation. I guess I'm hungry, too.

The cashier perks up when we approach. "What can I get you?"

Merlot scans the display case, her eyes lighting up. "I'll take a slice of supreme."

"And I'll do the meat lover's," I add, pulling out my wallet.

"Coming right up."

While we wait, she leans against me slightly, our shoulders touching. It's such a simple thing, but it feels intimate in a different way than what we shared back in the hotel room.

After I pay, the cashier slides our slices across the counter. Merlot grabs both paper plates and takes the food to an empty booth in the corner. I follow her. Instead of taking the seat across from her, I slid in beside her, close enough that our thighs touch.

She slides my plate in front of me, and I casually drape my arm across the back of the booth behind her, letting my fingers rest lightly against her shoulder. I grab my slice with my free hand, fold it New York-style, and take a big bite, closing my eyes at the explosion of flavors.

"This is so fucking cheesy," she jokes with a little laugh.

I raise an eyebrow, my mouth still full. After swallowing, I turn to her with a smirk. "The pizza or me?"

"Both," she replies, nudging me with her shoulder. "Definitely both. The arm reach—real smooth."

"I'll take that as a compliment," I say, pulling her a little closer. "Cheesy can be good sometimes."

I'm about to take another bite when I notice she hasn't even started eating yet. Instead, she's methodically tearing her supreme slice into small, bite-sized pieces.

"What are you doing?" I ask, even though it's painfully obvious.

She looks up, a pizza fragment between her fingers. "Eating?"

"That is absolutely not how you eat pizza." I gesture at her plate with my half-eaten slice. "You're committing a serious food crime right now."

"Says who?" Her eyebrows arch defensively. "There's no wrong way to eat pizza."

"Yes—yes, there is, and you're doing it. You fold it—" I demonstrate with my slice. "—or you pick it up whole."

She shakes her head in disagreement and pops a torn bit into her pretty mouth, a little sauce catching at the corner. I reach up and wipe it away with my thumb. I let my thumb linger on her lip a moment too long and notice a tiny dimple that appears when she smiles.

"So, what do you do?" I ask, the question slipping out before I can stop myself. "For work, I mean. Are you an artist?"

Her smile falters slightly. "We're doing that?"

"Doing what?"

"The whole get-to-know-you thing…" She takes another bite of her dismembered pizza. "I don't think—"

"Right," I say quickly, withdrawing my arm from behind her. "Sorry."

She sighs, setting down her pizza. "It's not that I don't want to talk. It's just… knowing too much complicates things."

Knowing not enough is complicating things as well. Especially when I've never wanted to know someone more than I do now.

"What's complicated about me knowing if you're an artist or a professional pizza destroyer?" I try to keep my tone light, but there's an edge of disappointment I can't quite hide.

"I'm a bartender, and I'm in school for art," she states. "That's all you get. "Your turn."

"I'm currently between jobs, business that is quite boring," I admit. "That's actually why I came to Boston. Doing some networking."

"Oh." She picks up another fragment of her pizza. She chews thoughtfully before asking, "So, are you thinking about moving here? To the States?"

I nod, wiping my hands on a napkin. "It's highly likely. The opportunities are better here than back home."

Merlot doesn't respond to that, just nods slightly, her expression unreadable.

I wonder what's going through her mind.

The silence stretches between us, not uncomfortable but filled with unspoken questions. I'm about to change the subject when Merlot's expression softens. She looks up at me through her lashes, a mischievous look in her eyes.

"You know," she says, "I have other food crimes."

"Oh?" I'm relieved at the shift in mood. "Do tell."

"Spaghetti. I cut it all up before I eat it," she confesses, her voice dropping as if sharing a scandalous secret. "With a knife. Into tiny little pieces so I can eat it with a spoon. And I bite into string cheese instead of peeling it."

"You monster," I say in mock horror. "What else?"

"I put ketchup on my mac and cheese."

"That's it. I can't be seen with you in public," I declare, but I'm moving closer to her as I say it.

I don't know who moves first, but suddenly her lips are on mine, soft and tasting sweetly of tomato sauce. I tangle my fingers in her hair as she shifts in the booth to press against me. Her tongue slides against mine, and I can't help the low groan that escapes me.

We're kissing like we're seventeen, hidden in the back of a movie theater. But I don't care who sees us. My hand slides to her waist, fingers dipping just beneath the hem of her shirt. I just want to touch her—feel her warm skin.

"Jesus," I whisper against her lips, my breath ragged. "The things you do to me."

She smiles against my lips, her hand now resting on my thigh, dangerously high. "I could say the same about you."

I pull back to look into her eyes, both of us breathing

hard. The connection between us is electric, undeniable chemistry that makes everything else fade away.

"I should confess something, too," I say, my voice breaking with huskiness. "I dip my french fries in milkshakes."

Her eyes widen in mock outrage. "You're kidding."

"Nope. Cold vanilla milkshake with hot, salty fries." I lean closer, my lips brushing against her ear. "Sweet and salty. Best combination in the world."

She shivers slightly at my proximity. "That's actually not the worst confession I've heard."

"I have another confession," I whisper, my hand sliding higher on her thigh. "I need you. Right now."

Her pupils dilate, and she bites her lower lip. "Then what are we still doing here?"

Grabbing her hand, I pull her from the booth with an urgency that makes her gasp. We practically run the two blocks back to my hotel, stopping to steal kisses against buildings a couple times along the way.

The elevator ride is excruciating. I pin her against the wall, my mouth on her neck, breathing in her scent: the remnants of her floral perfume mixed with me—our sexual sweat.

We barely make it through the door of my hotel room before we're tearing at each other's clothes. Her hands fumble with my belt, yanking it free with a satisfying snap of leather.

"Shower," I growl against her neck, already backing her toward the bathroom.

She nods frantically, stepping out of her jeans as I kick open the door behind us. I reach in to turn the water on, steam quickly filling the small space as we shed the last of our clothing. I pull her under the spray, and the hot water cascades over our naked bodies.

My hand roams over her, finding its way between her thighs. She's absolutely drenched, and not from the shower. I groan against her mouth as my fingers slide through her pussy.

"Fuck," she whispers, her head falling back.

I press her against the tile wall, lifting one of her legs to hook around my waist. The water pounds against my back as I position myself and thrust inside.

She feels incredible—tight, wet, hot, perfect. Her muscles clench around me as I thrust deeper, drawing a moan from both of us.

She captures my mouth with hers, and I plunge my tongue inside. I slide my hand between us to circle her clit, and she breaks the kiss with a sharp cry.

This connection feels impossibly right—not just the sex, but everything: the way we laughed over pizza, how she teased me. I want all of it. I want to know everything about her, despite her reluctance to share.

Her breathing quickens, becoming ragged as she gets closer to the edge. I increase my pace, driving into her, watching her face contort with pleasure.

"Look at me," I command.

Her eyes lock with mine, pupils blown wide. I can see everything there—the pleasure, the need, the unspoken connection. I thrust harder, deeper, wanting to leave my mark on her in ways that can't be seen.

I want every inch of her to remember this—to remember me. When she's with someone else, I want her body to betray her, to crave what only I can give her. The thought drives me wild, makes me grip her hips tighter.

She whimpers, her nails digging into my shoulders as I claim her. Every thrust is a promise, a reminder that even if this is only tonight, even if tomorrow we go our separate ways, her body will remember me. Every touch, every tongue-thrusting kiss, every whispered word will be burned into her memory, just as she's burning into mine.

Chapter Four

KIMBERLY

I TIPTOE SOFTLY through Connor's hotel room as I gather my clothes off the floor, putting on each item as I find it scattered throughout. I locate one boot under the desk, the other by the bathroom door.

Connor lies sprawled across the bed, one arm flung over his eyes, the other reaching toward the space I occupied minutes ago. His breathing is deep and steady.

I grab my purse from the nightstand, carefully lifting it to avoid the jingle of its contents. Last night's memories flash through my mind—his sexy smile, the way we'd connected.

The door feels impossibly loud as I ease it open, cringing at each subtle creak. I freeze when he stirs, mumbling something unintelligible before rolling over. The hallway light spills across his bare back, highlighting the scratch marks I left there. I grin to myself, proud of marking him as mine, even if only temporarily.

I slip through the narrow opening and pull the door

closed with agonizing slowness until it clicks shut. Only then do I exhale.

The empty hotel hallway stretches before me, accusing in its silence. Not only am I doing a walk of shame, but guilt eats at me for leaving—not saying goodbye. But I don't want to say goodbye. I'd rather leave and have him wake up questioning if it was only a dream. If I was even real.

In the elevator, I check my phone. It's 4:37 in the morning. I smooth my hair and fix my makeup using the shiny walls. I look exactly like what I am: a woman sneaking away from a one-night stand and looking wrecked. I am wrecked. He fucked me four times last night.

Between trysts, we shared little details about ourselves without revealing too much. Of course, I wanted to deepen the conversation and ask questions, but I was hesitant. I could see some glimmer of hope in his eyes, though. Hope that come morning, I'd give him my name, and he'd put my number in his phone. That's the reason I had to sneak out at 4 a.m.

I slip on my coat as I leave the hotel and step out onto the streets of Boston. The air is crisp and cold, so I pull it tighter and hug myself.

Usually, I stay with friends when I'm visiting. But that was kind of my tipping point when I bumped into Connor last night—they were all out of town for Thanksgiving. It put me in a bad mood. I know that is shallow, but I'm trying to save money, not spend it on hotels.

"Shit!" I curse out loud, stopping on the sidewalk. I realize I left my sketches in his hotel room. It's too late to get them now.

Fifteen minutes later, I walk up to the skilled nursing facility's main entrance. "Good morning, Kimberly. You're here early today," Glen, the night shift security guard, says after opening the door for me.

"Want to see mom before I head back to New York." I walk by him with a smile on my face. Glen has worked at this long-term care facility for about two years, almost as long as my mother has been here.

I fling open the swinging doors of the cafeteria, greeted by the aroma of freshly brewed coffee. Ah, just what I'm looking for. At the counter, I pour steaming coffee into a paper cup and add several spoonfuls of sugar, stirring until the crystals dissolve, hoping the sweetened caffeine jolt will help awaken my senses. I'll catch up on sleep during the four-hour train ride to New York City.

I nod to and greet more of the familiar staff and nurses as I make my way to my mom's room.

"Hey, mom." I sit in one of the uncomfortable chairs by her bed and set my coffee on the side table.

She's awake and watching reruns of what I call "old people shows" on the television hanging on the wall. She lays still against the white sheets, her frail body a permanent fixture on the mattress. A car accident left her paralyzed from the shoulders down, her once-active hands now resting limply at her sides. The only movement she can manage is the slight tilt of her head as she acknowledges my presence.

"Good morning, sweetheart," she says. "You're here early."

I touch up my hair self-consciously. "Got an early start today. I should get back to the city. I have a shift tonight."

"Okay sweetheart," she says, and I take her hand in mine. She can't feel our touch, but I know it still means a lot that I do the gesture. While most people might consider her fortunate to have survived, she often mentions she'd prefer death over living as she is now—as an invalid.

I'm grateful my mom is alive, but I can't help but feel guilty about wanting that, knowing that her reality is filled with unhappiness.

I taste my coffee, making a face when the bold sweetness of the sugar hits my tongue, then shrug off my coat, letting it fall behind my back in the chair.

"You look tired," she observes, her eyes sharp and alert despite her immobile body. "And your shirt's inside out."

I glance down and laugh. "Yeah, I was in a rush."

She raises an eyebrow. "From where exactly? You're never up this early unless you haven't been to bed."

"Mom," I groan, but there's no hiding anything from her. Even trapped in this broken body, her mind remains as perceptive as ever.

"I hope he was worth it," she teases with a knowing smile.

I take a sip of my coffee to hide my blush. "He was... interesting."

"Interesting?" she chuckles. "That's the best you can do?"

I smirk, grateful for these moments. Despite everything, we can still talk like this. Just mother and daughter, sharing secrets. It's almost normal, and I treasure that illusion of normalcy more than she could ever know.

"Well, he was tall. Handsome. Charming." I fidget with my coffee cup, digging my nails purposefully into the Styrofoam to cause dents. "But it was just one night."

"You deserve more than 'just one night', Kimberly."

I shrug, not wanting to get into it. If she knew the full truth—that I've been bartending at a club five nights a week and fake-dating a man in the mafia to pay for her care, that "interesting" men like Connor are my only escape from the exhaustion of it all—she'd be devastated. As far as she knows, I go to school full-time at NYU and work part-time at a cafe, living the life she always wanted for me.

"Did you meet him through a friend?" she asks.

"No, he was just some guy I met at a bar," I lie, leaving out the part where I cursed him out on the sidewalk. My mama's never liked that I have the mouth of a trucker, since she tried to raise me with good Midwest charm. It didn't stick—obviously.

I can almost hear her silent disapproval. She's always wanted better for me than random hookups in bars. After dad left, mom became obsessed with making sure I turned out "right." Like she thought his leaving was somehow her fault, that she hadn't created the perfect family environment. So, she doubled down on me, determined not to fail again.

I remember being six years old, coming home from school to find mom crying at the kitchen table. No dad. No explanation. Mom called the police, frantic, thinking something terrible had happened. Days later, they told her they'd tracked his credit card purchases—restaurant charges in Phoenix, gas stations in California, hotel charges in Seattle. He was alive and well; he just didn't want to be with us.

And her love life? One disaster after another. Dad abandoning us. Then there was Eric, who promised forever but barely made it three years. Next was Chris—whom she married—and everything was perfect at first, until he showed his true colors and openly beat his own son until he was black and blue. Mom turned a blind eye to it, saying that was how he disciplined his son. He eventually left mom for a younger woman. Then she finally met someone decent—Justin—only to have the accident take away any chance at that happiness, too. He visited for a while, then the visits grew less frequent, until they stopped altogether.

I look at my mom now, her body frozen but her mind still sharp. It's so fucking unfair. She should be traveling the world like she always talked about.

I push open the heavy metal door to Firefly marked "Employees Only" and give a slight nod to the security guard. My footsteps echo on the wooden floor as I head toward the women's locker room. Inside, the scent of perfume mingles with the stale traces of hairspray. As I reach my locker, I pull out a silky set of black lingerie. I slip out of my street clothes and into the lingerie, adjusting the straps, and check my reflection in the mirror once I put on my black stilettos. Bartending in heels fucking sucks.

Firefly is a popular club for New York City's wealthy elite, including families in organized crime. It's a sex club. We don't have a uniform, per se, but we have a requirement on the clothing, or I should say—lingerie—we can wear. We are allowed to go topless. It has definitely been proven that you will get more tips. But I choose to wear slightly more coverage, usually with nipple covers or pasties, depending on the outfit. More power to those who want to flaunt it, but that's not me. I just want the money, and it's good for me even wearing a one-piece lingerie set.

Employees are to be looked at—never touched. There is a no-fraternizing policy, although they make an exception for my fake boyfriend, Matteo Valentino. He got me the job here after meeting me as a waitress at a dump of a strip club.

I had been crying outside the club when he came to smoke a cigarette. He witnessed how patrons would grope me like pigs. In a moment of vulnerability, I shared with him that I needed the job for the money. He encouraged me to quit and offered to hook me up with a better one in the same industry, where men and women were classy and rich. He also proposed another deal, a lucrative one—pretend to be his girlfriend. Matteo seemed like the kind of man that few said no to, and I was desperate, so I said yes.

I didn't know then that he was involved with organized crime. Those things I learned while playing the role of fake girlfriend. And he has reminded me on more than one occasion that he pays me to play a part and keep my mouth shut—just sit there and look pretty.

It's a slow night. The usual Friday crowd is thin, probably because it's a holiday weekend. The few customers scattered throughout are nursing their drinks or in private rooms and don't require my attention.

I glance at the clock: 11:24. The night is crawling by.

"I'm going to restock," I tell Jasmine, the other bartender on shift. She nods, barely looking up from her phone.

In the back room, I sink down onto a crate of expensive vodka and pry off my heels with a groan of relief. My toes crack as I wiggle them against the cool concrete floor. The burning sensation gradually subsides as blood rushes back into my cramped feet. Christ, my arches are killing me.

I hear two men faintly speaking. That's not unusual, since the men's bathroom on the other side of the wall is connected to the air vents. But what catches my attention is when the name "Matteo" is said.

With my stilettos placed to the side, I carefully unfold a metal chair, its legs creaking slightly until it's completely set up. I step onto it, balancing cautiously as I position myself closer to the vent and eavesdrop the muffled voices.

"Did you hear that he tried to kill Killian Fitzpatrick's fiancée? Only to shoot Ryan Brady?" a man says. "Now Valentino has the Fitzpatricks after him."

"No. Fuck, Matteo is picking a fight with the wrong man," a second man states.

"All because this broad is Matteo's half-sister, and he doesn't want to share the inheritance with her."

Matteo has a sister?

"She's getting married to Fitzpatrick soon, and rumors are she's sleeping with Brady, too," the first man continues. "So, Valentino is fucking losing it. He's putting all of his men at risk for war."

"Isn't he older? Once he marries, he'll be fine."

I quietly gasp. *Is that why...?* I recall a recent conversation with Matteo, one that ended with me getting slapped, beaten, and told I was pretty much no use to him anymore.

"The Fitzpatricks will come after Matteo and everyone he cares about," one of them says.

Oh, fuck! Does that include me? Wait, no, he just said 'everyone he cares about.' Matteo doesn't care about me. *But do the Fitzpatricks know that?*

It becomes silent as the men leave the restroom.

It's hard for me to concentrate for the rest of my shift.

Should I stick to my role as the fake girlfriend and tell

Matteo what I overheard? Surely, he must already know the Fitzpatricks are gunning for him...

Or should I consider aligning myself with Matteo's enemy if this escalates into a war like those men think?

Or should I wash my hands of the whole situation and stay out of it entirely?

I might know things, and one thing I've learned from fake dating someone in organized crime is that the more you know, the higher the chance you might get killed for it.

And what if Matteo kills his sister? Is she innocent? I don't want that blood on my hands.

It's 2:30 in the morning, and though I'm conflicted, I'm sure Zach will pick up. He's the only one I trust to guide me through this. I hesitate, then finally make the call.

Chapter Five

ZACH

Fuck, Kim—what have you got yourself into?

I jab the elevator button for the lobby, cursing under my breath as the doors slide closed with painful slowness. It descends smoothly, the digital numbers blinking as I pass each floor. 12... 11...10... My foot taps impatiently, and my reflection in the metal wall looks like shit—dark circles under my eyes, hair disheveled from running my hands through it too many times this morning.

The elevator stops on the third floor, and I groan as two marketing interns step in, chattering about some social media campaign. They fall silent when they see me, straightening their posture.

I work here at Fitzpatrick Enterprises, too. But compared to their pristine suits and neatly styled hair, I look like I rode in on a Harley straight from a bar fight. My ripped jeans hang low on my hips, and my solid black tee does nothing to hide the sleeves of tattoos running down both arms. The intricate designs peek out at my collar, too, climbing up my throat.

When the doors finally open to the lobby, I practically shoulder my way past a delivery guy and make a right toward Blaze, the boxing gym. I'm searching for Killian Fitzpatrick and Ryan Brady, my bosses, who are here training for their upcoming fights.

Blaze occupies most of the first floor of Fitzpatrick Skyline Plaza, a skyscraper in New York City. This building leases to various shops and businesses but is the home office of Fitzpatrick Enterprises.

The smell of sweat and disinfectant hits me immediately—Blaze's signature scent. The gym is busy at this time of morning, with several fighters working the bags, and a sparring match happening in one ring.

I scan the room, looking for either of my bosses.

Blaze has a set of three practice rings along with several heavy punching bags hanging low from the ceiling. The wall's mirrors are ideal for working on form and footwork.

I spot Killian's red hair and find them both sitting on a bench outside one of the boxing rings, taking a break.

"Hey, boss," I say with a sigh. "There's something you need to hear."

"What's going on, Zach?" Killian asks as he and Ryan stand up to greet me, sensing my urgency.

"Remember how I mentioned that Kim, my ex-stepsister, started seeing Matteo Valentino a few months back?"

"She's the one who works at Firefly, right? Brown hair, about this tall?" Ryan remembers, speaking with his Irish accent and gesturing to her approximate height with his hand.

"That's her. Bartender," I confirm.

Killian nods. "You said you'd keep tabs on the situation."

"Yeah, and I have been since she refused to stay the hell away from him. She called me at two in the morning, freaking out. She overheard men talking about Matteo's most recent attempt to kill Cassie, and she wants to help. She may have information that could be useful."

Ryan steps closer. "Sounds convenient, doesn't it? Your ex-stepsister, who's dating Valentino, suddenly wants to help us?" His eyes narrow. "How do we know this isn't Matteo sending her to feed us bullshit or lead us into a trap?"

"It's not like that," I say firmly. "I know her. She has a good heart. She wouldn't be risking her neck calling me if she didn't genuinely care."

"You've been out of her life for years," Ryan counters. "People change."

"She's scared, man. I could hear it in her voice." I turn to include Killian in the conversation. "She knows approaching us puts her in danger. She's doing this for Cassie's safety—and her own. She wants out of this mess."

Killian, who's been watching our exchange silently, assessing the situation, finally speaks. "Set up a meeting with her. Tonight. Neutral location, somewhere public but private enough to talk."

"Tonight?" Ryan asks. "Kill, you're getting married tomorrow."

"We need to know what Kim knows. If there's even the smallest detail—something that could protect Cassie or bring Matteo down..." Killian states.

I look at Ryan, catching his reluctant nod. Despite his concerns, he'll back Killian. That's how it works between them—complete trust.

"I'll set it up," I say. "I'll text you both the details once I hear from her."

I leave them to finish their training session and head back toward the elevator. The ride up to my office on the sixteenth floor gives me too much time with my thoughts.

Memories surface like debris after a flood. Oklahoma. The flat, endless horizon. The double-wide trailer where dad and I moved after he married Kim's mom, Debbie.

For a while, it was good. Real good. When dad married Debbie, everything changed. The trailer park didn't feel so suffocating. Dad smiled sometimes. Debbie cooked actual meals, not just the microwaved crap I'd gotten used to. And Kim—she was twelve to my fifteen, all attitude and braces, constantly rolling her eyes at me.

Dad wasn't hitting me anymore. No more belt welts for getting C's in school. No more getting shoved against walls for "looking at him wrong." Debbie had somehow tamed that rage in him, redirected it. For the first time, I could breathe in my own home.

But good things never last in places like Stillwater, Oklahoma. When I turned seventeen, dad was drinking again. The beatings started back up, worse than before. Debbie tried to intervene once and ended up with a black eye herself. After that, she stopped trying to help, and I don't blame her.

The day I turned eighteen, I enlisted.

I remember Kim standing in the doorway of my bedroom as I packed, her arms crossed over her chest, about a blink away from either punching me or crying—maybe both.

I told myself I was doing them a favor by leaving. With me gone, dad would have one less person to rage at. Maybe he'd calm down. Maybe Debbie could handle him better without having to worry about me, too. And Kim could finish high school without the constant screaming matches.

Basic training was hell, but it was a different kind of hell. One with rules and order. For the first time, the surrounding violence made sense. Had a purpose. I thrived on it, channeling every memory of dad's fists into becoming the best. I served eight years in Afghanistan.

I wanted to reach out to Debbie and Kim—Kim especially —but by the time I could, when I wasn't in a war zone, I found out that Debbie and dad had gotten divorced. I was no longer family, didn't think I had the right to contact them. Instead, I imagined that Kim was probably living her best life; she'd most likely met a decent man who would tolerate her spitfire personality and stubborn attitude to settle down with and had at least one kid by now. That was what I hoped for her.

When my data security team brought me the intel they'd found on the new woman Matteo was dating, my eyes damn near bugged out of their sockets, seeing the name "Kimberly Stanton." The only Kimberly Stanton I knew was my ex-stepsister. There was no way she could be dating Matteo and working at Firefly—a sex club, of all fucking places.

I'd gone to Firefly with Ryan for a drink one night after work, intentionally looking for her, praying that it was another girl by the same name. But when *my* Kimberly stepped out from the stock room, I almost didn't recognize her. I stood there like an idiot, drink halfway to my lips. Gone was the fifteen-year-old with braces and a ponytail. In front of me was a confident woman. Her dark brown hair fell in soft curls past her shoulders. Her body, petite and curvy and filled out in all the right places, had only been covered in a lace teddy and thong set. I couldn't believe I was staring at the same girl.

My Kimberly was a tomboy, who used to follow me around, threatening to beat up the neighboring boys. She played football with me and begged me to play video games with her. This Kim had transformed completely.

I remember the way her eyes went wide when she saw me standing there at the bar. She nearly dropped the bottle of alcohol she was carrying. She had a visible look of embarrassment as she realized how little she was wearing and who was seeing her like that.

When her shift ended that night, she agreed to meet me at a diner down the street. We sat in a booth, catching up. I talked about the military, and she told me about going to school as an art major at NYU, mentioning that her mom was in Boston. She explained how she had gotten the job at Firefly, courtesy of her *boyfriend*, Matteo.

I didn't tell her who I worked for—that I knew who Matteo Valentino was. I couldn't. Not then.

When I asked her why she was working at a strip club, or sex clubs at all, she assured me it was never stripping and that she made good money bartending. She argued that living in New York is expensive. I wanted to tell her that Matteo has a shit-ton of money—he could help her. Of course, knowing Kim, I figured she wouldn't accept it. Too stubborn and independent.

But a week later, I couldn't take the thought of her with him anymore. It ate at me, knowing that she was involved with a selfish criminal, one with ties to human trafficking. I confronted her while she walked home after a late shift one night. I told her who I worked for and who Matteo was, and begged her to quit working at Firefly and break up with him. It was two in the morning and pouring rain. And for some reason, she chose not to take the train. She said something about not wanting to spend the money on it. We got into a heated argument after I offered to pay her expenses if she left Matteo. She scoffed, rejected my money, tried to deflect, and then said she felt abandoned when I left Oklahoma.

At that moment, yelling back and forth in the pouring rain, I wanted to take away her pain—from wherever it was stemming from. *So, what did I do?* I fucked her against my SUV.

I still remember every detail of that night. The way her wet clothes clung to her body, transparent in places, revealing glimpses of skin beneath. The heat of her anger turned into something else entirely when I pushed her up against the SUV, our faces inches apart. I hadn't meant for it to happen. But when her eyes dropped to my lips, a primal urge took over.

Her mouth tasted like mint and rain. My hands were everywhere, lifting her against the metal of the car door. Her legs wrapped around my waist, heels digging into my back as she pulled me closer. Water streamed down our faces, mingling with our impulsive kisses. I remember the sound she made when I entered her—half gasp, half moan.

She'd whispered my name against my ear, her voice breaking as I thrusted into her. It was angry, desperate, and so fucking good.

When she came, she bit my shoulder to keep from screaming, and I followed seconds later. Afterward, we stood there panting, foreheads pressed together, the reality of what we'd done slowly sinking in. She wasn't my stepsister anymore—hadn't been for years.

Immediately when our breaths had returned to normal, she'd pushed my chest back and called it a mistake. *That's not what it fucking felt like.* She reminded me she was with Matteo. I remember standing there, rain pelting my face, watching her pull herself together piece by piece.

I'll never forget what she said to me: "This never happened. We never happened." Her voice cracked on the last word. "Matteo would kill us both if he found out."

That is the moment I knew she didn't need me to tell her who Matteo was. She already knew. Then it hit me—she wasn't wrong. The thought of what he might do if he discovered what we'd done twisted my stomach into knots. I'd seen firsthand what he did to people who crossed him.

I decided to leave her alone—keep my distance. She was already caught in Matteo's web, and we didn't need to give him a reason to be pissed at her. I grabbed her phone and saved my phone number in her contacts under my childhood dog's name, Sandy—one she'd remember—and told her to call me if she needed anything.

And to my surprise, she called last night.

I step into my office and close the door behind me. My office at Fitzpatrick Enterprises isn't what most people expect from the head of security. It's not hidden in some basement bunker. Floor-to-ceiling windows line one wall, offering a panoramic view of Manhattan that would make most executives jealous. Killian insisted on it when he hired me— said he wanted security to have the best vantage point, to see threats coming from a mile away, metaphorically speaking.

A large mahogany desk dominates the room, usually covered with surveillance reports and background checks. Six monitors display various live feeds from around the building and our other properties.

I shuffle the folders on my desk to one side, clearing a space to work. Taking a deep breath, I pull out my phone and dial Kim's number. I drum my fingers on the desk as it rings once, twice, three times. By the sixth ring, her voicemail picks up.

"Hey, it's Kim. Leave a message, and I'll call you back. Maybe."

I hang up without leaving a message.

I toss my phone onto the desk and lean back in my chair, staring at the ceiling. But then it buzzes with a text notification.

> Can't talk. In class.

I type out a quick response:

> They want to meet tonight.

The three dots appear immediately, then disappear. Then reappear.

> I have classes late, then a shift at Firefly.
> Can they meet me there at nine-thirty?

> Yes.

> Thank you for doing this.

She doesn't respond.
I text Killian and Ryan the time and place.

Chapter Six

KIMBERLY

"Fuck!" I yell as I run up to the employee entrance at Firefly. "Shit!" I'm late, and one thing I've learned about dating—even fake dating—a guy in the mafia is that you don't keep them waiting.

I hurry and strip off my jeans and sweater, revealing the red lace bodysuit. I toss my tennis shoes into the locker, their laces dangling over the edge, and then slip on my matching stilettos. I slam my locker shut and walk over to the POS system to clock in and find the Fitzpatricks' assigned VIP booth.

I dash down the hallway, taking a deep breath, before pushing through the double doors into the main club area. The music hits me like a wall, bass thumping through my chest as multi-colored lights pulse across writhing bodies on the dance floor. I navigate around half-naked servers carrying trays of drinks, the crowd parting slightly as I move toward the VIP section.

My heels click against the floor, the sound lost in the music, but the vibration travels up my legs with each step. I can feel eyes on me—there are always eyes on me here. Classy but sleazy men and women eye me like fresh meat.

I spot the two men. The one I assume is Killian Fitzpatrick lounges back like he owns the place, one arm stretched across the back of the curved leather booth. Ryan Brady sits beside him, his attention locked on the floor until he notices me approaching.

Killian's eyes find mine as I walk up to him, lean down and yell in his ear over the music. "Killian?"

He nods his head.

"Come with me," I say and walk toward the circular stairs. Killian and Ryan follow behind me, but not too close. Upstairs, there are private rooms that are soundproof; we'll be able to talk freely there. I find one that is available by the green indicator light and open the door. They follow inside and close it, securing it with the lock. *Fuck, I can get into big trouble for this.* I grab a white robe, an amenity for guests, and quickly put it on before turning up the dimmer switch on the lights so that it's brighter. I'd rather not have this conversation practically naked in mood lighting. "My class ran over. I'm sorry I'm late."

"Thank you for meeting with us," Killian says, his voice smooth but authoritative. "Zach mentioned you might have some information that could be useful."

Ryan stands slightly behind him, arms crossed, expression unreadable.

I nod, adjusting the robe tighter around my body. "I don't know if what I have will help much, but maybe I could fill in some blanks for you."

I take a seat on the edge of the plush couch, crossing my legs.

"We'd appreciate anything you can give," Ryan says, stepping forward. I notice he has an Irish accent.

For a moment, I'm transported back to Boston—in Connor's hotel room—with his same accent whispering against my neck as our bodies tangle in the sheets. One night of reckless abandon with a stranger I met and had drinks with at a bar. My lips tingle in remembrance of his touch. And even in remembrance, I feel the intimacy of his kisses.

I shake the memory away, refocusing on the present situation.

"The truth is, Matteo and I aren't actually dating." I watch as their expressions shift—Killian's eyebrows raise slightly, Ryan leaning forward with interest. "He's paying me to pretend to be his girlfriend."

"Paying you?" Killian repeats, as he takes a seat across from me.

"Five thousand a month," I say with a nod. "I show up at events, business dinners, and act like the perfect girlfriend. I'm a student at NYU, not on a scholarship, responsible for my tuition and all my living expenses—I took his deal."

"How long has this arrangement been going on?" Ryan asks.

"About six months," I answer.

"Six months," Killian repeats, leaning back in his seat. His eyes narrow slightly as he studies me. "Were you ever intimate with him during this arrangement?"

I feel my face flush with embarrassment, but I meet his gaze directly. "No. Never. That wasn't part of our deal, and he never pushed for it."

"Not even once?" Killian presses, his tone skeptical.

I shake my head firmly. "The most physical contact was for show. A peck on the cheek when clients were watching, or he'd wrap an arm around my waist at events. That's it." I tuck a strand of hair behind my ear. "There's something else. About a month ago, Matteo approached me with... a different proposition." I take a deep breath. "He wanted me to marry him. For real. And have a baby." I pause, remembering how clinical he had been about the whole thing. "Through IVF, though—he was very specific about that."

They exchange a look I can't quite interpret.

"And you said no," Killian states rather than asks, his eyes studying my face intently.

I swallow hard, nodding. "I told him I couldn't do it— that I wanted to keep the original deal." My fingers trace the edge of the robe nervously. "He didn't take it well."

Ryan steps closer. "Did he hurt you?"

I close my eyes briefly, the memory still fresh and painful. When I open them again, I force myself to maintain eye contact despite the shame burning through me.

"He... he lost it. Completely." My voice wavers. "He grabbed me by the throat, slammed me against the wall, and said I was worthless to him."

Killian's jaw tightens, but he remains silent, letting me continue.

"He beat me pretty fucking badly." I blink back tears, refusing to let them fall. "When he finally stopped, I was curled up on the floor, sobbing. He just stood over me, breathing hard. Then he reached into his wallet, pulled out a hundred-dollar bill, and tossed it at me. It landed right next to my face, and he told me to buy makeup. Good makeup. Told me to cover the bruises I was going to have because we had dinner plans the next night with some important clients, and he needed me looking perfect."

Both men look at me sympathetically.

"You may be safe, for now," Ryan offers. "Matteo is currently in Argentina."

I breathe a sigh of relief.

Killian leans forward, resting his elbows on his knees, seemingly deep in thought. "So, he had the same plan as me," he mutters, looking toward the ground.

"Sounds like it," Ryan confirms. "Except Cassie wants to be with you, and she doesn't want to be with him."

I'm not exactly following, but I know not to ask questions either.

"I think..." I hesitate, lowering my voice despite the soundproofed room. "I think Matteo might be gay."

Both men freeze, exchanging confused glances.

"What makes you say that?" Killian asks.

"About three months ago, I met him at his penthouse. We had some gala that night. He stepped into the next room to take a phone call. He used speakerphone and left the door cracked open. I heard him talking to someone—a man. At first, I thought it was business, but then..." I lean forward slightly. "The way they were speaking to each other was... intimate. Matteo called him 'amore mio' and said he missed him. The other guy said something about wishing they didn't have to hide anymore."

"Did you recognize the other voice?" Ryan asks.

"No, sorry." I shake my head.

Killian rises to his feet, his expression softening slightly as he looks at me. "Thank you, Kim. Coming forward like this—

calling Zach, meeting with us—it took courage. If you remember anything else, even something that seems insignificant, call Zach."

Ryan nods, his face serious. "And if he reaches out to you, let him know."

"I will."

They move toward the door, Ryan unlocking it with a soft click. Then they're gone, closing it behind them. I pull my knees to my chest, the plush robe bunching around my legs. My hands are shaking. I didn't realize how tense I was until they left. I take a deep, steadying breath. Sitting here won't solve anything. I need to get back downstairs before I lose my job. That's the last thing I can afford right now.

Rising from the couch, I untie the robe and slip it off my shoulders. The air feels cool against my skin as I carefully return it to its hook. A quick glance in the mirror confirms what I already know—I look composed on the outside while everything inside is screaming.

The moment I step out of the soundproof room, the club's music slams into me. I make my way downstairs, weaving through the crowd. The music grows louder with each step until I'm once again surrounded by the pulsating rhythm and flashing lights of Firefly.

I slip behind the bar. Jasmine gives me a curious look as she shakes a cocktail.

"Where the hell have you been?" Chiara, my manager, appears beside me almost instantly, her face full of irritation. She taps her watch dramatically. "You're forty-five minutes late for your shift."

I reach for some glasses and start sanitizing them, dipping

them in each sink, before setting them out to air dry, trying to appear casual. "Sorry. I had to do something for Matteo"

Chiara's expression shifts immediately. "Oh. Okay." She nods. Without waiting for my response, she turns on her heel and strides away, already barking orders at one of the newer servers who's struggling with a tray of shots.

I exhale slowly, feeling the tension in my shoulders ease slightly. Matteo's name is like a get-out-of-jail-free card around here—the man drops thousands when he comes in and brings the kind of clientele that makes Firefly the hottest sex club in the city. His connection to me has me both protected and trapped.

I throw myself into my work, losing myself in the rhythm of pouring drinks, making change, and flashing just enough smile to earn decent tips.

Shake, pour, serve, smile, repeat.

As I walk home after my shift, an unsettling chill creeps over me, a sixth sense screaming that I'm being watched—stalked. My hand trembles as I reach for my phone, desperate to call Zach. But before I can dial, a force shoves me into a dark alley. The impact knocks the breath from my lungs, and a scream bursts from my lips, only to be muffled by a massive palm clamping over my mouth. The pungent tang of salty skin invades my taste buds.

With a swift, menacing motion, the man draws a shiny knife, cold steel pressing against my throat. My body freezes, terror rooting me to the spot as every nerve demands I listen.

"Scream again, and I'll slit your throat, bitch," he growls, each word dripping with malice. "Do you understand?"

I nod slowly, my eyes locked on his as he finally removes his palm, though the knife remains at my neck.

"What did you say to Fitzpatrick and Brady?" he asks, grinding the words out between his teeth.

"What?" I croak.

"Don't play stupid, you bitch," he snarls, his words slicing through the air with the same sharpness as the blade. "Matteo knows they came to visit you."

Fucking Chiara probably ratted me out!

"I didn't say a word about anything," I insist. "I don't even know anything. Matteo and me... our relationship isn't like that."

The man's eyes bore into mine, scrutinizing every twitch, trying to pierce through my façade. I lock onto his gaze, defiant and unflinching, daring him to call my bluff.

"If we find out you're lying, we will kill you... or worse."

What can be worse than being dead?

He yanks the knife from my throat, then draws his fist back like a coiled snake, only to whip forward, slamming into my stomach with the impact I would assume is the equivalent of a sledgehammer. I double over, gasping in agony, a cry of pain escaping my throat. In the haze of my suffering, I see him bolt, getting into a waiting sedan that screeches and tears away down the street.

"Are you okay?" an old man walking his little dog asks.

"I'm fine," I say and sprint off toward my apartment.

Once I get there, I lock the door. It's a fucking hole in the wall. The lock really won't do anything. A kindergartener can probably kick it in if they wanted to.

I let my purse fall to the floor and rush to the bathroom mirror, locking my gaze onto a tiny nick on my neck from where the knife pressed into my skin. Raising my shirt, I discover a bruise blooming beneath my red lingerie. I twist my body—a sharp pain shoots through me, and I hiss involuntarily. I guess I ran home on so much adrenaline I didn't notice it hurting before.

From the medicine cabinet, I pull out a bottle of old prescription pain meds. I unscrew the cap and dump two capsules in my palm before tossing them in my mouth. I turn on the sink faucet and lean to drink water from it, swallowing the pills.

"Fuck!" I yell out loud, standing upright. *Why does this shit happen to me?* I'm tough—I know I am strong, but there is only so much a girl can take before even the strongest-of-wills woman breaks.

I shouldn't have said anything. It was stupid to have them meet me at Firefly.

But you did the right thing, the little voice in my head reminds me.

I remove my clothing, even though it hurts, then get in the shower and wash away the day. It's almost three in the morning before I finally make it to bed.

At least tomorrow is Sunday, which means no school. I don't have a shift, either. I'll get out of town and go spend some time in Boston and visit my mom.

Chapter Seven

ZACH

KILLIAN AND RYAN debriefed me late last night. I would have gone with them to the meeting, but I was making final security preparations for the wedding today.

I concentrated on the wedding, making sure it went smoothly—which it did, mostly. We had prepared for the possibility of Matteo trying to stop the wedding, but he didn't. Instead, Victor Valentino surprised us all by showing up. Even though it was Victor who had sent his son to Argentina until the fight, he wants the families to make peace. Some sort of peace between the Valentinos and Fitzpatricks would be wonderful, in theory. But I'm still concerned about what Matteo might do to Kim.

I can't tell you how fucking relieved I was to hear that she'd been Matteo's fake girlfriend this whole time. I didn't enjoy hearing that he beat her up, though. That enraged me.

When I return home after Killian and Cassie's wedding reception, I pour myself a glass of whiskey, intent on unwinding from the long day. The Fitzpatricks have got me hooked. Only the Irish kind, though. I thought regular whiskey was good, but the Irish stuff is better.

I pull out my phone from my pocket and scroll to Kim's name. I get ready to call but hesitate. Part of me believes she won't even answer. I texted her last night after they told me about their conversation at Firefly, but she never messaged me back. And she's been silent all day today, too.

The strong, smooth taste of whiskey coats my mouth like a fiery kiss as I gulp it down, causing my nose to tingle and my throat to burn. A hint of oak and vanilla lingers on my breath as I grab my car keys and head back out of my apartment.

It's nearly midnight, but I don't care. I want to see her face to face.

Twenty minutes later, I pull up to Kim's building in a part of town even I—a trained military man—always avoid at night. The streetlights flicker ominously. Some of them don't work at all. The building itself looks like it's one strong wind away from collapsing.

As I step out of my car, a fat sewer rat scurries across the sidewalk, stopping to feast on a discarded box of Chinese takeout. The rodent doesn't even scatter when I approach, too comfortable around people.

The surrounding buildings are tagged with graffiti, and a nearby car sits on blocks, stripped of its tires.

Nope. I've seen all I needed to see, and she isn't sleeping here another night. I'll pull a Killian: move her shit out and tell her later if I have to. The thought of her walking alone here at night makes my stomach turn.

I silently curse Matteo. He could have at least put his fake girlfriend up in a nicer apartment. Goes to show he just wanted her as arm candy and really didn't care about her or her well-being.

Someone has wedged a brick in the building's security door to keep it open—not that it matters, since the lock is clearly busted. Inside, the hallway stinks of weed and something else I don't want to identify. I can hear arguing through the paper-thin walls as I make my way to the third floor.

I knock on 3C harder than I mean to. No answer. I knock again. Still no answer. *Where the fuck is she?* Firefly is closed on Sundays—she can't be working.

I pull out my wallet, get a credit card, and do an old-fashioned break in on this cheap lock. It works—easily.

The door swings open, and I'm hit with the full reality of Kim's living situation. The entire apartment is barely bigger than my bathroom at home. A twin mattress lies directly on the floor in one corner, covered with a flowery comforter. Next to it, a milk crate serves as a nightstand, holding a cheap lamp.

The "kitchen" is just a mini fridge, a hot plate, and a sink with rust stains. She neatly stacked the dishes, as if trying to maintain some dignity in this shithole. A folding table with one chair sits under the only window, which has a crack running through it, patched with duct tape.

The bathroom is hardly more than a closet with a toilet and shower stall. The ceiling above it has water stains that have left a pattern of concentric circles in yellow and brown.

She keeps everything organized, folded, and put away, like she's fighting against her circumstances. I can see her attempt to make it homier. A small potted plant sits on the kitchen counter, and she has her framed artwork hanging on the walls.

"Fucking hell, Kim," I whisper to the empty room.

At the end of the counter by the plant, there is a pile of mail. I grab a stack and flip through, noticing normal bills for rent and electricity. But there is one envelope that stands out, and it's from a long-term care facility. I unfold the papers inside. It's a charge summary. Her mother, Debbie Stanton, is the named patient.

Something happened to Debbie?

I look at the total on the fourth page, and my jaw drops at the cost of one month's care.

My head is spinning. Over sixty thousand dollars in past-due medical bills. How the hell is she managing this?

The door creaks behind me. "What the fuck are you doing here?"

I whirl around to find Kim standing in the doorway, her face a mix of shock and fury.

"Kim—"

"You broke into my apartment?"

"The lock's a joke. Just like this whole situation." I gesture around the room. "Why are you living this way? And what the hell happened to your mother?"

I slide the bill back into its envelope and toss it on the counter.

"Why are you going through my mail?" Her voice rises, cracking slightly. "You have no right!"

"Your mom is hurt—why haven't you told me?" I demand.

Her shoulders sag. "It's not your problem."

"Not my—" I rake my fingers through my hair, feeling frustrated. "Is this why you're working at Firefly and pretending to be Matteo's girlfriend? To cover bills?"

"Yes!" she shouts back.

"What happened to her?" I ask, my tone softening.

She refuses to look at me while she shakes her head, not speaking.

I close the distance between us. She tries to step back, but I gently pull her toward me, wrapping my arms around her shoulders. For a moment, she's stiff as a board, resisting the comfort I'm offering.

"Let me hold you," I whisper into her hair.

Something breaks inside her. Kim collapses against me, her arms finding their way around my waist as she buries her face in my chest. Her body shakes with each sob, tears dampening my shirt. I hold her tighter, one hand cradling the back of her head. Despite everything—the dingy apartment, the crushing medical debt, the situation with Matteo—it feels right to have her here against me. Like she belongs.

The familiar feeling of her embrace takes me back to our teenage years, when this was our language of comfort—usually after my dad beat me—but also when either of us just needed someone to hold onto. The last time I held her, truly held onto her like this, was the day I left Oklahoma.

"A drunk driver hit her," she confesses. "Two years ago. The bastard walked away without a scratch, but Mom..." Her body shudders. "She's been in long-term care ever since. Paralyzed. There's no recovery. She'll lay in a bed until the day she dies."

I tighten my arms around her, feeling her pain as if it were my own. "Why didn't you tell me? When it happened, or even when I found you at Firefly? I could have helped."

She pulls back slightly, tears still sitting on her eyelids. "You'd been out of my life for years. What was I supposed to say? 'Hey Zach, remember me, Kim—your former stepsister? I know you're busy with your successful military career, but my mom's hurt, and I'm drowning in debt?'" She shakes her head. "I couldn't do that."

"Yes, you absolutely could have." I cup her face in my hands, making her look at me. "You were there for me through the worst moments of my life. You think I wouldn't be there for you?"

She doesn't answer my question, but I see the look on her face and something shifts inside me. The woman I've known since teens, who held me when I was broken, is now breaking herself to keep her mother alive. Not anymore. Not if I can help it.

"Pack your things," I say, my voice steady with resolve.

She pulls back, confusion on her tear-stained face. "What?"

"You're coming home with me tonight."

"Zach, I—"

"This isn't a discussion, Kim. Look around." I gesture at the crumbling apartment. "This place—this part of town—is dangerous. That security door downstairs doesn't even lock. The window's held together with duct tape."

She crosses her arms. "I don't need your charity."

"It's not charity. It's what family does." I step closer. "Remember what you used to tell me? 'We've got each other's backs, always.' Well, I'm finally showing up to have yours."

I move to her closet and pull out a duffel bag, tossing it onto her bed. "And you're quitting Firefly."

"But the bills—"

"I'll help with your bills." The words come out quickly,

but I don't regret them. I'm paid very well by the Fitzpatricks. "I can handle it."

She freezes, staring at me like I've lost my mind. "That's... that's over ten thousand dollars a month. You can't just—"

"I can, and I will. And the Fitzpatricks have connections to excellent doctors and facilities. We can have your mom moved to New York, where you don't have to travel far to see her."

Her eyes widen in disbelief. "You can't solve all my problems."

"Watch me," I say, confidence dripping from my voice as I stride to her closet. I grab an armful of clothes still on hangers and drop them on the bed, then start removing them one by one, folding them neatly into her duffel bag. "I'm solving this problem right now."

She stands there watching me, her arms crossed. "This isn't some Hollywood action movie where the handsome hero swoops in, Zach. You can't just save me from the villain and fix everything with a dramatic gesture and a one-liner."

I pause, raising an eyebrow at her. "Handsome, huh?"

"That's not the point!" She throws her hands up in exasperation.

"Kim," I say, my tone softening. "I know this isn't a movie. Real life is messier, harder. But that doesn't mean you have to face it alone. Your mom was like a mother to me too, remember? Let me help."

Her resistance falters, and I can see the exhaustion behind her eyes—not just the physical kind, but the emotional kind as well.

"Besides," I say, trying to inject some lightness into the heavy moment, "aren't you graduating in, what, four months?

You're almost done with your degree. Soon you're going to be Kimberly Stanton, a hotshot artist, with galleries fighting to display your work. You won't need my help then—you'll be the one helping me pick out artwork for my sad bachelor pad."

She gives a forced smile and a tense nod in agreement. "I can pay you back," she says as her face brightens. "When I make those millions." She playfully punches my arm.

"Matteo. You need to end that, too. I assume he automatically deposits into your account?" I ask, and she nods. "Close it. I'll set you up with a new one."

"It's hard for me to accept this," she says, still trying to stay tough.

"I know."

"Thank you," she whispers.

A feeling settles in my chest as I look at her—a certainty I haven't felt in years. This is right. Having her close, keeping her safe—it's what I should have been doing all along.

Chapter Eight

KIMBERLY

WE FILL a duffel bag and a suitcase with my necessities, including my schoolwork and books in my backpack, and Zach takes me to his place.

It's an apartment in a building not too far from where he works at Fitzpatrick Skyline Plaza.

When I step inside his apartment, it already feels cozy, like a home. He doesn't have much, but he has more than I did. I look around and smile. One thing from Oklahoma he didn't leave behind was his country-raised personality, and it definitely shows in his space.

His living room is simple, but homey. A worn leather couch faces a modest TV that sits atop a wooden entertainment center. There's an American flag hanging on one wall, and a framed photo of his unit and medals on another. Neatly stacked in the corner beside an old record player are country albums by Johnny Cash, Garth Brooks, and some newer artists I don't recognize.

The kitchen is small but clean, with a few dishes drying on a rack near the sink. A magnetic notepad on the refrigerator has a grocery list in his neat handwriting. There's something charming about seeing "eggs, bread, whiskey" scribbled on it.

"Laundry room is down the hall," he mentions. "And this is the bedroom."

It's not fancy—just a queen bed with a royal blue comforter, a nightstand, and a tall dresser—but it looks like heaven compared to my previous situation.

"I know it isn't much," he says, rubbing the back of his neck. "I'll take the couch."

"That's ridiculous. I'll sleep on the couch. I don't want to put you out."

"Babygirl, I've slept on the cold hard ground in the military. The couch is a luxury and the bed even more so. I'll be fine."

Babygirl. He called me "babygirl." The casual endearment that he used to call me when we were teenagers makes my stomach flip.

Suddenly, I'm nervous. I try to focus on the conversation about sleeping arrangements, but my mind is already elsewhere. I think about that night he fucked me against his SUV, how good he made me feel at that moment. It was flesh against flesh, man against woman.

Zach was like an older brother, but there was a hint of something more. He's vulnerable with me. He was my sweet country boy. I was the tough tomboy who'd threaten to kick a kid's ass if they messed with *my* Zach.

I was happy for him and devastated at the same time when he enlisted. Happy that was leaving that place—his father—

but sad that it meant he had to leave me, too. He was my best friend.

I barely recognized him at Firefly. His ruggedly handsome face was vaguely familiar. He looked powerful, his chest broad and muscular. I felt an immediate and total attraction toward him. But I guess we both have changed physically over the years.

"I have to check in with my security team for tomorrow," he says before moving toward the door. "Make yourself comfortable." He walks out of the room.

I lay my luggage on the bed and pull out pajamas for tonight, along with my toiletries. I go into the connected bathroom and notice his grooming products. He's got cologne, hair gel, and a comb neatly placed on the counter, among other products. No doubt his strict time in the military taught him that.

I come out of the bathroom a little while later with my pajamas on, towel-drying my hair after a shower. I'm sitting on the edge of the bed when I hear a knock at the doorframe.

Zach appears, wearing gray sweatpants and an old faded Army t-shirt that hugs his broad shoulders. My breath catches slightly.

"Just need to grab some things," he speaks, moving toward his dresser. I catch a whiff of his clean and manly scent, and I take it in. "Then the room's all yours."

"Zach," I say, his name coming out before I overthink it. He stops, turns to look at me. "You don't have to sleep on the couch."

"Kim..."

"We can share the bed." I twist the damp towel in my hands. "We'd fall asleep watching movies all the time."

A small smile forms on his lips. "My Dad would've killed me if he knew."

"But he didn't," I say, returning his smile. "We were just kids then."

"We're not kids anymore," he indicates, his voice lower than before.

"I know. But it seems silly for you to be uncomfortable in your own home."

His expression is serious as he studies my face. "Are you sure?"

"I'm positive," I say, setting the towel aside. "Is everything okay with work?" I add, changing the subject.

He sits with me on the bed. "Yeah. Killian and Cassie got married today."

"What? Today?" My eyes widen in surprise.

"Yeah, it was a small ceremony followed by a reception. They're securely settled in the newlyweds' suite with Ryan. Tomorrow is still going to be hectic. I need to take Cassie and her classmates to a celebration after their ballet performance, and I'm organizing everything. After that, the three of them will be off on a week-long honeymoon. I'll finally have some free time."

"So, like, the three of them—they're together?" I ask, curious about the dynamic of Killian, Ryan, and Cassie's relationship.

He chuckles. "Yep, they are both with her. Somehow, they make it work. Me, I don't know if I could share a woman, especially with my best friend."

"You go, girl," I mutter under my breath, smiling at the thought of Cassie with her two men.

Zach catches my expression, and his lips curve into a grin.

"Well, well, Kimberly Stanton. Are you actually thinking about what it would be like? Being with two men?"

Heat rushes to my cheeks, but I don't back down. "Come on. Every woman has fantasized about having two male partners at least once in her life. Just, not all of us are lucky enough to partake."

He laughs, throwing his head back. "Is that so?" His eyes sparkle with mischief as he leans closer. "Men would rather have two women in their bed."

"Men are such pigs!" I shove his shoulder playfully. But I can't help laughing along with him before asking a question that's been on my mind. "How did you meet Killian and Ryan, anyway?" Organized crime and security teams weren't exactly part of the career path I'd imagined for the boy from Oklahoma. "I mean, you were military, then... what? How does someone go from serving their country to working for the Irish mob? Seems like quite a leap."

"It wasn't exactly a straight line," he says with a slight smile. "After my last tour, I was... struggling. You know how it is, coming back to civilian life."

I nod, though I don't really know. I've had my own personal life battles, but nothing like what soldiers face.

"I was working security at this shitty nightclub. Just muscle, really. One night, this fight breaks out. And there's this blond guy in the middle of it all, handling himself like he's been trained. I guess I recognized and appreciated it. But it was no ordinary bar fight," he continues. "Five men outnumbered him. At first, I thought they were just drunk idiots, but these guys were too coordinated."

I sit up straighter, pulling my legs under me, drawn into the story. "So, what did you do?"

"What any good Oklahoma boy would do—jumped right into the middle of it," he says with a laugh, and I grin at his storytelling. "I'd only been out of active duty about three months. Combat instincts were still fresh."

He repositions himself on the bed, turning his body to me.

"One guy had a knife. Another was reaching for something in his jacket—a gun. The blond guy was holding his own, but he was about to be in serious trouble." Zach's eyes get that distant look, like he's seeing it all play out again. "I took down the guy with the knife first and broke his wrist. Then the one going for his gun—caught him with an elbow to the throat."

"Jesus, Zach."

"Yeah, it got ugly fast. The blond guy and I ended up back-to-back." He laughs. "I was with a man I'd never met before. I was unsure who my opponent was or if I was fighting for the correct cause. Found out later they were part of the Sokolov crew—Russian mob trying to move in on territory in New York City. They were selling weapons to gang members, hoping to recruit them later for a territory war."

"That could've gone badly."

"Could've but didn't. We cleared the room together and afterward, he comes up to me, grinning. He sticks out his hand and introduces himself as Ryan Brady."

My jaw drops with a smile.

"Anyway, he thanks me, buys me a drink, and we get to talking. Turns out he's working with his stepcousin Killian Fitzpatrick, and he has all these sharpshooting skills. But he confessed he wasn't too good with combat."

"And then he... offered you a job with the mafia?" I raise an eyebrow.

"Not exactly. He introduced me to Killian the next day. This fancy restaurant downtown—a place I'd never be able to afford on my bouncer salary. He sized me up for what felt like forever without saying a word."

"That sounds intimidating."

"He called me a week later, said he valued how I stepped in to help Ryan without knowing who he was or what I was getting into. Said it showed character. He offered me a security position, better pay than I'd ever seen, and a chance to be part of something."

"Something illegal," I point out.

"Not everything the Fitzpatricks do is illegal, Kim. They are not like Matteo Valentino. They're businesspeople who sometimes operate outside of the law, yeah, but they have a code. But I knew what I was signing up for." He looks at me directly. "I wasn't interested in hurting innocent people— which is a value Ryan shares. But protecting someone like Cassie? Making sure Ryan and his men could do their job safely? That isn't so different from what I did in the military. Except the military saw me as a weapon, not family. They don't care about my well-being, just about one assignment to the next."

I hold his gaze, trying to reconcile this version of Zach with the boy I knew.

Looking at him now, I see a man who's found his purpose. The lost boy from Oklahoma with the abusive father and uncertain future has transformed into someone strong, principled, and sure of himself.

I don't even realize I'm moving until my arms wrap

around his broad shoulders, and I press my face against his neck.

"God, I missed you, Zach," I whisper, tightening my hold. "I missed you so much."

His arms circle me, tentatively at first, then pulling me closer.

"I missed you too," he says, his voice rough with emotion. "Every day."

There's so much time to make up for, so many years lost. But right now, in this moment, I'm grateful to have found him again.

"Look at you," I say. "The scrawny boy who used to hide behind me on the playground is now taking down the Russian and Italian mobs."

"I wasn't that scrawny," he defends.

Laughter bubbles up between us, the kind that comes from deep in your belly and makes your eyes water.

Our amusement gradually fades, leaving a warm, thick silence. His eyes drop to my lips for just a moment, and I feel my breath catch.

"Kim," he breathes.

Before I can respond, he leans in slowly, giving me every chance to pull away. I don't. Our lips touch in a gentle sensual kiss. It's brief, but it sends electricity through my entire body.

When he pulls back, his eyes settle on my face. "You should get some sleep."

I nod, pulling back from him reluctantly. I pull back the covers and slide underneath them, feeling the cool sheets against my bare legs. The mattress is firm but comfortable—definitely better than the couch.

"Oh, shit. Which side is yours? I ask, suddenly realizing I might be taking his preferred spot.

He stands at the foot of the bed, watching me with an unreadable expression. "The side you don't want," he states.

When he disappears into the bathroom, I settle deeper into the mattress.

I close my eyes, but sleep doesn't come. My mind drifts curiously. Two men. *What would it be like to be loved like that? To be the center of that kind of attention?* Keeping my eyes closed, I turn to my side, letting the fantasy take shape.

In my imagination, I'm lying on this very bed, but I'm not alone. Zach is there, his strong hands moving over my skin with the same confidence he showed that night against his SUV. But there's someone else too—another pair of hands, another mouth. In my drowsy state, the second man's face shifts between blurry features before settling on Connor's.

I imagine Zach's calloused fingers tracing my collarbone while Connor's lips press against my neck. Their bodies sandwich mine, warm and solid. The two of them working together to make me feel good. In this fantasy, there's no jealousy, no competition.

The vision grows hazy as I feel myself sinking deeper into the mattress. Connor's face blurs, and Zach's touch becomes more distant. The sensations that had felt so real just moments before begin to dissipate like smoke. My thoughts become disconnected, fragments rather than complete images.

I struggle to hold on to the fantasy, to keep both men with me in my mind, but consciousness slips further away. My last coherent thought is of Zach's lips against mine, that brief kiss we shared, before darkness claims me completely.

In art class, I meticulously sketch out the details of my next project. The scene depicts a book, its pages being torn out with a sense of urgency and desperation. Each page seems to flutter in the air, frozen in a moment of chaotic beauty. A small smile creeps on my face as I remember Connor—the moment we bumped into each other, my sketches flew out of my hands.

The task assigned to us was to create an image evoking powerful emotions in the viewer, and I believe this piece effectively does so. The sketch invites contemplation, raising far more questions than it provides answers.

For me, it represents my life. The book is my life, and maybe the chapters are ones I wish to erase, start over, or simply forget. It's chaos.

"Good job, Kim," my teacher, Professor Peterson, says softly from over my shoulder.

"Thank you."

"Come see me during office hours, okay?" she suggests, a gentle smile lighting up her face.

"Yeah, I will."

As she walks away, I feel a flutter of nerves twisting in my stomach. What could she possibly want to discuss with me?

A few hours later, I knock on my professor's door, which is already open.

"Come in, Kimberly." Professor Peterson waves me into her office from where she's sitting behind her desk. The space reflects her artistic sensibilities—walls covered with student artwork and shelves packed with art history books.

I take a seat in the leather chair across from her, my sketchbook clutched to my chest.

"Your work has been exceptional this semester," she says, pushing her glasses up the bridge of her nose. "Particularly your recent pieces—they show a depth of emotion and technical skill that's rare in undergraduate students."

"Thank you," I say, feeling my cheeks flush with the unexpected praise.

She leans forward, resting her elbows on her desk. "Which is why I wanted to speak with you about an opportunity."

My heart skips a beat. "An opportunity?"

"The Vanguard Gallery downtown is looking for a student curator for their summer exhibition series. It's a paid position," she adds and looks around on her desk before picking up a piece of paper, handing it to me—an application. "That's a foot in the door. I think you should apply. I'll write an excellent recommendation letter."

I look through the multi-page application. "It includes an essay?" I ask, noting the requirement. "I'm flattered you'd consider me, Professor, but..." I hesitate, fidgeting with the corner of the application. "Essays aren't really my thing. I've never been good at English or writing. Art is how I express myself because the words never come out right when I try to put them on paper."

She nods thoughtfully. "Many artists feel that way. That's why you're an artist—you communicate visually."

"In high school, I barely passed my English classes," I admit, embarrassment heating my face. "I can't organize my thoughts into paragraphs and thesis statements. It's like my brain... freezes. I mean—why do you think I'm twenty-six and still in college?"

It's true. Other than deferring a year to take care of my mom right after her accident, it's taken me longer than most to successfully complete school.

She takes the application from my hands and looks at it again. "The essay portion is meant to gauge your understanding of contemporary art movements. You get to choose the topic. I suggest writing something that moves, that you can be passionate about, that might drown out any technical flaws in the paper."

"Okay," I say, the idea growing on me. This opportunity might be what I need. If I can secure it, I could help with my mom's hospital expenses while pursuing my passion.

"If someone deserves it, it's you." Her eyes meet mine. "I may not know you personally, but your work speaks for itself. You put a lot of yourself into it."

"Thank you so much, Professor. I can't tell you what this means to me. I'll start brainstorming topics for the essay tonight," I promise. "I won't let you down."

As I walk out of her office, application in hand, I feel something I haven't felt in a long time—hope. After years of struggling, of watching my mother's health deteriorate while trying to balance school and work and endless hospital bills, maybe things are finally turning around.

Chapter Nine

ZACH

"Kim, you home?" I call as I walk through the door, then hang my jacket in the coat closet.

I find her sitting by the window in the bedroom with the curtain pulled back.

She doesn't respond, so I pause in the doorway, reluctant to disturb her. She's completely absorbed in her work as the afternoon light streams through the glass, bathing her in a golden hue that makes her skin luminous. Her pencil moves with confident strokes across the sketchpad balanced on her knees.

It's mesmerizing, watching her create. Her brow furrows slightly with concentration, and her lips press together in that particular way they do when she's deep in her artistic zone.

"Sorry," she apologizes, suddenly glancing up. "I didn't hear you come in." Her smile is apologetic, but her eyes still hold that dreamy, faraway look.

"Don't apologize," I say, moving closer.

"How was work?" She sets her sketchpad aside, tucking her pencil behind her ear. "You're home a little early."

I sigh and drop onto the bed across from her chair. The weight of the day feels heavier now that I have to share it. "It was... complicated. It involves you, actually."

"What?" she asks, confused.

"Apparently, Killian's ex-whatever got ahold of some footage from Firefly—you know, when you met with them."

She nods slowly, her expression growing concerned.

"Well, she somehow convinced Cassie that the three of you hooked up in one of the private rooms," I state.

"But that's not what happened."

"I know that. Killian and Ryan know that. But they never told Cassie they met with you at all."

Her eyes widen. "No way..."

"Yeah, it's bad. She left them—moved into Victor's brownstone."

"Can I do something? I can talk to her, lay out the truth, woman to woman."

"No, you should definitely stay out of it. They're already confronting the ex."

"I feel terrible about this."

"It wasn't your fault." I rub my temples, feeling a headache forming. "They could have avoided this whole mess by being upfront with Cassie from the beginning. What were they thinking, keeping your meeting a secret?"

"Maybe they didn't think it was important."

I lean back against the couch cushions. "If they'd just mentioned to Cassie, 'Hey, we're meeting Kim to discuss your psycho half-brother,' the ex wouldn't have this ammunition now."

She nods, pulling her legs up underneath her. "You're right. Secrets have a way of causing more damage than the truth ever could. Do you think they'll be okay?"

"I hope so. I've never seen them happier than they are with her." I reach over and take her hand. "Enough about them. Working on something for school?" I ask, pointing to her sketchpad.

"No, this one's for fun."

"Can I see?"

She turns the sketch toward me. It's the inside of a bar, and there are patrons sitting on stools. I lean in closer to examine the drawing. I immediately focus on a figure seated at the bar—undeniably Kim. But beside her sits a man. He's leaning toward her, his face partially turned in profile, with features rendered in careful detail. There's an intimacy to their positioning—not overtly romantic, but familiar in a way that makes something twist in my chest.

My guess is that she knows the guy who is sitting next to her in the sketch.

I don't think she's seeing anyone. She goes to school and returns home or visits her mom. But she might still be hung up on someone. We haven't discussed our past relationships.

"I'll get out of your way." I say, handing her back the sketchpad.

"No, please, sit with me," she insists, her eyes pleading. "You're gone so much."

"I have a job that I'm serious about," I explain. "It's demanding, but I wouldn't have it any other way."

"I admire you for being dedicated to your work. But remember, you need to make time for yourself," she reminds me. "Work-life balance is key."

"Are you following work-life balance?"

"I am now. Thanks to you, I have more time to sketch." She beams with an appreciative smile.

"Good. I'm glad to hear that."

She sets her sketchpad on the chair cushion, her eyes never leaving mine. With a graceful movement, she rises and crosses the small space between us. Before I can react, she's settled herself on my lap.

My hands instinctively find her waist, steadying her. The gesture feels both natural and startling—like we've done this a hundred times, yet it's entirely new territory.

"What's this about?" I ask, my voice lower than I intended.

She shrugs, a small smile playing on her lips. "Just missed you today."

As she shifts slightly to get comfortable, I'm struck by how easily we've fallen into this domestic pattern. For weeks now, we've been sharing space, sharing meals, sharing evenings—all while maintaining this careful dance around what we actually are to each other. Playing house, essentially, innocently—no more kisses since her first night. But that doesn't mean I haven't woken up with a hard-on for two weeks straight, since we seem to drift together in our sleep.

The routine has been comfortable—predictable in the best way. Morning coffee prepared just how she likes it. Evening debriefs about our days. The occasional brush of hands when passing dishes. All innocent, all safe.

We stare at each other, the air between us charged with unspoken tension. I can feel her breath on my lips, see the slight parting of hers. Time stretches, elastic and infinite.

Something inside me snaps. I surge forward, crushing my

mouth against hers. Her lips are soft, and I'm lost in the sensation. I force her lips open with my tongue. She tastes faintly of coffee and something sweeter—distinctly Kim. Fuck, I could make out with her all fucking day.

She responds instantly, her arms wrapping around my neck as she presses closer.

My hands, no longer content with just her waist, begin to explore—tracing the curve of her back, the slope of her hips. She sighs against my mouth.

My fingers find the hem of her shirt, hesitating a moment before slipping underneath to feel the warmth of her skin. When my palm cups the soft fullness of her breast, I can't help but groan against her mouth. She's perfect—the weight of her tits filling my hand completely. I squeeze, feeling her rosebud nipple harden instantly against my palm. Fuck, I love that she never wears bras.

But something makes me hesitate. I pull back, breaking our kiss. My breathing is ragged, and I rest my forehead against hers, my hand still beneath her shirt but now motionless.

Her eyes flutter open, confusion and desire battling in her gaze. "What's wrong?"

"I want to take you out tonight," I say, my voice husky. "That new place on Seventh Street just opened. I've heard the chef is incredible. I can use Killian's name and get us a VIP table and top tier service."

She shifts on my lap, her fingers playing with the collar of my shirt. "Dinner?" she asks, a hint of reluctance in her voice. "We could stay in instead," she murmurs, shifting closer. "I'm not really hungry for food right now."

Her hips rock subtly against mine, and I have to stifle a groan.

"Kim..." I start, but she silences me with another heated kiss, deeper and more insistent than before.

Pulling back, she reveals swollen lips and flushed cheeks. "We've been dancing around this for weeks," she whispers against my mouth. "Can we just fuck?"

Can we just fuck?

I offer to take her out because she isn't just some woman I want to screw, and she just wants to fuck me.

This isn't how I pictured this happening between us.

I gently place my hands on her shoulders, creating enough space to think clearly.

I bow my head, searching for the right words—how to tell her what she means to me—how the past few weeks have meant to me. But I also need to prepare myself. Maybe she doesn't feel the same.

Before I can formulate a response, my phone buzzes insistently in my pocket.

I check it, and the screen illuminates with a message from one of my men, something about work.

"Forget dinner," I mutter. "I have to go."

She slides off my lap to a stand. "Oh, okay. Another time?"

"Yeah," I say flatly before leaving the bedroom.

I grab my jacket back from the closet and put it on, ignoring her as she follows me to the door. The distance between us feels like miles now, though she's only a few feet away.

"When will you be back?" she asks.

"I don't know. Don't wait up," I say, not meeting her eyes when the words come out colder than I intend.

"Zach—" she starts, but I'm already closing the door behind me.

I stand in the hallway for a moment, my forehead pressed against the cool wall. *Fuck. What happened in there?*

The elevator ride to the main floor is excruciating. I keep replaying her words in my head: *"Can we just fuck?"*, Not *"I want you"* or *"I've been thinking about us."* Just a casual, "Can we just fuck?" Like that's all she wants from me. No strings. No emotions.

Outside, the cold winter air hits my face, but it doesn't clear my thoughts. I start walking, hands shoved deep in my pockets.

Is that all I am to her? Merely the guy who's giving her a place to stay until she sorts out her future? A convenient roommate, a potential fuck-buddy she wouldn't mind sharing a bed with? After all we've shared over these past weeks—the deep late-night talks, the way she nestles against me during movies, those peaceful breakfasts... I thought we were building toward something.

I'm unsure of where we stand, and whether all those moments meant as much to her as they did to me.

Chapter Ten

KIMBERLY

I FUCKED UP YESTERDAY. Zach offered to take me to dinner, and I told him I just wanted to fuck. Ugh, I'm so stupid.

The look on his face when I said it. God, I can't stop seeing it—that flash of hurt.

I roll over in bed, staring at the ceiling fan as it spins above me. He came home late last night after I cried myself to sleep. But then when I woke up, he was gone again without a word. My phone sits silent on the nightstand. No good morning text. No funny meme. Nothing.

I didn't suggest it because I didn't want to go to dinner; my hesitation was because I didn't want him to spend more on me when he was already doing so much. He's paying my tuition, my mom's care, a roof over my head, and food.

In my attempt to give him what I thought he wanted by suggesting we skip to the physical part, I completely misjudged the situation. I realized he genuinely wanted to take me out, not just for me, but for himself as well. His intentions were so thoughtful, and I can't seem to navigate this without messing up.

I decide to get some coffee and text him.

My fingers hover over the screen. What do I even say? Something casual, something normal.

> Heading out for coffee. Want me to bring you anything?

I hit send before I can overthink it. God, this is ridiculous. I'm terrified of a text message. Three little dots appear almost immediately, making my heart jump.

> Black, two sugars. Thanks.

I exhale slowly. At least he's answering me. It's not warm, but it's not cold either. Just...neutral. Which is better than nothing.

I pull on a hoodie and head downstairs. There is a coffee shop around the corner, or I could get some at Fitzpatrick Skyline Plaza—closer to him. While I try to decide which shop to go to, I'm also trying to formulate what I'm going to say when I see him. An apology? A joke to break the tension? Nah, that doesn't feel right.

My phone buzzes; it's mom's new care facility here in New York sending their weekly update email. I make a mental note to visit her tomorrow.

The morning air is crisp against my face as I walk, rehearsing apologies in my head.

I'm a few blocks away from the shop when I notice them —two large men in dark suits walking toward me. Something about them seems off. They're scanning the sidewalks methodically, not strolling casually like most pedestrians or on their way to work or tourists with their phones out. One nudges the other and nods my way.

My pace falters. I decide to cross the street abruptly, pretending to be interested in a shop window.

They change direction, too.

My heart rate kicks up. I pull out my phone, pretending to take a call while watching their reflection in the storefront glass. They're definitely following me.

Shit!

I spin around and break into a run, fingers fumbling with the screen of my phone to find Zach's contact. My thumb is hovering over the call button when I hear the screech of tires behind me. A dark, windowless, van swerves to the curb, its door sliding open.

"Hel—!" I scream, but my voice is cut short as two men—different from the ones who'd been following me—leap from the vehicle. One grabs my arm while the other clamps a hand over my mouth.

Is anybody fucking seeing this? I hope a pedestrian—a witness—calls 9-1-1.

I struggle against their grip, kicking wildly as they haul me into the van. The door slams shut, plunging me into dim light. My heart hammers in my chest as I try to orient myself.

That's when I see him.

"Matteo." I gasp, my voice barely a whisper.

He sits across from me, legs crossed casually, wearing a satanic smile that spreads across his thin lips.

The van jerks as it speeds away.

"Hello, Kimberly," he says.

My eyes dart to a man beside him—lean, with dark-rimmed glasses. He adjusts his glasses, glancing at Matteo with a fondness that's unmistakable.

"I haven't seen or heard from you in weeks," I state, finding my voice as the adrenaline sharpens my senses.

"I've been out of the country," he scoffs. His eyes narrow suddenly. "But you knew that already, didn't you?"

The van takes a sharp turn, throwing me into the side of one of the two bulky men I'm sitting between. I steady myself, planting my feet on the van's floor.

"Don't bother denying it," he continues. "You're not a good liar."

"I—"

"I know you closed your bank account and moved in with Fitzpatrick's security beefhead."

My stomach drops.

The phone in my hand buzzes, and before I can even look at the screen, one of the men sitting next to me snatches it from my grasp.

He swipes at the screen, frustrated when the lock screen appears. His eyes dart to mine, a cruel smile spreading across his face.

"Hold her," he barks at the man on my other side.

Rough hands grip my head, fingers digging painfully into my jaw, forcing me to look forward. I struggle against his hold, but he only tightens his grip.

"Stay still," the first man hisses, raising my phone to my face.

The phone unlocks, facial recognition betraying me. *Fucking technology!* The guy tosses my cell phone to Matteo.

"Well, well," Matteo says, scrolling through it. "It was your boyfriend. One of them, anyway. I'm learning that the Fitzpatrick clan likes whores."

What does he mean by that? I shoot him a confused look.

"Don't insult my intelligence. Boston."

Oh, fuck. I stare at him, my heart pounding in my ears. *Does he know about Connor?* My thoughts race, trying to connect how he could possibly know about that one-night stand. He must have someone following me everywhere.

He sighs dramatically, his attention already drifting as he slides my phone into his jacket pocket.

"Your boyfriend is quite the busy man," he says, examining his manicured nails. "Texted you about an emergency at work. Poor Cassie has been kidnapped." His tone is flat, unconcerned. "He's working with Killian and Ryan, trying to track her down."

"Cassie? Who else would—?"

The man beside Matteo—his boyfriend?—laughs.

"Oh my God," I whisper, the realization hitting me. "You took her, too."

Matteo's smile widens, satisfaction gleaming in his dark eyes. "Smart girl. Though not smart enough to stay loyal, were you?" his voice drops to a dangerous purr. "You're going to be my girlfriend for one more night. My fight is tonight, and I need you there. Looking pretty. Hot. Convincing." He continues, his tone shifting to something darker as he leans forward, his eyes boring into mine. "And after the fight, after I win, I have a surprise planned for you. Fitting end for a disloyal whore."

My stomach twists with dread. "What are you talking about?"

"You'll see," he says with a grin, then his eyes flick to the burly man sitting beside me. "Shut her up. I'm tired of her voice."

The man yanks a roll of silver duct tape from his jacket pocket. I try to twist away, but one of the goons pins my arms to my body while the other's fingers hold onto my jaw, forcing my head still. The tape makes a sickening ripping sound as he tears off a strip.

He slaps the strip across my mouth, pressing it firmly against my skin. The adhesive pulls at my face, and I struggle to breathe through my nose as panic rises in my chest. My arms are still pinned, so I'm unable to remove it myself.

Matteo turns to the man with glasses. "Charlie, I need you to stay at the warehouse with Cassie."

Charlie's expression shifts, disappointment evident on his face. "But I thought I was coming to the fight."

"Plan changed," he informed, his tone leaving no room for argument. "I need someone I trust to handle Cassie."

"What exactly am I supposed to do with her?"

He leans closer, his voice dropping to a murmur. "Kill her after I win. Prove to me you can do this—be with me and in my world, Charlie."

His face pales slightly, but he gives a jerky nod. "I can do that."

Then, as if remembering something, Matteo reaches into his jacket pocket and pulls out a sleek black phone—not mine, but his own. His fingers move across the screen before he holds it to his ear.

My eyes widen as I watch his face transform. The cruel smile melts into something almost pleasant, his posture relaxing as he waits for the call to connect.

"Killian," he greets warmly, as though greeting an old friend. "Or should I call you brother-in-law?"

I pull against my restraints, desperate to make any noise that might alert Killian to what's happening. One of the men beside me notices and presses his forearm against my throat in warning.

"Patience, Killian," Matteo continues. "Whether you get her back or not is up to you."

His eyes narrow as he listens to whatever Killian is saying on the other end of the line. His fingers drum against his thigh.

"Here's the deal," he says. "Win the match, and I'll kill her. Lose it, and I'll give her back, maybe with just a few bruises." He pauses, a cruel smile playing on his lips. "I'm curious what you'll do. How much does she mean to you? Will you lose for her?"

Charlie shifts in his seat, watching Matteo with undisguised admiration.

"Good, then tonight is the night. And no forfeiting." Matteo holds up a finger when Charlie tries to whisper something to him. "Fake losing it. Let's give them a show."

He ends the call, placing his phone back inside his jacket pocket.

The van pulls up through an alley behind a building downtown that I'm unfamiliar with.

The driver cuts the engine. The sudden silence feels heavy, suffocating—a doom—as I'm about to find out what's happening next.

"Charlie," Matteo says, his voice low and commanding. "Go straight to the warehouse. Wait for my call."

Charlie's face falls. "But—"

"No buts," Matteo interrupts, reaching out to stroke Charlie's cheek with disturbing tenderness. "When I call you —and only when I call—you kill her. Understand? Not before. I want Killian to think he has a chance to save her."

Charlie hesitates, then nods, his expression hardening with resolve. "I understand. I won't let you down."

"I know you won't," he murmurs, leaning in.

Their lips meet for a kiss. Charlie's hand slides to the back of Matteo's neck, pulling him closer as if I'm not even here, bound and gagged between two thugs. The kiss lingers, becoming more heated, more possessive—an obvious display of power and intimacy meant to unnerve me further.

When they finally break apart, Matteo signals the two men I'm sitting between with a nod.

The men roughly haul me out, the tape still firmly sealed over my mouth as I'm marched through a service entrance and up a flight of stairs. My mind races, trying to memorize the route, searching for any distinguishing features I could relay to Zach—if I ever get the chance.

We enter what appears to be a private dressing room. The space is small but luxurious, with a vanity table, a plush couch, and a clothing rack filled with dresses.

Matteo dismisses his men with a flick of his wrist. "Wait outside."

Once we're alone, he rips the tape from my mouth in one swift motion. The pain makes my eyes water. But he ignores me, walking to the clothes rack. After flipping through several hangers, he yanks free a dress—if you could even call it that. It's more like scraps of shimmering black fabric held together by impossibly thin straps.

"Put this on," he says, throwing it at me. The garment lands against my chest before falling into my hands.

"Could you... turn around?" I ask. I know he's gay, but still...

He laughs, settling himself on the couch directly across from me, crossing his arms. "No." His eyes gleam with cold amusement. "I'll watch. I'm not leaving you alone."

My stomach churns. I glance toward the door, calculating my chances of escape.

"Don't even think about it," he says, reading my expression. "My men are right outside."

I swallow hard, fingers trembling on the dress's thin straps. Slowly, I turn my back to him, though I know it won't provide much privacy. I peel off my hoodie, hyper-aware of his eyes on me.

"Hurry," he snaps. "You'll still need makeup."

I remove my t-shirt and jeans, trying to change as quickly as possible while maintaining some shred of dignity. The dress is even smaller than it looked on the hanger, covering just the essentials.

"Stop acting so prudish," he says with a bored sigh.

The fabric strains across my hips as I shimmy into it, the material clinging to every curve of my body. It's at least a size too small. The hem barely covers my ass. I tug at it uselessly, trying to stretch it lower.

"Jesus, you've gotten fat." He sighs.

I have been eating more—proper food, healthy meals that Zach prepares. Not the ramen noodles and dollar menu items that were my staples before. For the first time in years, I haven't been saving pennies or sacrificing food to make rent.

"Beefhead must be feeding you well," he continues, as if

reading my thoughts. His eyes narrow. "Fattening you up like a prize pig."

I bite back a retort, one that begins with my favorite curse word, knowing it won't help my situation. Instead, I focus on breathing, on staying calm.

Matteo checks his watch, impatience flashing across his face.

"Sit," he commands, pointing to the vanity.

I obey, settling onto the small stool in front of the mirror. My reflection stares back at me, hair disheveled from the struggle. He places a makeup bag on the vanity's table, unzipping it to reveal an assortment of high-end cosmetics.

"Make yourself presentable," he orders. "You know how I like it. We have a luncheon and interviews before the fight. Snap, snap."

My fingers tremble slightly as I reach for the foundation. I apply it to my face, and a question burns in my mind, one I've been afraid to ask since the moment I realized what kind of man Matteo truly is.

"Would you have killed me, eventually?" I ask, my voice steadier than I expected. Our eyes meet in the mirror. "Even if I'd taken your deal—gotten married, had your child?"

His stiff expression doesn't change.

"Eventually," he admits with a small shrug, as if discussing the weather. "Once the child was born, you would have outlived your usefulness."

The mascara wand hovers near my eye. My hand freezes.

"I would have been the perfect wife for you," I whisper, trying to control my shaking as I resume applying the mascara. "Isn't that what you told me? The perfect arrangement."

A bitter smile spreads across his face as he watches me in

the mirror. "You would have been. That's why I chose you." He moves behind me, placing his hands on my shoulders. His fingers dig painfully into my skin. "Your independence, your self-sufficiency—it was ideal. You didn't need emotional attachment. You were practical. Focused on survival."

I continue applying makeup with precision, trying not to flinch under his grip.

"I thought you'd understand the business proposition," he continues. "A marriage of convenience. You get financial security; you wouldn't have had to work another day for the rest of your life. You could do your shitty art and hang out with your vegetable mother." My heart feels like it was stabbed by his insults—not of me, but of my mother. "I get respectability and an heir. But it's too late now. You turned down the deal. Made your choice. I don't need you anymore. I've moved on to plan B."

"So why am I here?" I ask, meeting his eyes in the mirror. "Why not just kill me?"

Matteo's laugh is deep and hollow. He leans closer, his breath hot against my cheek. "Because tonight isn't just about the fight and showing you off. It's about making allies."

Chapter Eleven

CONNOR

TONIGHT, my brother and Killian are going to take down Matteo Valentino, and I'm here in New York City, ready to help. I've brought from Dublin a few of my best sharpshooters.

En route to the United States, I learned Cassie was kidnapped. It makes me even more determined to be here for Ryan. I know how deeply he loves her.

The shock on his face when I arrived at Fitzpatrick Skyline Plaza was something I'll never forget. He stood there, mouth open, like he'd seen a ghost rather than his older brother. I hadn't given him any warning—just showed up. The initial surprise gave way to relief almost immediately. His shoulders had slumped as he pulled me into a fierce hug.

We've never been close. Not since our father first started grooming me to take over the family business. Father wanted Ryan to use as a weapon, training him to be a cold-blooded killer—someone Ryan most definitely isn't.

I used to resent Ryan for it. While I was stuck in endless meetings, learning the intricacies of our legitimate businesses and the ins and outs of our underground empire, Ryan got to be... Ryan. Father demanded perfection from me—every decision scrutinized, every failure magnified.

I'd watch him through windows, target shooting, and envy the simplicity of his purpose. He was a tool—I was the heir.

The weight of the O'Brady legacy pressed down on my shoulders alone. When I made mistakes, there was hell to pay. When Ryan made them, father would shrug it off—"He's just the bastard boy," he'd mutter. The irony wasn't lost on me—I was trapped by my legitimacy while he was free because of his lack of it.

Watching Ryan now, seeing the dark circles under his eyes and the tension in his shoulders as he worries about Cassie, I realize how petty those old grievances seem.

Blood is blood. And tonight, I want to be the brother I should have been all along.

Something changed in me the day Ryan brought her to Ireland. I remember standing at the window of my father's study, watching their car pull up the driveway. He had never brought a woman home before. Not once in all our years.

She stepped out of the car with a quiet confidence, her blonde hair catching the rare Irish sunlight. Ryan's face—I'd never seen him look at anyone that way, like she was the center of his universe.

Upon meeting Cassie, father called her a whore. She kept her composure, but I could see the hurt in her eyes. Ryan though, slugged our father, punching him in the jaw.

I watched my brother stand tall before the man who'd belittled us both constantly, and something inside me broke free. I was done—completely and utterly finished with the old man and his poison.

For years, I'd been the dutiful son, seeking his approval, sacrificing my own desires. But what had it gotten me? A hollow existence in a cold mansion, trapped with my father who didn't give a shit about my happiness, and surrounded by loneliness instead of love.

I wanted what Ryan had found—not Cassie specifically, but that look in his eyes that told me he was in love. That certainty that someone in this world saw him completely and chose him anyway.

I walked out of that room without a word, leaving my father clutching his jaw. That night, in the solitude of my office, I began making plans: arrangements for my departure, transferring funds to accounts he couldn't touch. I wanted to leave Ireland—go somewhere with enough space to breathe, to discover who I was.

Boston had been my first stop after leaving Dublin. I needed to build relationships with our American connections —men who might prove valuable when I cut ties completely with the O'Brady name. I don't know if I'll change my name like Ryan did—dropping the 'O' from O'Brady. I'll gauge how potential partners respond and go from there.

Father always underestimated the importance of our stateside operations, dismissing them as "peripheral interests." But now, his short sightings have become my opportunity.

I'd spent a week in Boston, meeting with dock workers, union representatives, and the men who controlled the flow of certain goods through the harbor. Men who might do business with Connor O'Brady, not Prince O'Brady, the heir.

And then there was Merlot. I hadn't planned on meeting

anyone—certainly not a feisty woman who would make me forget my own name for a few precious hours. It had been a chance encounter. And for an evening, I forgot about family legacies and criminal empires.

That night with her showed me what was possible. That I could feel something genuine, something that wasn't tangled up in duty or expectation. The way she looked at me—not as an O'Brady, not as anyone's son or brother or boss—just as a man she wanted.

Watching Ryan now, his face tight with worry for Cassie, I understand what he's fighting for. What I could fight for, too, someday. Not just business interests or family honor, but a connection that makes everything else fade into background noise.

However, whenever I envision my future, every woman I picture myself with has Merlot's face.

After Ryan won his boxing match against some amateur fighter, he met up with Zach and our teams at an abandoned building. It's across from where we believe Cassie is being held based on the location of the van that she was taken in.

We gather in what was once a corporate office, now a skeleton of cubicles and broken windows. The scent of mildew and neglect fills the air entirely.

"All right, listen up." Ryan's words cut through the silence, commanding attention without raising his voice. The team of nine men, all dressed in black tactical gear, form a semicircle around him. "This isn't just another extraction. This is Cassie."

He unrolls a detailed blueprint of the warehouse building on a dust-covered desk. His finger traces the outline of the rooftop.

"Connor, I want you and the Irishmen positioned here, here, and here."

I nod. The roof offers clear sightlines into the warehouse with plenty of angles.

"We'll have three-sixty coverage," I confirm, mentally placing my shooters.

"Zach," Ryan says. "Stay with Connor and spread your men in the corner offices."

"Johnson has the northeast corner, Woods'll take the west, and Sides will hold the southern approach backing the main entrance," Zach tells his team. "We'll set up in a staggered position. My men can maintain watch on all entry points."

"No one takes a shot until my signal," Ryan emphasizes.

With our orders, we break away, get in position, and wait.

I settle into mine on the rooftop while my team fans out, each man finding their designated spot. Peering through my scope, I can see the warehouse windows, most darkened, but a few show movement inside—shadows passing like ghosts.

I adjust my earpiece, listening to the soft breathing of my men as they set up. Earlier, we gave Killian an earpiece, too, so that Ryan can communicate with him and confirm Cassie is alive. Killian is a thousand percent willing to lose his fight against Matteo, but first, he needs to know she's alive.

Zach is to my right, already in position, with his tablet propped against a ventilation unit. The glow from the screen lights up his face as he taps furiously at his cell phone.

His brow furrows, and he lets out a quiet curse under his breath. I watch as he types into his phone, then waits, his jaw clenching tighter with each passing second. He types again, more forcefully this time, then shakes his head.

"Everything all right?" I ask quietly, keeping my voice low enough that it won't carry beyond us.

His head snaps up, almost as if he'd forgotten I was there. He quickly locks his phone screen and puts it in his pocket.

"Yeah, hopefully. My gir—Kim—she's not responding to my texts."

Women problems. Right, I'll stay out of that. I've got my own. When I left Boston and went back to Ireland, my attorney had the divorce papers ready, and my wife happily signed them. Now, if I can only get Merlot out of my head...

I'm considering going to Boston to find her. I need to look into every university, technical college, and bar, since all I definitely know is that she's a bartender and going to art school.

The comm in my ear goes off. "I have direct sight to the man holding Cassie," Ryan confirms. "Kill, you will not believe who it is...It's fucking Charlie."

"Who the fuck is Charlie?" I mouth to Zach.

"Her friend from school," he answers.

"Ryan—" I say, as I watch from my point of view—this Charlie guy picks up a gun.

"I see him," Ryan says steadily.

I continue to keep my eyes locked on Charlie and he's about to point the gun at Cassie.

"I'm lining up my shot," he confirms.

The crack of his rifle shatters the air. Through my scope, I observe Charlie's head snap back, a spray of blood misting the air behind him. He drops to the floor, the gun he'd been holding clattering to the ground beside her.

"Confirmed hit." Zach's voice comes through the comm.

"Connor, maintain overwatch. Anyone approaches that isn't us, take them out," Ryan orders.

"Copy," I respond, adjusting my scope to scan the perimeter.

"Zach, I need you to get her," Ryan says.

I'm sure Ryan wants to be the one that saves Cassie, but his talents are most helpful here, using a sniper rifle.

Zach takes off as we begin a shootout on Matteo's men.

The night erupts into chaos as we hold our positions. I cover Zach as he makes his way into the warehouse. I track the first man through my scope. These men are scrambling like ants whose hill has been kicked. They're disorganized and panicking. Amateurs. I exhale slowly, letting my crosshairs drift ahead of his path, leading the target by a hair.

"Connor, I've got movement on the east side." Ryan's voice crackles through my earpiece.

"Copy that." My response is automatic as I squeeze the trigger.

The rifle bucks against my shoulder. My suppressor dampens the sound, but I still feel the concussive force ripple through my body. The man drops.

I adjust my position slightly; the crosshairs settle on a man who's crouching behind a rusted-out delivery truck. He's young, probably hasn't seen his twenty-first birthday yet. Won't see his twenty-second, either.

The rifle echoes in my ears as the young man's body slump forward. There's no time for remorse. I shift my position, scanning methodically through my scope for the next threat.

"Movement at the main entry point," Johnson announces through the comms. "Vehicle approaching."

That's when I see it—a sleek black sedan screeching around the corner, tires smoking against the asphalt. It skids to a halt directly in front of the warehouse entrance, the driver executing a perfect J-turn that positions the car as a barrier.

"We've got company," I report, adjusting my scope for a better view of the new arrival.

Ryan's voice comes through my earpiece, tense but controlled. "It's Matteo."

That means the match between him and Killian is over. Killian should be here shortly, too.

The driver's door of the car swings open, and Matteo emerges, dressed in a hoodie and boxing shorts.

"I need a clear shot," I mutter into the comm, readjusting my placement. The sleek contours of the sedan create a perfect barrier between my crosshairs and Matteo's chest.

I watch as the warehouse door bursts open. Zach appears, but Cassie isn't with him.

"I have visual on Zach," I report, my breath fogging the edge of my scope in the night air. "He left Cassie inside, holding off Matteo from entering."

"Fuck," Ryan hisses through the comm. I can hear the helplessness in his voice. "I don't have a shot. His car is blocking my line."

I track Zach through as he engages with Matteo and his men. Three hostiles converge on him from different angles, forcing him toward the loading bay. He pivots, dropping one man with a double-tap to the chest. But there's a calculation in the way Matteo's men are moving—they're not just shooting wildly. They're herding him away from the entrance.

"Zach's being flanked," I report. "They're boxing him in."

Through my crosshairs, I watch Zach register the trap too

late. A burst of gunfire forces him to dive behind a stack of abandoned pallets.

Matteo seizes his opportunity, like a predator sensing weakness as he moves toward the warehouse entrance.

"Matteo's moving to the entrance," I report, my finger tensing on the trigger. "I don't have a clean shot."

"Connor!" Ryan's voice explodes in my ear, raw with desperation. "Cover me! I'm going in!"

"Copy that," I respond, shifting my position to get a better angle.

I track Ryan, peering with my scope. His body stays low, using the shadows between streetlights as camouflage.

I center my crosshairs on a man positioned near the loading dock, his attention fixed on Zach's position. The distance is roughly four hundred meters—a challenging shot for most, but routine for me. I control my breathing, letting the world narrow down to just my heartbeat and the target. I pull the trigger softly, and not a second later, he drops to the ground.

"We've got another vehicle approaching hot." Side's voice crackles urgently through the comm. "Southeast entrance, moving fast."

The sound of screeching tires, the high-pitched wail of rubber burning against asphalt, cuts through the night. A black Dodge Charger comes hurtling around the corner, headlights off. The vehicle fishtails wildly, the back end swinging out in controlled chaos before the driver rights it, sending a spray of dust into the air.

"Hold your fire!" I bark into the comm, my finger easing off the trigger. "That's Killian!"

The driver's door flies open before the dust has settled,

and Killian emerges like a dark apparition, sprinting toward the warehouse door.

I swing my rifle to the warehouse, searching for any sign of movement. The crosshairs slide across broken windows and crumbling concrete until I catch it—a flash of motion. Ryan —but he's not alone.

Through my scope, I see Cassie in his arms, her blonde hair unmistakable. Ryan holds her protectively, his arms wrapped around her as she presses her face to his chest. Relief floods through me.

Matteo's body lies sprawled on the concrete, his hoodie now dark with a spreading stain as the blood saturates it. His eyes stare sightlessly upward, mouth slightly open in what might have been his final gasp. Either Ryan or Cassie must have shot him.

I watch as Killian sprints toward them. He reaches them in seconds, enfolding both Ryan and Cassie in his embrace.

The sight of their reunion sends a wave of relief through me, so powerful it's almost dizzying. But I can't afford to relax, not yet. Not until I know everyone's status.

"All teams, check in," I say into the comm, my voice steady despite the adrenaline still coursing through my veins. "A team, report condition."

"Johnson here. I'm good."

"Woods, all clear."

"Sides checking in. No injuries."

"B team, report condition," I say.

One by one, my Irish sharpshooters respond.

"Doyle. I'm fine."

"Sullivan. All good, boss."

"Flanagan. Ready for a pint, but otherwise intact."

I allow myself a small smile at Flanagan's typical response. Even during a gunfight, he never loses his sense of humor.

"Zach?" I call, scanning the area where I'd last seen him pinned down.

"I'm good," he replies, his voice a bit winded, but still reassuring. "Just a scratch. Nothing worth mentioning."

"Then why'd you mention it?" I chuckle, a mixture of relief and amusement in my tone.

"Dick," he retorts playfully.

I laugh again. Despite having met the man today, I feel an unexpected camaraderie with him. There's something about facing death together that forges bonds quickly. My Irish team meshed seamlessly with his American crew—professionals recognizing professionals. No ego battles, no territorial pissing contests. Just men doing what they do best.

It's rare in our world. Usually when families or crews come together, there's tension, suspicion. But Zach's men follow his lead without question, just as mine follow me. And watching him move—the precision, the calm under pressure—I know why. He's earned their loyalty the same way I've earned mine.

Chapter Twelve

CONNOR

Bodies litter the warehouse perimeter, and the cleanup team moves with practiced efficiency—dissolving evidence, collecting shell casings, and removing any trace of our presence. The interior has been cleared except for Victor and Cassie, having their private moment of closure with Matteo's body.

Through the grimy window, I watch Victor's shoulders shake as her hand rests on his back.

I can't imagine what's churning inside him. His own son orchestrated this entire nightmare—not just to seize power, but to systematically eliminate his own family. His sister first, then Victor himself.

Victor kneels beside his son's body, but I recognize the complexity in his grief. He's not mourning the man his son became. He mourns the little boy he dreamed would carry his legacy with honor.

I turn away from the window, letting them have their

moment. My phone buzzes with a message from our extraction team—five minutes until we need to clear out completely.

Zach strides over to the black sedan that was Matteo's, yanking open the driver's door to check the interior. He whistles low, running his hand appreciatively over the leather dashboard. "What should we do with the car?" he asks, looking back at Killian and Ryan.

Killian walks over, his face still flushed from the exertion of his fight. "We need to get rid of it completely. Chop it up. Last thing we want is this vehicle being tracked back to us." He kicks the tire with distaste. "The problem is, our guy's shop is closed until after New Year's. We'll have to store it until then."

"That's two weeks away," Ryan says with disappointment in his voice.

I step forward, an idea forming. "Actually, I've got an option. There's a steel barge leaving for Dublin tomorrow night. Customs has already cleared the cargo's manifest." I pull out my phone, scrolling through my contacts. "My guy Liam runs the loading dock. If we can get this to the shipyard by morning, he'll make sure it gets crushed and buried in the hold."

Ryan glances at Killian. "What do you think?"

Killian nods decisively. "Do it. That car needs to disappear." He turns to Zach, who's still admiring the vehicle's interior. "Follow Connor to the pier and give him a ride back once he's done."

"Sure thing, boss," he accepts, stepping away from the sedan. He tosses me a casual salute. "I'll be right behind you."

"I'll make the call on the way," I say, already dialing Liam's number as I slide into the driver's seat.

The leather interior still holds his scent—expensive cologne mingled with the metallic tang of blood and sweat from his boxing match. I grimace, rolling down the window to let in the cool night air. The engine purrs to life with a satisfying rumble. The dashboard lights up with a soft orange glow.

He answers on the fifth ring, his voice thick with sleep. "Connor? It's two in the bloody morning."

"I need a favor," I say, pulling away from the warehouse, checking my rearview mirror to confirm Zach is following in his vehicle.

"A favor at this hour better involve either a beautiful woman or a lot of money," he grumbles.

"How about a beautiful car?" I reply, accelerating onto the empty streets. "Need a luxury sedan to disappear. Permanently. Can you get it on tomorrow's Dublin shipment?"

There's a pause, then a heavy sigh. "Loading starts at seven." I hear rustling on the other end—sheets being pushed aside, feet hitting the floor.

"I'm on my way now. I'll make it worth your trouble," I promise, taking a sharp turn toward the shipyard. "Double your usual rate."

Liam chuckles. "For you, O'Brady? Triple. And I want a bottle of Midleton Very Rare."

"Done," I agree without hesitation, knowing he won't take my money anyway. I will bring him that whiskey another day, though. "I'll be at the east gate in twenty minutes."

"See you there," he says, fully awake now. "Slip seventeen."

I hang up and toss the phone onto the passenger seat, letting my mind drift as I navigate the empty pre-dawn streets.

The job's done. Matteo's dead. Cassie's safe.

I'm torn between staying in New York to strengthen the bond with my brother and moving on. On the one hand, the idea of building something meaningful with him is enticing. We've lost so many years over my resentment toward him. On the other hand, he and Killian are still navigating their new relationship with Cassie, creating a life together, and I don't want to become an intrusive "fourth wheel" in their lives.

Miami's an option. But the relentless sunshine would wear me down. I'm not used to that much sun.

California's got better weather balance, but the west coast scene is too crowded with people looking to reinvent themselves.

Then there's Boston and the hunt to find Merlot.

A soft thump interrupts my thoughts.

I frown, glancing in the rearview mirror at the empty backseat. There it is again—a dull, rhythmic sound coming from behind me.

I ease my foot off the accelerator, rolling up the window to block out the street noise. The thumping continues, more distinct now. Knocks, followed by silence, then repeated. Surely it can't be anything wrong with the car. I didn't think it got hit with bullets, but maybe I missed it on inspection.

The sound comes again.

It's coming from the trunk.

My hand instinctively moves to the holster under my jacket, fingers wrapping around the grip of my Glock. I check the mirror again—Zach is still following two car lengths back, his headlights steady in the darkness.

The thumping grows more insistent—louder.

"Shit," I mutter, pulling the car to the side of the road. This is the last complication we need tonight.

Someone's in the fucking trunk.

The trunk's pounding intensifies—whoever's trapped inside knows we've stopped.

I open the driver's door, getting out of the car just as Zach pulls up and gets out as well. He starts to ask what I'm doing, but I silence him with a curt signal.

I press my finger to my lips, then point toward the trunk. His eyes widen as he draws his pistol and moves to the passenger side, creating a crossfire position.

We communicate silently with hand signals—three fingers, then a closed fist. A countdown.

Three.

Two.

One.

I press the trunk release button on the key fob, my gun trained steadily on the opening lid. The hydraulics hiss as the trunk door slowly rises.

My finger eases slightly on the trigger, but I maintain my aim as it fully opens.

Curled inside, her wrists and ankles bound with zip ties, is...

"Merlot?" I say, at the same time Zach says "Kim!"

Kim?

For a moment, time freezes. My brain can't process what my eyes are seeing. The woman from Boston—the one I haven't been able to forget—is bound in Matteo Valentino's trunk. And somehow Zach knows her.

Before I can even react, Zach holsters his weapon and pulls out a tactical knife, rushing forward. "Jesus Christ. I've been texting you all day." His voice breaks with emotion as he saws through the zip ties binding her wrists.

The moment her hands are free, her fingers instinctively dart to the thick tape sealing her lips. With a determined tug, she peels it away, a muffled whimper escaping from her throat.

I remain rooted in place, my gun still half-raised, mind reeling. She blinks against the sudden streetlight, her eyes adjusting to the darkness. When she recognizes me, her expression shifts from fear to confusion.

Tell me about it. You're confused? I'm fucking confused.

She winces as circulation returns to her limbs. Despite everything, she looks relatively unharmed. Her makeup is smudged around her eyes where mascara streaks her cheeks from dried tears. She's wearing a short black dress that's torn at the neckline and hem, revealing a few scratches on her upper thigh. But there's no blood—physically, she seems intact.

Zach reaches into the trunk, sliding one arm beneath her knees and the other around her back, lifting her out. As her bare feet touch the pavement, she sways unsteadily, her legs numb from being confined in that small space for who knows how long.

"I've got you," he says, steadying her with his hands on her waist. She takes a tentative step, wincing.

He pulls her against his chest, his arms circling her protectively. She melts into him, her body shuddering with what might be relief or delayed shock, but her eyes—those eyes I'd dreamed about for weeks—remain locked on mine over his shoulder.

I holster my weapon, suddenly feeling like an intruder in an intimate moment. My throat is dry, words failing me entirely.

"How did you—" Zach starts, pulling back just enough to look at her face while keeping his arms firmly around her waist. "Matteo had you? This whole time?"

She nods, her voice hoarse when she finally speaks. "He grabbed me when I left for coffee this morning." Her eyes widen. "Cassie? Is she—"

"Safe," he confirms. "With Killian and Ryan. Matteo is dead."

The relief on her face is palpable, like someone who's been holding their breath underwater and finally breaks the surface.

Then her eyes find mine again. "Connor," she whispers, my name escaping her lips like a desperate plea, ragged with emotion.

The woman I'd spent one unforgettable night with in Boston—thinking she was just Merlot, a beautiful stranger—is somehow tangled up in all this. In my brother's world. In Zach's life.

"You two know each other?" Zach asks, his voice sharp with sudden suspicion as his eyes dart between us.

I clear my throat, struggling to find words that won't make this situation awkward. "We've met," I say carefully, the understatement of the century.

"In Boston," she adds quietly. "When I was visiting my mom. How do you know Zach?"

"I'm Ryan's brother," I answer.

"Oh," she says softly.

My mind races with questions. How does she know Zach? What's her connection to Matteo? To all of this?

"Why would Matteo kidnap you?" I ask, my voice coming out rougher than intended. The coincidence seems impossible —that she would end up in his trunk on the night we take him down.

Her eyes dart to Zach, then back to me. She shifts her weight, wincing slightly as she does.

"I was Matteo's girlfriend," she mumbles. "*Fake* girlfriend," she adds.

Zach's arm tightens around her waist. "She called me after she heard about Matteo's attempt to kill Cassie where Ryan got shot—wanted to help."

A wry, humorless smile twists her lips. "Turns out he's not big on disloyal girlfriends, even when the entire relationship was just for show." She brushes a strand of hair from her face with trembling fingers. "Who knew crime lords were so sensitive about fake breakups?"

Zach's brow furrows. "What do you mean?"

"He wasn't just angry that I talked to Killian and Ryan," Kim replies. "He found out I closed the checking account. And that I had..." She glances at Zach, something vulnerable flickering across her face. "That I had moved in with you. He had someone watching me."

His expression softens, his thumb unconsciously tracing circles on her arm.

She turns to me. "He knew about Boston, too." Her voice drops to barely above a whisper. "About us."

Us. The word echoes in my mind, stirring up memories of tangled sheets and whispered confessions in a hotel room.

Is there really an "us" to speak of? When I woke up the

next morning to an empty bed and no note, I'd assumed she wanted to forget it had ever happened. Now she's acknowledging what happened between us openly in front of Zach.

She's not hiding it. Not trying to pretend it never happened. But why bring it up now, with her... boyfriend? Partner? Whatever he is to her standing right beside her?

Zach's expression darkens as the implication of her words sinks in. His arm drops from her waist, and he takes a half-step back.

The tension between us thickens. She shivers in the night air, wrapping her arms around herself.

His jaw works as he processes everything, then his expression softens. He steps forward, closing the distance he'd created between them.

"Hey," he says, his voice gentle as he takes her hands in his. "Matteo's dead. He can't hurt you—or anyone—ever again." His thumbs brush over her knuckles. "It's over."

Her shoulders slump with visible relief, but there's still a tremor in her body that speaks of shock and trauma. A tear escapes down her cheek, which she quickly wipes away.

"We should get you to a hospital," Zach continues, his eyes scanning her body for injuries. "You need to be checked out."

"No." She shakes her head immediately, pulling back slightly. "I'm fine, really. Just some bruises and—I just want to go home, take a shower, and forget this ever happened." Her voice cracks on the last word.

"Kim," his voice is firm but kind. "You were bound in a trunk for hours. You should be examined."

"He's right," I interject. "Shock can mask serious injuries. You should get checked out."

"Okay," she whispers. The fight seems to drain out of her all at once.

"Let's drop the car off at the dock as planned, then I'll take you both to the hospital," I say, my eyes meeting Zach's over her head. An understanding passes between us—Kim's well-being.

He nods, his jaw tight. "We'll follow in my car."

He guides her to his sedan, his hand protectively at the small of her back. As he opens the door for her, she hesitates, glancing back at me.

"Thank you," she breathes, the words meant for me alone.

I nod, not trusting myself to speak. As she slides into the passenger seat, I glimpse her profile illuminated by the dashboard lights—the same delicate curve of her cheek that I'd traced with my fingertips that night in Boston. The memories crash over me with renewed intensity—her contagious laughter, her whispers, the way she'd looked at me like I was the only man in the world. *But I'm not the only man in the world—am I?*

I slide back into the sedan, gripping the steering wheel until my knuckles turn white. The engine starts, but I sit motionless for a moment, watching in the rearview mirror as Zach closes the door and walks around to the driver's side.

His expression is unreadable, but the tension in his shoulders tells me everything I need to know. Whatever relationship exists between him and Kim—it's complicated.

I pull back onto the deserted street, with Zach following close behind. My mind races faster than the car I'm driving, piecing together what I've learned. She's involved with Zach somehow—living with him, apparently—but a detail of their interaction strikes me as oddly platonic. There was concern and protection, but not the passionate reunion I'd expect between lovers during a crisis.

They hadn't kissed. Not once. Just embraced, like... friends.

Something clicks into place inside me, a decision forming with the kind of certainty I haven't felt since walking out of my father's study that day in Dublin.

I'm staying in New York.

The way she looked at me, the way she'd said my name— there is still something there, something unfinished between us. One night in Boston wasn't enough. I want more. I need more.

Chapter Thirteen

KIMBERLY

"Home sweet home," Zach says, flicking on the lights and stepping aside to let me in.

I manage a smile and walk past him, clutching the paper sack of prescriptions we picked up at the all-night pharmacy. The doctor had assured me nothing was broken—just bruised.

I drag myself toward the bathroom. The moment I close the door behind me, I catch my reflection in the mirror. A stranger stares back—hair matted with sweat, mascara smudged.

The water hisses as I turn the shower to its hottest setting. Steam fills the small space, and I peel off my clothes, wincing at certain movements. Every inch of my body aches from being crammed in that trunk, my muscles still remembering the contorted position I'd been forced into for hours.

Under the scalding spray, I scrub until my skin turns red, but I can't wash away the memories. The image of Killian and Matteo circling each other in the boxing ring—being forced to watch a fight between two of Matteo's big goons, knowing the whole time that he had been planning to kill Cassie from the beginning. The image of Matteo grabbing my arm and dragging me to the parking lot—but this time, he wanted me to get in the trunk, not the passenger seat where I always sat, including earlier tonight. I protested and pleaded for any humanity in him to not put me in there. And with a silent nod to his goons, they stuck me with a needle. I woke up bound by zip ties and with tape over my mouth.

I turn off the water because it's beginning to run cold.

The truck—the darkness, the suffocating heat. The way my lungs burned with each labored breath through my nose.

But I'd never felt such a surge of adrenaline. One moment I was half-dead, the next I was trying to kick and claw my way out like a woman possessed. My body hurt everywhere, but something inside me had snapped back into place. A switch had flipped. I would not be a victim anymore.

The car had come to a stop. Suddenly, I was second-guessing myself. *What the fuck was I planning to do with my hands and feet tied? Stupid Kim.* I should have figured that part out before kicking the car and letting the driver know I was awake.

But it was too late. I listened carefully as I heard the car door open and two sets of footsteps approach. Then there was light, blinding and harsh, as the trunk popped open. But my eyes didn't adjust to see Matteo's ugly fucking goons like I expected. Instead, I saw Zach's face, then Connor's.

I wrap a towel around myself, a small smile crossing my lips. A part of me had hoped Zach would come for me. And he did—he found me, even by accident.

But Connor? That was a shock. I'd convinced myself I'd

never see him again. Not that I wouldn't want to see him again. That was the lie I'd been telling myself all along, that I shouldn't see him again.

I press my forehead against the cool bathroom mirror, trying to sort through the tangle of emotions between Zach and Connor.

A knock startles me.

"Kim? Are you okay in there?" It's Zach's voice, concerned.

"Yeah, I'm fine," I call back. "I'll be out in a minute."

I slip into the T-shirt and shorts I grabbed earlier. Taking a deep breath, I open the door.

His hair is damp and tousled, and he's wearing fresh clothes. The scent of his soap mingles with the steam from my shower. He must have used the guest bathroom while I was lost in thought during mine.

"Hey," he mumbles.

Without thinking, I take his hand. "Come here."

I lead him to his bed, my bare feet padding across the hardwood floor. When we reach the mattress, I gently tug him beside me. The mattress dips under our weight as we lie facing each other, close enough that I can see the flecks of gold in his blue eyes.

"I never thanked you properly," I say, my fingers finding his.

"You don't have to—"

"No, I do." My voice strengthens. "You saved my life tonight, Zach. You found me when I thought I was going to die."

His eyes soften, but a hint of amusement plays at the corners of his mouth. "Finding you was pure dumb luck."

He told me earlier that they were on their way to get rid of the car for good. They would have crushed it into a metal cube and shipped it to Ireland with me inside.

If Connor hadn't noticed my kicking, I would have been one very compact—and dead—Kim.

I squeeze his hand, smiling despite the morbid thought. "Maybe it was luck. But you still found me. I think... maybe you were meant to." He raises an eyebrow. "Fate, destiny, whatever you want to call it." I shrug.

His expression shifts, his eyes darkening with what looks like guilt. He sits up slightly, running a hand through his damp hair.

"Kim, I... I'm so sorry." His voice is thick with emotion. "I was so fixated on Cassie, on finding her for them. I just assumed..." He trails off, then meets my gaze directly. "I thought you weren't texting me back because you were mad at me for canceling coffee. It never occurred to me that Matteo would take both of you. I should have realized you were in danger, too."

"Zach, stop." I shake my head. "You couldn't have known."

I take a deep breath, knowing I need to clear the air between us.

"Besides, I'm the one who should apologize. About the other night—" I pause, gathering my thoughts. "It was all a big misunderstanding. When you asked me to dinner, I acted weird about it." I look at our still-intertwined fingers. "I wanted to go—I really did. I just didn't want you to feel like you had to take me out because you were already doing so much for me."

"I was just thinking that after all the shit you've been through, a nice night out of the house would have been good."

I nod. "Yeah, I could've used that. We both could've."

The silence settles comfortably between us for a moment before Zach shifts, his expression curious.

"So... Connor," he says, his tone casual but interested. "What's going on with you and O'Brady?" His eyes search mine, not accusatory, just genuinely wanting to understand.

Heat rises to my cheeks, and I sigh. "A one-night stand. I bumped into him on the street—literally. Let him buy me a drink at a bar. I never gave him my name."

"Wait, what?" He props himself up on one elbow.

"I told him to call me Merlot," I say with a cringe. "So, he's used that and a couple of other wine varieties."

I can't control the grin that takes over my face as I think about our time together.

"You like him," he says. It's a statement, not a question.

I swallow hard, then nod my head, unable to deny it. My heart races as I gather my courage to speak. "But I also like you, Zach. Actually, I love you— and the thought of loving anyone, that scares the hell out of me," I whisper, unable to meet his eyes. My fingers tremble against his.

Zach stays silent, giving me space to continue.

"I've never had a real relationship before," I admit, my voice barely audible. "Twenty-six years old, and I've never been in a relationship. Not one. I've had flings, one-night stands, casual things that never went anywhere because I made sure they didn't. I always kept people at arm's length because..." I pause, swallowing hard. I don't finish my sentence because I truly don't know why I'm like this. I finally look up at him, my eyes stinging with tears I refuse to let fall. "I don't know if I'm ready for what this could become, Zach. But that doesn't change how my heart races when you walk into a room, or how safe I feel when you're near me, or our obvious attraction."

He shifts closer, his warmth radiating toward me. His eyes hold mine with an intensity that makes my breath catch.

"Kim," he whispers, "I love you, too." His thumb traces the outline of my jaw. "I think a part of me has always loved you, even before I understood what that meant."

My heart hammers against my ribs as his words sink in.

"I'm not going anywhere," he continues, his voice steady despite the emotion I can see swimming in his eyes. "There's no rush, no timeline. I'll wait as long as you need—months, years, whatever it takes. I just want to be in your life, however you'll have me."

The sincerity in his voice makes my throat tighten. "I'm not asking you to wait for me." But even as I say that, I don't like the thought of him being with anyone else, which is hypocritical because I can see myself with Zach, but also Connor.

"I know." He smiles, that crooked smile that makes my stomach flip.

Something changes in his expression. Without a word, he shifts, positioning himself above me, his weight supported on his forearms. His hand gently cups my cheek.

"Is this okay?" he whispers, his breath warm against my lips.

I nod again, and he nudges my legs apart with his knee, settling his hips between my thighs.

"You're mine, Babygirl," he murmurs, his lips hovering

inches from mine and his voice low and rich. There's no jealousy or possessiveness in his tone—just raw desire.

I want to be his. But before today, I thought I'd never see Connor again. Fate keeps bringing me these two men, and now I feel like I have to choose.

His lips crash against mine, soft at first, then hungrier as my body responds to his touch. My hands find his shoulders, then his hair, threading my fingers through the short, damp strands. His tongue teases the seam of my lips before delving inside, exploring with deliberate strokes. I arch into him, feeling the weight of his body pinning me deliciously to the mattress.

"Wine names, huh?" he murmurs against my mouth, pulling back to see my face. There's a playful glint in his look. "What did he call you? Riesling?"

I roll my eyes but can't help smiling. "Rosé, actually."

"Fancy," Zach comments, dropping slow kisses along my jaw. "Did you let him call you that while he touched you?" His fingers trail down my side, slipping under my shirt to caress the bare skin of my waist. "Did he touch you like this?" he taunts and moves his hand underneath my pajama shorts, fingering my pussy.

I gasp, half from his touch and half from his words.

"And what did he do to make such an impression that you're still smiling about it weeks later?"

His tone is light, teasing, but there's something possessive in the way his fingers are moving in and out of me.

"Exactly what you're doing now," I whisper, remembering how Connor was so skilled. Apparently—Zach is too. "You're both good with your fingers."

"Fuck," he says, his touch making me temporarily forget my name—where I'm at—the shit that went down tonight.

"Just my fingers, huh?" he whispers, his breath hot against my ear. His fingers curl inside me, finding a spot that makes me grip the sheets. "What else did he do that got you so worked up?"

I close my eyes, embarrassed but aroused by his teasing. The way he's talking about Connor while touching me feels forbidden—exciting. His thumb circles my clit with precise pressure, making it impossible to think straight. I bite my lip, trying to hold back a moan.

"Did he make you come like this?" he asks. "Or is he one of those guys who's all about himself?" His lips brush against my neck, leaving a trail of goosebumps.

"He was..." I start, but my words dissolve into a whimper as Zach increases his tempo.

"He was what?" he presses, slowing his movements deliberately, denying me the orgasm I want. "Did you scream his name while he fucked you?"

My breath catches in my throat. The way Zach is talking—it's not jealous or angry. There's something darkly arousing about how he's using Connor to push me closer to the edge.

"Zach, please..." I beg.

"My girl knows who's touching her now, doesn't she?"

I nod my head rapidly. "Fuck, Zach, let me come."

"You will," he declares, his fingers slowing, and it frustrates me further internally. "But on my cock."

In one swift movement, he pulls out of me, and I whimper at the loss that leaves me feeling empty and aching. His hands move to the hem of my shirt, pulling it over my head in one fluid motion. The cool air hits my bare skin, making my nipples harden instantly. His eyes darken as he takes in the sight of me.

"Fuck, you're beautiful," he breathes, lowering his head to take one peaked nub into his mouth.

I gasp, arching into him as his tongue swirls around the sensitive bud. My hands fumble with his shirt, desperate to feel his skin against mine. He helps me, breaking contact just long enough to pull it off before returning the attention to my breasts.

"I need you," I whisper, my fingers tracing the defined muscles of his abdomen, feeling them tense under my touch. "Please, Zach."

He hooks his fingers into my shorts, dragging them down my legs along with my underwear. The cool air of the bedroom hits my exposed skin, making me shiver—or maybe it's anticipation.

He strips off the rest of his clothes with hurried movements, revealing the hard planes of his chest and a canvas of detailed tattoos, along with the trail of dark hair leading to his impressive cock. I gasp as he lowers his body over mine and pushes himself inside me. My back arches off the bed, my nails digging into his shoulders as my body stretches to accommodate him.

"This body—" Thrust. "Your pussy—" Thrust. "Is mine," he growls, his voice raw with desire, with another thrust. "Say it, Kim."

"Yours," I breathe, my fingers gripping his thick, muscled waist. "I'm yours, Zach."

He withdraws almost completely before slamming back into me, setting a rhythm that has me seeing stars while the headboard knocks against the wall. Each thrust is deliberate, claiming, marking me from the inside out. The sound of skin against skin fills the room as he sets a punishing pace. My legs wrap around his waist, pulling him deeper as my heels dig into his back.

"No one gets to see you like this—fuck you like this—unless I say," he tells me, his breath close to my ear. His words are a raw act of possession.

I smile up toward the ceiling, thinking about his words. He didn't tell me I couldn't be with anyone else. Just unless he says...

"Harder," I breathe out, rushed.

Something primal flashes in his eyes, and he somehow gives me what I want despite his already rough thrusts.

I'm lost in sensation as he drives into me, his powerful thrusts making the entire bed shake. My fingernails rake down his back, leaving marks I know he'll wear proudly tomorrow. The pressure builds inside me, a coiling tension that threatens to snap with every movement of his hips.

"I'm close," I pant, my voice barely recognizable to my own ears.

Zach slows unexpectedly, his rhythm changing from frantic to deliberate. I whimper in protest, my body aching for release. But then he shifts his weight to one arm. His free hand cups my cheek, thumb brushing across my lower lip with unexpected tenderness.

"Look at me," he orders softly. "I want to see your eyes when you come."

I force my heavy lids open, meeting his intense gaze. What I see there catches me off guard—beyond the possessiveness is a man who's vulnerable.

"Come for me," he commands, his voice strained. His

movements pick back up, and he grips my hips, fingers digging into my skin. "Come around my cock."

I shatter beneath him, crying out his name as my body clenches around him and my orgasm pulses through me. He follows moments later, his rhythm faltering as he buries himself deep inside me, groaning my name against my neck as he comes.

We collapse against each other, our breathing ragged, bodies slick with sweat. He rolls to his side, taking me with him. He doesn't withdraw, keeping us connected as he wraps his muscular arms around me. His fingers trace idle patterns on my damp skin, and I nestle my head against his chest, listening to his heartbeat slowly return to normal.

For a while, we lie there, limbs tangled, exchanging soft kisses that gradually slow as exhaustion claims us. The weight of everything—Matteo, the kidnappings, the emotional revelations—is lifted after much-needed, mind-blowing sex.

I study his face, the sharp angles softened by sleep, his dark lashes fanned against his cheeks. In sleep, the hardened protector dissolves, leaving behind a vulnerability that makes my heart ache.

I trace the outline of his jaw with my fingertip, barely touching, not wanting to wake him, this man who saved me in more ways than one. This man who wants me to be *his*?

"I love you," I whisper to a sleeping Zach.

Chapter Fourteen

ZACH

Morning sunlight filters through half-closed blinds, casting golden stripes across the rumpled sheets. I slowly regain consciousness. My arm is draped over something warm —someone warm. Kim. Her dark hair is spread over the pillow, her breathing deep and peaceful.

For a moment, I simply watch her, tracing the delicate curve of her shoulder with my gaze. Memories of last night flood back—vividly.

While I'm confident she wants me—she's admitted that she loves me— she's interested in Connor, too. *But what does that mean?*

I feel a tightness in my chest at the thought. Jealousy? Fear? I'm not sure.

He's charming, with his easy smile and self-assured swagger.

That's not me. I'm all rough edges.

When I walk into a room, people notice—not because I

command attention like he does, but because something in their primitive brain says "danger."

I glance at the intricate sleeve covering my left arm, the black ink stark against my white skin. Each tattoo marks a moment, a memory, sometimes a mistake. I wonder what Kim sees when she looks at them. Does she find my roughness appealing, or is it just a novelty compared to Connor's clean-cut charm?

I run my fingers lightly across the skin of her back, feeling the contrast between her softness and my calloused hands. Would she prefer his touch?

She stirs beside me, her eyelids fluttering. I hold my breath, not ready for this moment to end.

She stretches like a cat waking from a nap. Her eyes open slowly and focus on me. "Hey," she whispers, her voice still husky with sleep.

"Morning," I respond, pushing my insecurities down where they belong.

She reaches up to trace the inked patterns on my chest, following the dark lines with curious fingertips. "What are you thinking about? You look serious."

I consider lying, but something about the vulnerability of the moment makes me honest. "Just wondering what you see in me."

She props herself up, drawing the sheet around her like armor and creating a barrier between us that wasn't there moments before.

"What's wrong?" I ask, trying to keep my voice level despite the sudden knot of anxiety in my stomach.

"Nothing," she says. "Are you thinking that because you're regretting it?"

Me? She thinks I'm the one regretting it? I give her a look of confusion, and maybe she can sense my uneasiness, but that is about something else. "I genuinely want to know, and I thought you'd be the one regretting it."

"Oh," she says, her straight-lined lips curling into a smile. "You really want to know?"

I nod, not trusting my voice.

"I see someone who doesn't pretend," she states. Her hand returns to my chest, palm flat against my heartbeat. "When you're angry, you're angry. When you care, you care completely. There's no filter, no games. I love and appreciate that about you."

I swallow hard. "Some people call that just being an asshole."

She laughs, the sound warming me from within. "Your asshole moments speak to mine. I know many people who would label me a bitch." Her face goes serious, then her eyebrow raises. "I guess growing up like we did hardened us."

I nod in agreement.

"Kim..." I clear my throat. "I want to talk about Connor. You never thought you'd see him again. But now, you have."

Her fingers freeze against my chest, and I can feel her heartbeat quicken through her palm. A heavy silence stretches between us, thick with unspoken truths.

"No, I didn't think I would," she finally admits, her voice barely above a whisper. She shifts away slightly.

"That doesn't mean you never thought about him." I say, remembering the pictures she drew of a bar. That had to be Connor.

I swallow hard, waiting for her to continue, afraid to interrupt whatever confession is about to pour from her lips.

"When he and I were together that night in Boston," she continues, "it was intense and unexpected. We connected in a way I hadn't expected. Actually—I probably shouldn't speak for him. I connected in a way I hadn't expected," she admits, almost looking disappointed at the thought that he may not have thought as much about her as she did about him. Her gaze drops to the twisted sheets between us. "I was involved with Matteo, and it was a risk. But then I got back to New York—and as fate would have it—back to you. I—I'm torn, Zach. I feel I'm not in the right place for a relationship with anyone. You or Connor. But I find myself drawn to you, and I don't want to be without you, either."

She wants to be with me, but she also doesn't want to be with me. *I guess in the heat of the moment, I can call this woman mine, but she really isn't mine at all, is she?* I want to call Kim mine—no question. But she won't commit. I meant what I said about waiting for her. *But what if she chooses him?*

"Last night was..." she says before biting her lip, hiding a smile.

"Amazing?" I offer.

"Yes," she whispers. "And I realize that I'm not giving you any clarity. But I know I want to do that again..." She trails off before taking my lips with hers.

My phone beeps on the nightstand, interrupting us.

I sigh and turn around to look at it. It's a text message from Killian.

Debrief in thirty. My office. Bring Kim.

I take a deep breath, turning back to Kim. "We have to go meet Killian for a debrief of last night."

She groans before snuggling into me some more. "Do we have to?"

"I wish we didn't." I would stay in bed all day with her if I could.

When we get up to Killian's office, Connor is standing outside his door.

"Well, if it isn't my favorite Cabernet," he jests, his eyes lighting up when they land on Kim.

"Connor." She breathes his name like it's something precious.

Her cheeks flush a delicate pink, and her smile—that smile —it's different from the ones she gives to everyone else. A smile I've seen only given to me. I watch as her eyes dart to the floor, then back up to his face, like they can't decide where to settle.

I stand beside her, suddenly hyper-aware of the space between us, of how we're not touching when just an hour ago we were wrapped around each other with nothing between our skin.

"Ah, Zachary," he says, finally acknowledging me, using my full name with a nod. "Good to see you again." His voice carries the perfect balance of friendliness and professional distance, making it impossible to detect any hint of rivalry or tension.

An awkward silence falls over us. I'm acutely aware of how she is standing slightly closer to me than to him, but her body is angled toward him. Maybe I'm overthinking it.

Before I can respond, Killian's door swings open. He

stands there in his crisp suit, looking more like a Wall Street executive than the head of an organized crime family. "Good, you're all here," he says, stepping aside to let us in. "We have matters to discuss."

We settle into the chairs across from his large wooden desk, Kim in the middle chair while Connor takes the far right one, stretching his long legs casually.

"Kim, glad to see you are okay," Killian says. "I'm sorry that you got mixed up in all this."

"That's what I get for sleeping with the enemy," Kim jokes, but instantly looks embarrassed. "Fuck—that's not what I meant." She looks between the three of us. "I never slept with him. It's an expression? Shit... I'm going to shut up now." She sinks into her chair.

"How is Cassie?" Connor asks.

"She's good. Sleeping in with Ryan," Killian confirms.

"I'm glad everything worked out, and Matteo is gone," Kim says.

"About that," he says, his voice dropping to a more serious tone.

He taps a few keys on his computer, and the monitor screen switches to the news headlines from various outlets:

MATTEO VALENTINO, HEIR TO VALENTINO FORTUNE, DISAPPEARS WITH LOVER, NO SUSPICION OF FOUL PLAY

Killian rises from his chair and moves to the window, standing in front of it in the sunlight. "Officially, as far as the public world is concerned, Matteo Valentino has disappeared, along with his lover, Charlie," he explains, turning back to face us. "Not dead—disappeared. There's an important distinction there that we need to maintain. Victor gave his blessing. This is how he wants us to roll with it. But in our world, other crime families will know that it's fake—see right through it. That makes this a vulnerable time—"

"Depending on how big of balls your enemies have," Kim mutters under her breath, though it was still clearly heard.

I smile at how sassy and blunt she is. I look over at Connor and he seems to appreciate it, too, with a smirk on his face.

"Yes, exactly," Killian acknowledges with a hint of a smile. "Everyone should still be on high alert. At least for a while, to see if anyone tries to overthrow Valentino's place or gain the territories."

Killian moves back to his desk, his fingers grabbing a slim black folder and opening it, laying it out on the desk. There are photos—paparazzi shots of Kim and Matteo at various events, their staged intimacy captured from all angles.

"This is where it gets complicated," Killian says, spreading the photos across the desk. "The story we're putting out is that Matteo is taking some time away from public life to deal with personal matters. No foul play, no drama—just a wealthy businessman who needs space."

Kim leans forward, picking up one photo of her and Matteo at a charity gala, his arm possessively around her waist, her smile perfect but never reaching her eyes. Her fingers tremble slightly before she sets it down. A bad memory, perhaps?

"And what's my role in this fairy tale?" she asks, her voice steady despite the tension in her shoulders.

"You're the heartbroken girlfriend, since you have been seen with him out in public. The story is that you and Matteo were in a committed relationship that ended amicably the night of his... disappearance. The one who had no idea he was planning to step away with a secret lover. You noticed nothing unusual about his behavior, no indications of trouble. As far as you knew, he was just a normal businessman with normal business concerns."

She nods in agreement. This is a lot of responsibility for her, but we need to be prepared in case the police or someone else, maybe a business associate of his, comes looking for Matteo.

Connor clears his throat. "And how would you explain the fact that she is living with Zach?"

"Kim is my stepsister," I throw out there. "Even though our parents divorced years ago, she's staying with her stepbrother because her current living situation is bad. She never lived with Matteo."

Connor smiles, taking in this new information. "Fair enough."

Killian nods, satisfied with my explanation for Kim's current housing. His attention turns to Connor.

"Now, Connor," Killian says, in a tone he uses when assigning critical tasks. "Your role is perhaps the most important of all."

Connor straightens in his chair. All traces of his earlier flirtation with Kim vanish as he shifts into professional mode. The transformation is remarkable—his eyes sharpen, his posture becomes more alert. Even his breathing seems to change. This must be his Prince O'Brady persona.

"You're our connection to the Irish," Killian continues. "Victor found messages between Matteo and the O'Malleys. Matteo was planning on selling a few of his warehouses and businesses to them, who have been asking questions about the territory for months now. With Matteo gone, they'll be the ones we should watch carefully."

His jaw tightens slightly. "They're friends of the family. I wonder if my father knows about this. He refused to work with O'Malley, so I guess he got his foot in somewhere else. What exactly do you need from me?"

"Similar to how Kim put it... get in bed with the enemy," Killian states, and Kim smiles.

"That's a risky move," I state. "He's not one of us. No offense."

"None taken," Connor mutters, sitting back in his chair.

"He still hasn't officially left O'Brady," I say.

"Which makes it even better," says an accented voice behind us. Ryan is standing in the doorway. "Father is furious with him for coming to the United States and helping us. He can use that to his advantage by letting the O'Malleys think that he wants to overthrow Father—because he's on the outs. Of course, O'Malley is going to want to work with Prince Connor O'Brady."

Kim's head snaps to Connor. "You're a fucking prince?"

Fuck, there it is. I guess I just lost this competition if there was one. She wasn't aware of his title. Even though he's an unofficial prince, the people of Ireland still treat his family like royalty. How can I compete with a prince?

"I'll explain later—another time," he says to her in a hushed voice.

Ryan steps fully into the room, closing the door behind him with a soft click. He looks tired but alert, his eyes scanning each of our faces before settling on me.

"Zach," Ryan says, leaning against Killian's desk. "You're the bridge we need."

I shift in my seat. "The bridge?"

Ryan nods, a half-smile playing on his lips. "You're going to pose as the man Victor brings in to run Valentino's operation. After Connor and the O'Malleys make a deal, they will go to you looking for a deal, but both of you are already working together, and we'll come up with a plan to stop them once we have more info on O'Malley."

"And you trust him?" I ask, referring to his brother, someone I thought he wasn't close to at all.

"You don't?" Ryan asks. "Last night you made a great team. What's changed?"

I look away from Ryan to Connor—then Kim.

Killian catches my gaze. "Is there something we should know?"

I feel a knot forming in my stomach as she shifts uncomfortably beside me. Her eyes dart between Connor and me, and I can see her mind working, processing, calculating what to say.

Just as Kim goes to speak, I do before she can. "No," I say firmly, breaking the silence. "Nothing's changed. We're all professionals here." I don't want to admit what's really going on—that I'm letting personal feelings get in the way of work.

But even as I say it, my voice lacks conviction. Ryan raises an eyebrow, clearly not buying it. Killian's look is penetrating, missing nothing.

"Look," Connor interjects, "I understand the hesitation. Trust is earned, especially in our line of work. I'm willing to prove myself, however necessary."

His words are directed at Killian, but his eyes flick briefly to Kim and me.

Killian sighs, running a hand through his red hair. "The

fact remains, Connor's our best option for infiltrating the O'Malleys. He has the background, the connections, and most importantly, a plausible reason for reaching out to them now."

"We'll work together, then," I state simply. Fantastic—I'm being forced to work with a guy who very recently slept with the same woman I have. Do I really have an issue with Connor? No, not really. I thought he was a good guy until I realized he was my competition.

And may the best man win.

Chapter Fifteen

KIMBERLY

KILLIAN DISMISSES us from his office. Now that we're up to speed, Killian and Ryan want to go rest with Cassie.

"Zach," Connor says as the three of us walk down the hallway. Zach turns to face him. Connor extends his hand, a peace offering hanging between them. His eyes, usually bright with confidence, now hold a plea. "Look, man," he says, his voice lower than before. "I know things got weird in there, but I want to help. I'm serious about leaving Ireland and finding my own path."

He's leaving Ireland. I smile internally.

Zach stares at the outstretched hand for what feels like an eternity. I notice his fingers twitch at his side—hesitant.

"Is this because of me?" I ask, and both men look at me, seemingly confused, but we all know it is.

"Kim," Zach says.

"Please, Zach. People's lives are at stake. We need to be a team, or this could all go wrong." Connor will have to get close to this O'Malley guy, and Zach has to be the bait. I don't want either man to be sidetracked and hurt—or worse, killed.

Zach takes his hand, gripping it firmly—perhaps a little too firmly. Their handshake lasts precisely three seconds. At least it's something.

"And these are for you," he says as he pulls out a set of rolled papers from the inside pocket of his suit jacket and hands them to me.

My sketches. My fingers brush against his as I take them, a moment of contact that sends an unexpected current through me.

"You kept these? I thought for sure you'd have thrown them away."

"I found them after you left in a hurry. Something told me to hang onto them."

A flush creeps up my face as I continue flipping through the stack. Something's missing.

"Wait," I say, looking up at him. "The footprint one isn't here."

His hand moves to the back of his neck, rubbing at it. "About that," he says, clearing his throat. "I hope you don't mind, but I kept it."

"You kept it?" I repeat, surprised. "But it had your shoe print on it."

"It's still my favorite."

I can't help but smile. It was a whimsical fairy sketch, hastily drawn on that rainy afternoon at the hospital when visiting mom. I'd snapped at him on the sidewalk after he stepped on it.

"You kept it." My voice comes out softer than I intended.

Connor nods, his usual confidence momentarily replaced

by something more vulnerable. "It's framed, actually. In my suitcase."

Warmth spreads through my chest at the thought of him preserving that imperfect sketch, dirty footprint and all.

"It reminds me that first impressions aren't always right," he says, holding my gaze. "And sometimes the most beautiful things come from unexpected collisions."

Isn't that the truth?

The hallway suddenly feels too small, too warm. I'm acutely aware of Zach standing beside me, his breathing slightly heavier than normal.

"Well, I have to get to class," I state nervously, giving Connor a hug. It feels too good to have his arms wrapped around me again. Then I turn to Zach and give him a hug too with equal contact, but I add a quick peck on the cheek, knowing that the moment between Connor and me may have been awkward for him—hopefully it will give him some kind of assurance.

I go to the elevator and push the "down" button on the wall.

"Have a good day at work, and try not to kill each other," I say as the metal door opens. They are both wordless as I get inside and press the button for the lobby, and the doors close behind me.

"Shit." I whisper as I complete the ride. Those two men make me feel things with both my heart and my body.

I want them both. I'm fucked.

I can't believe that I'm in class the day after being kidnapped. If I had any excuse not to go to school, that would be my best one. But I can't let mafia shit ruin my life—my chance at making something for myself. Especially being so close to graduating.

The art history classroom feels surreal after everything that's happened. Professor Leighton's voice drones on about the Renaissance while I try to focus on my notebook, but my pen keeps hovering above the page, unmoving.

After class, I go straight to the campus library and find a quiet corner to work in.

I stare at my laptop screen, the blinking cursor taunting me while the red marks on my printed essay draft mock me. This is the essay Profession Peterson asked me to write for the curator internship. She recommended I use the guidance of Professor Leighton, who is qualified to teach both art history and English. I slump into the chair. Professor Leighton's feedback is brutally honest: "Your analysis lacks depth and original perspective. Reconsider your topic entirely."

I groan, rubbing my temples. My original topic on contemporary street art seemed perfect. It's accessible, relevant to my skills—but apparently too "derivative," according to Leighton. The clock is ticking. Without this paper, there's no chance of an internship, no future beyond this mess I'm in.

"Focus, Kim," I mutter to myself, maybe a little too loud, earring a glare from a student at the next table.

I scroll through my bookmarked articles. Female Renaissance artists? Too broad.

What about art forgery? The technical precision required, the history of famous fakes throughout art history? No, too close to my current reality. I'd rather not write about criminal enterprises while actively involved in one.

What if I wrote about art as a coping mechanism—the way artists throughout history have documented trauma, violence, and healing? I could incorporate my own experiences.

That's it.

I sit up straight, fingers flying over the keyboard as I type out a new title statement: "Healing Through Art: Non-Verbal Documentation of Trauma and Healing."

It will examine how artists have documented and healed from trauma through their art. I have a few of those artists in mind, but I'll do some more research to find the best examples. I could even incorporate some of my work— sketches I made after Mom's paralysis, when the hospital waiting room became my studio.

My heart races as I scribble notes on a blank sheet of paper, ideas coming faster than I can capture them. I'll write about how art creates space for healing when words fail.

I pull out my phone and compose an email to Professor Leighton and copy Professor Peterson, outlining my new direction for guidance. My fingers hover over the send button for a moment before I press it.

"I'll have a chicken wrap. Extra dressing," I say to the deli attendant. "And a water cup, please."

He presses some buttons on his POS, then looks at me for payment. "That'll be eight seventy-five."

I reach into my purse, fingers searching for the familiar

shape of my wallet. Nothing. I dig deeper, pushing aside my sketchbook, phone, and the stack of returned drawings. Fuck! Panic rises in my chest as I rummage more frantically.

"I, um..." I stare at the deli attendant, whose patient expression is quickly morphing into annoyance. "I forgot my wallet."

I'm about to apologize and step aside when a familiar Irish voice speaks from behind me.

"I've got this."

Connor appears at my shoulder. He slides a sleek black card across the counter before I can protest.

"Make that two wraps," he adds smoothly. "And two bottles of water, not water cups." He's dressed more casually than when I saw him this morning—dark jeans and a navy button-down with the sleeves rolled up to his elbows, revealing sexy manly forearms I've caught myself staring at more than once.

The attendant's demeanor instantly changes, his eyes widening slightly at Connor's commanding presence—or maybe it's the black card that carries no limit.

"Connor," I whisper with a smile. "My fucking hero. What are you doing here?"

His mouth quirks into that half-smile that does something strange to my insides. He reaches for our order as the deli worker hands it over, then guides me toward an empty table away from the late-night rush crowd that has a little more privacy by the window.

"Zach mentioned you'd be here," he shares, unwrapping the packaging from his food. "Said you were working on an important paper." His eyes meet mine, amusement dancing in them. "He thought I should check on you."

"Really?" I ask, feeling a complicated warmth spread through my chest. "Unless he's tied up somewhere, and you made him tell you where I was," I tease.

His expression shifts, almost imperceptibly. "He thinks we need to talk. And believe me, he emphasized the talking part." He takes a bite of his wrap, chewing thoughtfully before continuing. "Let's just say we've reached a temporary truce. You have one hell of a protective former stepbrother." He winks at me as he teases me, knowing that Zach is more to me than a former stepbrother.

We eat in a comfortable silence for a few minutes, although he shakes his head and laughs as a witness to another food crime—I dip my wrap in the cup of extra dressing rather than pouring it on the bite I'm about to take.

"You know," Connor says finally, setting down his wrap and wiping his hands on a napkin, "seeing you again was a pleasant surprise. The circumstances were unfortunate. But after Boston...." He pauses, searching for words. "When you left, I thought that was it. I didn't expect to find you here, of all places."

I swallow a bite that suddenly feels too large. "Neither did I."

"I don't know. Maybe it was fate or something equally ridiculous." He laughs softly, almost self-consciously. "I've never been one for believing in that sort of stuff."

My heart does a strange little flip in my chest. I take a sip of water to hide whatever expression might be betraying me.

"The thing is," he continues, leaning slightly forward, his eyes locked on mine, "I told myself that if I ever saw you again, that I would do anything I could to keep you—make you stay. Now that I've found you, I don't want to let go. But

I'm afraid I might be too late, and you belong to someone else."

He's thinking about Zach. I can see the vulnerability in his look.

"Connor," I say and look away.

"Tell me I'm not too late, Merlot."

The deli's fluorescent lights suddenly seem too harsh, too revealing. Like a spotlight when being interrogated by police. When I look up again, he still watches me, waiting for an answer I'm not sure I have.

"It's not that simple," I finally say, my voice barely above a whisper. "My life is... complicated right now."

Connor leans back slightly, his expression cautious. "Complicated how?"

How? Is he serious? Oh yeah, he lives in a world full of complicated days. There are probably levels of complicated days, like a scale. Do these men ever not have a normal day?

I laugh, but there's no humor in it. "Where do I start? I was Matteo's fake girlfriend—which, other than being kidnapped recently, I still have to be careful of the fallout from. I've got an essay due to be considered for an internship after college. My mom sits paralyzed in a long-term care facility, and I have a mountain of her medical debt and my school debt. And then there's..." I trail off, gesturing a triangle vaguely between us.

"Me?" he finishes for me.

"You, and Zach," I add softly.

A muscle in his jaw tightens, but he doesn't look away. "Are you and he...?"

I shake my head, twisting my paper napkin between my fingers. "I'm not with Zach, not in the way you think," I continue. "I've never been in a relationship before. I don't know if I can give myself completely to any man. Not to him. Or you. The truth is, I'm barely holding myself together right now." I pause as a group of laughing students pass by the window. "These past few weeks, with everything that's happened—the kidnapping, the threats, all of it."

He reaches across the table and takes my hand in his. His touch is warm, steady. For a moment, he holds my hand, his thumb tracing small circles against my skin. The simple gesture feels more intimate than it should.

"Kim," he says, his voice gentle but firm. "You don't have to handle everything alone. You talk about your life as if you are being a burden, as if your problems are some heavy weight that will crush anyone who comes near you."

"That's exactly what they are," I whisper. "My mother's care, my financial problems, school commitments... I can't drag anyone else into that mess."

Connor shakes his head slowly. "That's not how relationships work. Not real ones." He leans forward. "When I say I don't want to let you go, I don't mean just the fun parts, the easy parts. I mean all of you. Your struggles, your fears— everything that makes you, you. And I'm sure Zach feels the same way. Let someone in."

I feel a warm tear roll down my cheek. "I'm a hot mess," I joke. "I'm not worthy of you guys."

He reaches out and brushes away the tear. "Let us decide who we're worthy of. Kim—you have two men who'll practically get down on their knees for you. You must be someone special."

Two men want to be with me. The thought is as terrifying

as it is exhilarating. But the concept feels so foreign, like trying to decipher a language I've never studied.

My phone vibrates against the table, cutting through the moment. I instinctively reach for it, grateful for the interruption that breaks the intensity between us.

"Sorry," I mutter, breaking eye contact with him to check the notification. "Oh my god," I breathe, scanning the email twice to make sure I'm not hallucinating.

"What is it?" he asks, leaning forward.

"Professor Leighton," I say, my voice rising with excitement. "He actually likes my essay idea. Says it has 'profound potential' and wants to discuss execution details after next class." I look up at Connor. "He never approves ideas this quickly."

I feel overwhelmed emotionally—first Connor's assurance that I'm not alone and now this. I'm starting to cry, but happy tears this time. *Fuck, Kim, get it together.*

His face lights up with a genuine smile. "That's fantastic. What was the idea?"

"Using art to heal," I explain, feeling a spark of creative energy. "How artists document suffering and healing through visual expression."

"Sounds like something you know a thing or two about," he says softly.

I nod, suddenly feeling lighter. "It's personal, which is probably why it resonated."

"You know, having someone in your life to share these moments with is a good thing. I'm glad that I got to be here when you received this news. It makes me happy to see you happy," he says, and my heart squeezes.

I'm about to respond when the bell above the deli door

chimes. I glance up reflexively, and my heart stutters. Standing in the entrance, scanning the room with narrowed eyes, is Zach. His leather jacket hangs open over a dark T-shirt. His hair is slightly windswept, as if he's been running his hands through it—something he does when he's worried.

The moment his eyes land on our table—on Connor's hand still resting on mine—his entire body stiffens. He moves toward us with deliberate steps, navigating between tables with the measured control of someone trying very hard not to lose their composure.

Chapter Sixteen

ZACH

"WHY HAS SHE BEEN CRYING, CONNOR?" I ask as I reach the table. My eyes flick to their hands, touching on the tabletop.

He leans back in his chair with that familiar mask of cool confidence sliding into place. "Zachary," he acknowledges with a slight nod.

They break their hand-holding, and Kim stands up and gives me a long hug, wrapping her arms around me. Her short body reaches up and she whispers "thank you" in my ear.

I have no idea what she's thanking me for.

I pull back. "Everything okay? I didn't send him here to make you cry."

"No, I'm fine," she says with a smile, wiping away one last tear. "I'm beginning to understand that it's okay to let people in."

Oh. "Yeah, it is. You're not alone."

She smiles brightly, a beam I haven't seen in years. "And my professor loves my idea for my essay."

"That's great, babygirl."

"These are happy tears. I'm going to freshen up." She squeezes my forearm lightly before walking toward the bathroom.

I watch her walk away, and the weight that's been pressing down on her shoulders seems to have lifted somewhat. As she disappears into the women's room, I slide into the booth across from Connor where she was sitting.

"Damn, man," I say, shaking my head in genuine amazement. "You must have a way with words to get her to understand she's not alone in her troubles. I've been trying to tell her that for a while now."

"You're welcome," he says with a smug grin. There he is— the asshole confidence I know. "Sometimes it's not what you say, but when you say it," he adds, spinning his water bottle between his palms. "People need to be ready to hear the truth. And sometimes it means more coming from someone who isn't as close to the situation."

I lean forward, elbows on the table. "What exactly did you say to her?"

He hesitates, as if deciding how much to share. "Nothing special," he replies, eyes drifting to the bathroom door and back to me. "Nothing you probably haven't said as well."

Fine. He doesn't want to take credit, playing it cool. As long as she's okay. I sent him here hoping they'd talk about their feelings for one another, wanting them to sort through that. And if I'm a betting man, she gave him the same excuse she gave me—non-committal, because her life is chaotic. That's my independent, stubborn Kim. Maybe since I've been in organized crime for a while now, I've gotten used to the chaos. When there is no chaos, that's when shit gets eerie.

The bathroom door swings open, and Kim reappears, her face freshly washed, eyes still a little puffy but clearer now. She touched up her makeup, but not enough to hide that she had been crying. She's got her bag slung over her shoulder and something determined in her stride.

"I'm ready to head home," she announces, glancing between Connor and me. "The essay can wait until tomorrow after I talk to my professor. I'm..." She exhales. "Drained."

I stand immediately. "I'll walk you back."

Connor rises too, draining the last of his water from the bottle and tossing it into the nearby trash with perfect aim. "I'll come too," he says.

The three of us step out into the night. The air has a winter chill that seeps through clothes, and she hugs herself slightly. Connor shrugs off his coat and drapes it over her shoulders.

My leather one may have been warmer, but okay...

The walk to my place is quiet, but not uncomfortable. Kim walks between us, her petite frame bundled in Connor's oversized jacket, looking like a child playing dress-up. The streetlights catch in her dark hair, creating halos of amber light as we pass beneath them.

I steal glances at Connor, trying to read his expression. His face is contemplative, serious in a way. Whatever passed between them in that deli has changed something fundamental. I wonder if I should feel threatened by it, but strangely, I don't.

We're halfway to my apartment when the first fat raindrops begin to fall. They splatter against the concrete, creating dark polka dots that spread and merge as the rain picks up intensity.

"Shit!" Kim squeals, laughing as she pulls Connor's jacket over her head. The three of us break into a run, splashing through puddles already forming on the uneven sidewalk.

There's a covered bus stop ahead, its plastic shelter gleaming under the streetlight. "In there!" I shout over the downpour, pointing.

We dash toward it, shoes squelching, clothes nearly soaked through. Kim reaches it first, and she collapses onto the bench inside, breathless with laughter. Connor and I pile in after her. He shakes his head like a dog, sending water droplets flying everywhere.

"Connor!" she protests, still laughing as she shields her face.

I lean against the plastic wall, catching my breath as the rain drums against the roof of the shelter. For the moment, I smile. I was questioning how this could work, if by some miracle she decided to be with one of us—both of us. Could I do that? Share her? Seeing them right now and the undeniable chemistry that mirrors my own with her—separately in other ways... She's laughing and genuinely happy. He's doing that for her, and I'm okay with that.

***

I'm at the office—been here for hours, in our security room reviewing footage, when Connor enters.

I give him a nod, acknowledging his presence but not saying anything.

"Everything is a go for O'Malley," he says, standing beside me. "They took the bait."

I hear him, but I mindlessly continue to look at the video. At this point, I'm literally watching leaves blow on the ground like they are going to suddenly change into criminals doing criminal things.

"Look," he starts, then stops. Takes a breath. "I was wondering—" He breaks off again, pacing a few steps before returning to his original spot.

I raise an eyebrow. "Spit it out."

He leans against the desk, trying for casual but achieving something closer to awkward. "It's about Kim."

A pressure tightens in my chest. "What about her?"

Connor's eyes meet mine directly now. "I want to take her out to dinner."

I huff.

Tried that—asking her on a date and she rejected me. My generosity is hard for her to take. But would she reject him?

Suddenly I realize he asked me for permission or my blessing. "Go for it," I say and look back at my monitors. I doubt she'd agree anyway—her pride and all.

I see him looking at me curiously out of the corner of my eye, as if he expected a fight.

"Okay. Can I have her number?"

I roll my eyes, reaching out my hand. "Give me your phone."

He pulls his cell from his pocket, unlocking it before handing it over. I pull up his contacts and quickly tap in her number, saving it under her name.

"There," I say, giving it back. "But don't be surprised if she says no."

He takes the phone, a small smile playing on his lips. Without hesitation, he taps her contact and hits the call button, then immediately switches to speaker. The ringing echoes through the security room.

I widen my eyes, making a "what the hell" gesture at him. I wasn't expecting him to call her right now, asking her out with me sitting right here.

She answers on the fourth ring. "Hello?" Her voice sounds cautious, probably uncertain about the unknown number.

"Hey, it's me." He maintains steady eye contact with me as he speaks.

"Oh! Hi." Her tone shifts immediately, warming.

"Listen, I was thinking about dinner tonight. I want to take you out. Actually, Zach and I want to take you out."

I shake my head vigorously at Connor, pointing at him emphatically. What the hell is he doing? I mouth "NO" silently, making a cutting motion across my throat. The last thing I want is to be a third wheel on their date, watching them make heart eyes at each other. I don't know why, but the sharing-spaghetti scene from *Lady and the Tramp* comes to mind.

"Actually," she says, and I know it's coming—the part where she says no—"that sounds perfect. But Connor, I want to make this extra special for Zach. I owe him." She has no clue that I can hear her. "Can we go to his favorite place?"

My jaw drops. I stare at the phone in disbelief. She said yes? And she wants to eat at my favorite spot?

His eyes gleam with triumph as he watches my stunned expression. "Absolutely," he says. "We'll make it a night he won't forget." He winks at me. "How about I pick you both up around seven?"

"Perfect," she replies, and I can hear the smile in her voice. "I'll see you then."

After they hang up, he pockets his phone with a self-satisfied grin that makes me want to punch him. Or thank him. I haven't decided which.

"What the hell was that?" I demand, keeping my tone low despite the empty room.

"That," he says, pushing himself off the desk, "was me solving our problem."

"Our problem?"

"Yeah. You want her. I want her." He points out like it's the simplest equation in the world. "She clearly wants both of us. So why fight over her when we can share?"

I stare at him. "And you're okay with that? Sharing?"

He shrugs, his shoulders lifting in a non-committal answer that doesn't say one way or the other.

"You've got to admit," he says instead, a subtle smile curving the corner of his mouth, "our girlfriend is pretty sweet, thinking about your favorite restaurant."

"She's not our girlfriend yet," I point out.

"The keyword is 'yet.'" He drops into the computer chair next to me. "You see, I've read about manifesting, you know, kind of like dressing for the job you want... so by calling her my—" I raise an eyebrow at him. "—*our* girlfriend," he corrects, "I'm manifesting, so it'll come true."

I roll my eyes at him.

"Look," he continues. "All I'm saying is, tonight we focus on her. Make her feel special. Show her what it would be like with both of us in her life. No pressure, no expectations."

I nod, considering his approach. "No pressure. I like that."

The concept fits. Kim's been under enough stress lately. "Let her set the pace, see where things go."

He looks pleased with my agreement. "So, what is your favorite spot, anyway? Where are we taking our girlfriend tonight?"

A devilish grin spreads across my face. "Food Truck Alley."

His expression falls momentarily before he breaks into a laugh. "Food trucks? Seriously? I was thinking it would be more along the lines of bar food."

"Trust me," I say, spinning back toward the monitors. "She loves it. Best damn tacos in the city, Japanese food that'll make you cry, and this one dessert truck with fried Oreos that..." I kiss my fingertips dramatically. "It's going to change your life," I assure him.

"All right, all right," he says, holding up his hands in surrender. "I trust you." He glances at his watch again and stands. "I should let you get back to work."

"Yeah," I agree, returning to the monitors. "I'll finish up here."

"Seven at your place, then?" he confirms, heading toward the door.

"Seven," I repeat.

He pauses with his hand on the knob. "Oh, and Zach? Wear something nice. Not your usual black-on-black biker bar look. Do you own a polo?"

Before I can retort, he's gone, the door clicking shut behind him.

I turn back to the monitors, but my mind isn't on security footage anymore. The room falls silent except for the hum of the electronics. I recline in my chair, staring at the ceiling, contemplating what had just happened. An official date with Kim... and Connor?

I've heard of arrangements like this before—polyamorous relationships, they are called.

Killian and Ryan are in one with Cassie. I consider that this might actually work—the three of us. If they can do it, so can we. We just need to get Kim on board.

The thought doesn't scare me as much as it probably should. In our world, conventional rules don't always apply. We've all seen enough to know that happiness comes in different packages, and you grab it when you can.

I pull out my phone and text Ryan.

> Need some advice. About poly relationships.

His response comes quickly.

> I knew it!

> Knew what?

> That there was something going on between you and my brother with Kim.

> How did you know?

> The way you both looked at her in Killian's office. Not exactly subtle.

I stare at his message. Before I can respond, another text pops up. It's Killian. Ryan added him to our chat.

Killian: It works if everyone's honest. No secrets. Talk about everything. And I mean EVERYTHING. Trust me.

Ryan: Understand it's not a competition between you and Connor. You're both bringing different things to the relationship for her.

I lean back in my chair, contemplating their advice.

She hasn't even committed to either of us yet. We're taking her out to dinner tonight. See where it goes.

Ryan: Don't assume Kim wants this just because you and him might be cool with it. She might need more time.

Killian: Tonight, show her what's possible. You guys have to be on the same page about this—a hundred percent. If you two can't get along, if there's tension, like there was in my office, it won't work.

Ryan: Also—If she's not into both of you equally, it won't work.

How do I know if she is?

Killian: You'll know. I brought Ryan into my relationship with Cassie, and I could see it on both of their faces. But it didn't change the way she acted or felt toward me.

> Ryan: And heads up, if you haven't already... that first time you see Connor kiss her or take her to bed... you'll feel something. It can be good, bad, or something in between. Acknowledge and deal with it.

My stomach tightens at the thought, but not entirely in a bad way.

> And you guys don't get territorial?

> Killian: Fuck yeah I do.

> Ryan: Just not with each other.

> Ryan: You know, Zach, Killian got VERY possessive at the wedding when all you did was give Cassie a hug.

> Killian: Seriously, Ryan? (Zach, don't hug my wife...)

I laugh out loud. Killian is very much a jealous and possessive guy when it comes to Cassie.

> Ryan: But honestly, if you guys do this, it's not about sharing like she's property. It'll be about the three of you being in a relationship together. Different dynamic than you're used to.

They have given me a lot to think about.

> Thanks for the advice. I'm going to get back to work and try not to overthink this whole thing.

Ryan: Good luck.

I pocket my phone.

Don't overthink it. Right.

I force myself to focus on the task at hand, clicking through different camera angles, checking for any blind spots or suspicious activity.

But thoughts of tonight keep creeping in. What to wear. What to say. How to act around both of them. And Kim can't even commit to one of us—how will she commit to two?

Fuck. I'm overthinking it already.

I push back from the desk and stand up, needing to move. Pacing the small security room, I roll my shoulders to release the tension building there. I'm Zach fucking Warren. I've stared down the barrel of a gun more times than I can count. I've built a reputation that makes hardened criminals think twice before crossing me.

And I'm feeling anxious about a date?

I stop pacing and face my reflection in the dark monitor screen. My distorted image stares back at me, and I point a finger at it.

"Listen up," I mutter to myself. "This is just dinner. Food trucks. Your territory. Your comfort zone. You've got this."

I straighten my shoulders, squaring them.

"Kim loves you. She said yes to this date. She specifically asked for your favorite place." I nod at my reflection, conviction building. "And Connor? He's not your enemy here. He's... an ally."

The word feels strange on my tongue, but not entirely wrong.

"You're both on the same team now. Team Kim." I almost laugh at how ridiculous that sounds. "This isn't about ego or competition. It's about making her happy. And if that means sharing... then that's what you'll do."

Okay, pep talk over.

Chapter Seventeen

CONNOR

I CAN'T HELP but feel a mix of excitement and nerves. After trying on three shirts, I chose a navy button-down; it's casual enough but still looks like I put in effort. I check myself in the mirror, running a hand through my hair one last time.

"Damn, Connor," I mutter to myself with a smirk. "Might want to dial it back a notch. Poor Zach won't stand a chance if you show up looking this good."

I laugh at my own joke, but then pause, my smile fading slightly. Kim agreed to this weird three-person date, and she didn't do it just for my benefit. She must see something in him, too. That quiet confidence he has, or maybe his dry humor that catches you off guard. He's not exactly GQ material, but I guess there is a certain appeal about him. Dependable. Manly. And then there's their history. They grew up together. Years of shared memories I can't compete with.

I spritz on cologne—just enough, not a cloud—and check my phone. Still thirty minutes before I need to leave.

I grab my keys and wallet, trying to shake off the sudden weight in my chest. This wasn't supposed to be a competition, but standing here, I'm realizing it could be. And I might be the one at a disadvantage.

My phone buzzes in my hand, startling me out of my thoughts. Ryan's name flashes on the screen, indicating a text message.

> Need you at Fitzpatrick Enterprises' boardroom ASAP.

I frown at the message. Whatever it is, it must be serious.

> On my way. Is everything OK?

> I'll explain when you get here.

Great. So much for my carefully planned evening. I check the time and sigh, then pull up a new text for Zach.

> Hey man, hate to do this, but something's come up. My brother needs me for an emergency meeting. Can we push dinner back about an hour? I'll text when I'm heading over. Or you two can go and I'll meet you there.

I slip the phone into my pocket, grab my jacket, and head out the door.

The elevator doors slide open with a soft ding, and I step inside, jabbing the button for the floor I want. Ryan's penthouse apartment sits forty floors up, making the Fitzpatrick Enterprises boardroom conveniently close. Small mercies, I suppose.

As I descend, I check my phone. No reply from Zach.

The elevator comes to a halt. I pocket my phone as the doors open to reveal the sleek, modern hallway of Fitzpatrick Enterprises. As I navigate the corridors, my mind races with possibilities about what he might need. Is it something with O'Malley?

As I round the corner, I spot Zach striding purposefully toward me from the opposite end of the hallway, his brisk pace mirroring my own, suggesting we are both headed to the same destination. He's alone.

I slow my stride. "What are you doing here?"

He looks as surprised as I feel, eyebrows raised in a way that would be comical under different circumstances.

He comes to a stop a few feet away from me. "Killian texted me to come to the boardroom. Said it was urgent."

"Killian?" My confusion deepens. "Ryan's the one who messaged me."

"I don't know what's going on," he admits.

I shrug, glancing toward the boardroom door. "Let's find out."

Together, we approach the frosted glass doors. Through the translucent panels, I can make out shadowy figures moving inside. Zach and I exchange a last look, his expression mirroring my uncertainty, before I push open the door.

Killian and Ryan sit next to each other on the far side of the long conference table, their expressions serious.

Zach takes a seat across from them, and I follow, sitting in a chair next to him.

"What's going on?" I ask.

"Victor received a video message and sent it to us," Killian states.

Ryan pivots the sleek silver laptop on the table, angling the screen toward us. "You need to see this," he says.

The video player has already been queued. Ryan taps the spacebar, and the recording begins to play.

The man who appears on screen makes my skin crawl instantly. He's older, maybe in his sixties, with steel-gray hair and cold grey eyes. But what catches my attention is the jagged scar that runs from his right temple down to his jawline, like a lightning bolt carved into his flesh.

"Victor Valentino," he begins. "My deepest condolences for your tragic loss." His expression remains completely unchanged as he speaks of Matteo's death, the practiced sympathy so hollow it's almost insulting. "You may call me Deveraux," he continues. "Your son and I were in the midst of what I believed to be a mutually beneficial arrangement before his... unfortunate departure. I understand the Fitzpatrick family has been quite industrious lately." His jaw tightens slightly. "Particularly in dismantling certain operations I had established. Operations your son had guaranteed would remain untouched."

I glance at Killian, whose face has hardened into stone.

"This represents a significant financial setback for my organization," Deveraux continues, as he speaks formally and articulately. "But—" He waves his hand dismissively, his expression shifting to one of casual indifference. "—these things happen in our line of work. One must be prepared for occasional disruptions."

The nonchalance with which he discusses the destruction of his human trafficking operation makes my stomach turn. He straightens his already immaculate suit jacket, eyes glinting with something predatory.

"Your son, however, offered me a valuable gift as a gesture of goodwill for my considerable troubles. One that he was supposed to deliver the night of his death." Deveraux's thin lips curve into what can only be described as a smile. "A woman. Kimberly Stanton."

My head snaps toward Zach so fast I nearly give myself whiplash. His face drains of all color, mirroring the shock I feel coursing through my body. Our eyes lock in mutual horror. Kim—*our Kim.*

"It's come to my attention that Ms. Stanton is currently under the protection of yours and Fitzpatrick's organization."

Next to me, Zach's breathing has become audible, his hands gripping the edge of the table so tightly his knuckles have gone white.

"I respect territorial claims, Victor," Deveraux continues, his tone deceptively reasonable. "I always have. But a deal is a deal, and your son made one with me. The fact that she now shelters behind your walls—and those of your new allies— does not nullify that deal."

"Turn it off," Zach growls, his voice barely recognizable.

Ryan ignores him, allowing the video to continue playing.

"I expect the exact merchandise that was promised to me. Not a substitute. Not money. I want Kimberly Stanton." He leans closer to the camera, the scar on his face pulling taut against his skin. "That is non-negotiable."

It feels like someone removed all the oxygen from the room. I look at my brother, whose jaw works silently, a muscle twitching in his cheek.

"You have forty-eight hours to deliver her to me. When the clock runs out, I will personally come knocking on doors— yours, the Fitzpatricks', wherever she might be hiding—and I will eliminate anyone who stands in my way." His voice remains eerily calm, making the threat all the more chilling. His cold eyes stare directly into the camera. "I have my ways of finding things out. I also know that it was your daughter who killed Matteo."

Fuck. How does he know Cassie killed him?

"I will not hesitate to bring this information to light if you don't give me what I want, Mr. Valentino. I'll send detailed instructions for the handover shortly." The screen goes black.

For several heartbeats, nobody speaks.

"Where is Kim now?" Ryan asks, his tone unnervingly businesslike.

I whip around to confront my brother, fury igniting in my chest like a match thrown on gasoline. "You're not seriously considering handing her over?" I snarl, half-rising from my chair.

Ryan's face remains impassive. "Connor—"

"We will protect her," Killian interrupts, his voice quiet but firm. "That's not even a question. She's under Fitzpatrick's protection, and she'll stay that way."

Zach exhales sharply beside me, some of the tension leaving his shoulders.

"I wasn't suggesting otherwise," Ryan says. "I asked where she is because we need to move her immediately."

"She's in my office," Zach states, his voice tight with strain. "I told her to wait there while I came to this meeting."

Killian shakes his head firmly. "Your apartment is not secure enough. We need the girls to stay here in the building where we can implement proper security protocols until we come up with a solid plan."

Ryan drums his fingers on the table. "She can stay with Connor."

I nod without hesitation. "Of course."

"Fine," Zach agrees, almost reluctantly. Does he not trust me to protect her?

Killian stands. "Ryan and I need to contact Victor and strategize our response." He glances at his watch. "We'll reconvene in a couple of hours."

Zach and I hang back in the corridor as Killian and Ryan stride away, already deep in conversation.

"I'll go get her now," he says, his voice still tight with tension. "Pack up some of her things from my place and bring her over." He runs a hand through his hair, looking suddenly exhausted. "Christ, I don't even know how to explain this to her."

"Yeah," I say, the reality of the situation hitting me all at once. "Looks like our dinner plans are officially canceled, huh?" I attempt a weak smile. "Think those food trucks deliver to a building under lockdown?"

The joke falls flat, but his expression softens slightly. Then his jaw tightens as he meets my gaze. "I should have seen this coming."

"We couldn't have known," I say.

"This isn't just some business threat," he says, his voice dropping to a near-whisper. "You saw that video. The way he spoke about her—" He breaks off, swallowing hard.

Yeah, I noticed that. He definitely is treating her like a hot commodity.

"We will not let him anywhere near her," I say firmly, gripping his shoulder. "Not a chance in hell."

"Agreed. Whatever it takes."

"Whatever it takes," I echo. For the first time since meeting Zach, I feel a sense of true alliance forming between us. A common goal—a pact.

He nods once, decisively, then turns to leave.

"Zach," I call after him. He pauses, looking back over his shoulder. "Pack a bag for yourself, too."

He says nothing at my offer to crash at my place, just rotates and walks away.

I step into Ryan's apartment, my temporary home, and suddenly become aware of the state it's in. What had felt perfectly livable for a bachelor now looks like a disaster zone.

I grab a garbage bag and start collecting the trash, hurrying. "Shit," I mutter, taking in the empty whiskey glasses on the coffee table, the pile of laundry draped over an armchair, and the stack of takeout containers by the sink.

The dishes get a quick wash, and I wipe the counters with a spray cleaner I find.

I've cleared the visible mess and am stripping the sheets off my bed. I rummage through Ryan's linen closet and find a spare set that looks and smells clean. As I tuck the fitted sheet around the mattress, I realize I'm making up the master bedroom for Kim. Where exactly am I planning to sleep? The couch, obviously. Zach can take the spare bedroom—unless—do they sleep together in the same bed now?

I shake the thought from my head. We have more important things to worry about.

I smooth the comforter over the bed and fluff the pillows, feeling oddly domestic.

With the apartment now presentable, I glance at my watch. It's been almost two hours since the meeting. I pace around the living room, checking my phone every few minutes for updates. Nothing from Zach, nothing from Ryan.

I've just started rearranging the throw pillows on the couch for the third time when I hear three quick knocks on the door.

My heart jumps as I cross the room in a few quick strides. When I pull open the door, Kim and Zach stand there. Her face is pale, her eyes rimmed with red. She's clearly been crying. Each clutches a suitcase, hers a sleek carry-on with a floral pattern, his a battered military duffel.

"Hey," I say, stepping aside to let them in. "Come on in."

She walks past me. I catch a whiff of her perfume, the floral one, as she moves by. Zach follows, his eyes scanning the apartment before he sets his bag down by the wall.

"You okay?" I ask her once I've closed the door behind them.

I realize that was a dumb question. Of course she's not okay.

She nods stiffly. "Zach explained everything." Then she looks between us, her composure remarkable despite the fear clear in her eyes. "One of Matteo's guys told me that if I wasn't honest that I'd be dead or worse. I guess Matteo chose worse. I just didn't realize that it meant giving me to someone else to be pimped out." She lets out a non-humorous laugh. "Fuck!" Kim shouts toward the ceiling. "Why does this shit keep happening?"

I glance at Zach, giving him a worried look. We just got her to a good place, and now she's slipping.

Her hands shake as she sinks onto the couch, her fingers raking through her dark hair. I move quickly to her left side, taking her trembling hand in mine.

Zach takes her right, our bodies creating a protective barrier around her.

"Hey," I say softly, placing my hand over hers to still the trembling. "Look at me." Her eyes, glassy with unshed tears, meet mine. "We won't let anything happen to you," I tell her, my voice low but firm. "You understand?"

He nods, his jaw set in determination. "You're safe here. This place is like Fort Knox. Killian's got men stationed at every entrance, and the security system would make the Pentagon jealous."

She pulls her hand away, standing abruptly. "You don't get it," she argues, pacing the length of the living room. "I've met this Deveraux guy. He collects people—women—like their trophies. A girl he brought to a dinner meeting was extremely strung out on drugs. He told Matteo how he keeps them high because they're more compliant. She was sitting there like a fucking zombie. Me—I'm a stubborn bitch. How much drugs will he pump me with until I'm as compliant as he wants?"

"Stop. Kim, he's not going to get you," I say. She's talking like he already has her.

"The entire Fitzpatrick security team is at our disposal," he adds.

"We're not just two guys trying to protect you. We have teams of people working on this right now. The best security experts, former military, intelligence analysts—all focused on keeping you safe."

The look on her face says she's not happy about that. And she might be the only one who would be. She feels guilty knowing people are taking time out of their day to help her.

"Before you say anything, you are worth it," Zach says.

The tension in her body eases with his reassurance.

"Thank you," she whispers. "Can I go lie down? I just want to sleep."

She doesn't even wait for a response before wandering down the hallway.

⚊⚊⚊

I've never been one for teamwork, not since I was a kid when group projects inevitably meant I'd end up doing all the work while someone else took half the credit. But as I sit next to Zach in the dimly lit tech lab of Fitzpatrick Enterprises, I realize this situation demands something different from both of us.

We got Kim into bed and went downstairs to work. He focuses intently as his fingers fly across the keyboard, the rapid clicking creating an almost hypnotic rhythm. It's past midnight now, but neither of us has mentioned leaving.

"I've got something," he mutters. He shifts his chair slightly, allowing me space to see his screen.

We got a tip that Deveraux is already in the city, having arrived yesterday.

The image that appears is grainy. It's a surveillance from a pizza joint by some docks. Most shady businessmen in organized crime use boats to get from point A to B because it's the most low-key and lavish. No crime boss wants to drive cross-country, even in the most expensive cars.

Deveraux's yacht is massive—gleaming white against the dark water, at least seventy feet long. The timestamp in the corner reads 2:17 AM.

"Zoom in," I say, leaning closer to the screen.

He taps a few keys, and the image enlarges, pixelating

slightly but still clear enough to make out the figures descending the gangplank.

The first man is him—the scarred bastard from the video. Even in the dim lighting of the dock, that facial disfigurement is unmistakable. He's dressed in what looks like a tailored suit, his movements confident and unhurried. Behind him, a woman follows, her steps uneven and faltering. She's beautiful —or was, before whatever they've done to her—with long blonde hair that hangs limply around her shoulders. Her head lolls slightly as she walks, and twice she nearly stumbles off the narrow gangplank.

"She's drugged," he states, confirming Kim's recount of how Deveraux manages women.

The second man follows, shorter but no less menacing, with a shaved head. He's half dragging another once-beautiful woman of his own.

I shoot him a look. "We should go stake it out."

"I was thinking the same thing," he agrees, already pushing back from the computer. "If we leave now, we can scope it out before dawn." He checks his watch. "We should probably tell Drake we're heading out, though."

I nod, standing up and stretching my stiff muscles.

The elevator ride up to my temporary apartment is silent, both of us lost in our own thoughts about what we just saw. Those women were paraded off Deveraux's yacht like merchandise. That will not be Kim.

Drake, a mountain of a man with close-cropped hair and shoulders that barely fits through doorways, rises from his position on a chair near the entrance. He acknowledges us with a subtle nod.

"Everything quiet?" I ask in a hushed voice.

"Yes, sir. Ms. Stanton hasn't moved since you left. I've been checking on her every half hour as instructed."

"We're heading out for a few hours. Going to do some reconnaissance. Let us know when she wakes up."

Drake nods firmly. "I'll hold down the fort. She's in good hands."

"Thanks," I say, clapping him on the shoulder.

As Zach and I step back into the elevator, I find myself thinking about Kim. Despite everything she's been through—Matteo's abuse, the constant fear, and now this nightmare with Deveraux—she's still standing. Bent but not broken. Her resilience is rare, a toughness that's unteachable.

"She's going to get through this," I say quietly as the elevator begins its descent.

He glances at me, then nods. "Yeah, she is. Kim's the toughest person I know. Has been since we were kids."

"She's stronger than anyone gives her credit for," I continue. "Even herself, it seems."

"Doesn't mean she has to do it alone," he states, his voice firm with conviction.

"No," I agree. "She's got us."

Chapter Eighteen

KIMBERLY

THERE IS a knock on the door, and I start to open it. My hand hesitates on the doorknob. I'm not expecting anyone, and Drake will usually just come inside to check on me. Zach and Connor have been doing recon work on Deveraux since early this morning.

Drake's enormous frame fills the doorway. At six-foot-five with muscles that strain against his black T-shirt, he's an intimidating presence. But there's a woman beside him who catches my attention—a petite blonde whose head barely reaches his shoulder. Her brown eyes sparkle, and when she smiles, dimples appear in her cheeks.

"Hey, Kim," she says. "I'm Cassie."

I stand up straighter. *The Cassie?*

"It's nice to meet you finally."

The apartment is a mess behind me—magazines scattered across the coffee table, a bowl of cereal with milk settling on the bottom, and Ryan's DVD collection from where I'd raided it. I'd been pacing between the TV and the bookshelf for the last hour, unable to settle on anything that would quiet my racing thoughts.

"Come in," I say, stepping aside. "Sorry about the..." I gesture vaguely at the surrounding mess. "I wasn't expecting company."

She steps inside, her movements graceful. I catch Drake's eye, giving him a small nod of acknowledgement. He returns it then backs away as I close the door.

"I apologize for showing up like this," she says, glancing around the apartment with curious eyes rather than judgment.

"Not at all," I reply, feeling strangely relieved to have company. "I was just..." I trail off, not sure how to explain what I was doing. Waiting? Worrying?

We move to the couch, and I hastily clear away some magazines to make room for her. The silence stretches between us for a moment.

"So," we both say simultaneously, then laugh.

"You first," I offer with a warm smile since she's the one visiting me. There must be a reason.

"Actually," Cassie says, tucking a strand of her golden hair behind her ear, "I wanted to meet you properly. I've heard a lot about you."

I shift uncomfortably on the couch. The way her blonde waves catch the light makes me instantly self-conscious about my hair, which I haven't even bothered to brush today.

"All good things, I hope?" I try to joke, but my voice sounds strained as I hear it. And since I'm nervous around her, I immediately blurt out shit, like this... "I'm not a homewrecker, I swear."

She laughs, and it's genuine. "Yes, I know."

I cringe. "I should apologize," I say, fidgeting with the hem of my shirt. "About meeting Ryan and Killian at Firefly. I mean, of all places, I was selfish and asked them to meet me where I worked."

She shakes her head, her expression softening. "You don't need to apologize. Really. I appreciate the thought, though." She leans forward, elbows resting on her knees. "If anyone should apologize, it's those two idiots of mine. And trust me, they have. Extensively."

"Matteo used me to hurt you, and it worked."

Cassie nods slowly, her eyes darkening at the mention of her half-brother. "He knew exactly how to hurt all of us." She brushes imaginary lint from her jeans before meeting my gaze again. "But I'm so relieved that nightmare is finally over. Though now..." She sighs, "we're facing a different monster with Deveraux." A small, confident smile curves across her lips. "I have complete faith that Connor and Zach will take him out. Especially with Killian and Ryan backing them up. Those four together? He doesn't stand a chance."

"You're right," I agree. "Though I'm almost more worried about Connor and Zach killing each other before they get to Deveraux."

We both burst into laughter, the tension in the room finally breaking.

"God, those two," she says. "Ryan says they're like oil and water."

I fidget with a loose thread on the couch cushion. "I'm curious... How do you do it? With Killian and Ryan, I mean. Having a relationship with both of them." The moment the words leave my mouth, heat rushes to my face, and I press a palm against my forehead. "I'm sorry. That was incredibly personal and rude. We just met, and here I am prying into your love life."

Cassie's laugh is warm, and she waves away my embarrassment with a gentle smile. "It's okay. Really." She settles deeper into the couch. "It helps that they are best friends. They've always had this bond that's unbreakable. When feelings developed between us, there was already a foundation of trust."

"That makes sense," I say, relieved she didn't take offense. "Though from what I've seen, apart from their mutual love of Irish whiskey, Connor and Zach are complete opposites. In the real world, they'd probably never even be friends."

Her lips curve into a knowing smirk, her eyes twinkling with mischief. "Good thing we don't live in the real world, then, isn't it?" She leans closer, as if sharing a delicious secret. "In our world, a man who wears three-piece suits can absolutely be ride-or-die with a guy covered in tattoos." She gives me a playful wink that makes me laugh.

"But Connor and Zach..." I shake my head, struggling to articulate what I'm feeling. "When I'm with them, it's like they both reach something inside me I didn't even know was there. Not physically—though that's..." I feel my cheeks warm. "But it's deeper than that. Like they speak to my soul or something." I cringe at my own words. "God, that sounds so cheesy when I say it out loud."

Cassie's expression softens, her eyes lighting up with recognition. "No, I get it. I absolutely get it." She leans forward, suddenly animated. "That's exactly how I feel about my guys. They each touch different parts of who I am."

"Yes!" I exclaim, feeling a wave of relief that she understands. "The thing is, I've been pushing guys away for a long time. It's not just them. This has been my dance for years —finding reasons why it won't work with any man who gets too close. But at the same time, my life has always been chaotic, so those reasons are easy to find."

"Self-preservation," she says softly.

"Yeah, but it's exhausting." I pull my knees to my chest. "I've never been in a relationship at all, but I want one. I think I'm ready. But I don't want to choose. So, to go from none to two relationships..."

"And that scares you?"

"Terrifies me," I admit. "But it's like they're both standing outside this fortress I've built, and instead of trying to break down the walls, or just giving up like most men do, they're... waiting. Patient. Like they know, eventually I'll open the door myself."

Cassie watches me with her perceptive eyes, not rushing to fill the silence.

I grin, feeling a weight lift off my shoulders by admitting that out loud.

"You know...I actually agreed to go on a date with them, but then this whole lockdown thing happened," I tell her.

She looks disappointed for me. "I'm sure there will be another chance."

Reaching over, I grab her hand. "I appreciate you coming over. I needed this... girl talk."

"Of course," she says, her smile warm and genuine. "When Drake mentioned you were here alone, I thought maybe we could use some girl time. It's not easy being in our position."

"No, it's definitely not," I agree, nodding. "God, I'm so rude," I say suddenly, jumping up from the couch. I notice my empty wine glass on the coffee table and grab it. "Can I get you something to drink? I've sat here talking your ear off without even offering you anything." I walk to the kitchen area, opening a cabinet. "Ryan has a decent wine collection. There's a fantastic cabernet, or if you prefer white, he's got this amazing Sauvignon Blanc that I've been stealing sips of all week."

Cassie shakes her head, her hand moving to rest on her stomach. "No alcohol for me, thanks. Water would be perfect."

My eyes widen as I register the gesture. "Oh! Are you...?"

Her cheeks flush slightly as she nods, a small secret smile playing on her lips. "It's still early."

"Congratulations!" I exclaim, genuinely delighted for her. I fill a glass with water and bring it over. "That's wonderful news."

"Thank you," she says, accepting the drink. "It's still surreal, to be honest. But we're thrilled about it."

I study her as she cradles the glass, the way her face glows with that special kind of happiness that comes from within. She has this brightness about her, this natural bubbly energy. Looking at her now, I can already tell she's going to be an amazing mother—warm, patient, loving. The mom who bakes cookies and doesn't mind getting finger paint on the walls. The kind who listens.

"You know," I say, settling back onto the couch, "I'm an artist." I fidget with my hands, suddenly feeling shy. "I sketch and paint. I'm no professional or anything, but..." I trail off, then gather my courage. "If you guys have a theme planned for the nursery, I'd love to contribute something. Maybe a mural or some custom pieces for the walls?"

Cassie's eyes widen. "Are you serious? That would be

incredible! We haven't settled on a theme yet, but I'll let you know. We're waiting to find out the gender. But we've been tossing around a few ideas already. Ryan's pushing for this sophisticated prince or princess theme—animals all wearing gold crowns." She rolls her eyes affectionately.

"That sounds cute, actually."

"It does," she agrees. "But then Killian wants this whole woodland adventure theme with foxes and bears and little camping scenes. He even wants to hang tiny lantern nightlights that look like they're hanging from branches."

"That's adorable," I say, genuinely charmed by the concept.

"And I'm kind of leaning toward a vintage storybook theme—you know, with watercolor illustrations from classic children's books. Peter Rabbit, Winnie the Pooh, that sort of thing." She sighs happily. "So basically, we have no idea what we're doing."

"All of those sound amazing," I tell her. "I could definitely work with any—"

A sharp knock interrupts us, and Drake's deep voice calls through the door. "Kim? Are we still on for your mom's hospital visit?"

"Shit, I completely lost track of time," I say.

She rises, draining the last of her water. "Don't apologize. I'm the one who showed up unannounced." She moves to the kitchen and places her empty glass in the sink. "I should get going, anyway. The guys will wonder where I disappeared to."

I grab my jacket from the back of a chair and quickly slip it on. "This was really nice. We should do this again." The words tumble out of me in a rush, but I mean every one of them.

Her face lights up. "I'd love that." She eyes me curiously. "They know you're leaving the building?"

"Yes, they do. They fought me on it, but it's my mom... and Drake will be with me."

"I don't think it's a good idea, but I'd risk it to go see mine, too."

I hesitate. "Actually, it's not just about seeing my mom," I admit, feeling suddenly vulnerable. "Tomorrow's my birthday."

"What? It is?"

"It's not a big deal." I shrug, but the way my voice catches betrays me. "But every year, I've spent my birthday with mom. When I was little, birthdays were difficult. My dad left right before I turned seven, and money was tight. Mom would save for months to make each birthday special." Cassie watches me with genuine interest. "There was this one year—my eleventh birthday—when she couldn't afford a cake. So, she took a day off work, which she never did, and we spent the entire day making paper flowers together." I smile at the memory. "Paper flowers filled our apartment. Hundreds of colorful paper flowers hung from the ceiling, taped to the walls... It was fucking magical." I gasp. "Excuse my language—if you haven't heard, I have the mouth of a trucker."

"That sounds beautiful—the flowers, not the vulgar language." She laughs.

I smile to myself, marveling at how comfortable I feel with Cassie after such a short time. There's something about her that puts me at ease, making it impossible not to open up. Most people I meet get the carefully constructed version of Kim—the tough bartender with the sharp tongue who keeps everyone at arm's length. But with her, those walls came down without me even noticing.

"You know," I say, "I feel like I've known you forever." I laugh softly. "Is that weird to say?"

"Not at all. I feel the same way." She reaches out and squeezes my hand. "I'm really glad you're not a frigid bitch." We giggle a little.

Another knock at the door, more insistent this time.

"I better go. I hope you have a wonderful visit with your mom," she says, her voice warm with sincerity. She pauses with her hand on the doorknob, a mischievous twinkle lighting her eyes. "And maybe we can figure out something special for tomorrow. No one should spend their birthday without a proper celebration."

I stand there for a moment, staring at the closed door with a small smile spread on my lips.

I just made a friend.

Chapter Nineteen

KIMBERLY

"Happy birthday!" Cassie yells as we enter the dark room and she flicks on the lights.

I blink against the sudden brightness, and that's when I hear them.

"SURPRISE!" Zach and Connor shout in unison with huge smiles on their faces.

I stand frozen beside Cassie, my jaw slightly open as I take in my surroundings. It's a small lounge venue. Soft lighting casts a glow over the plush booth seating that lines the room. In the center, several round tables with elegantly folded napkins and flickering tea lights are clustered together. A wooden stage occupies the far end, complete with a dance floor in front of it.

"Where are we?" I ask curiously.

Cassie links her arm through mine, giving it a gentle squeeze. "We're at your birthday celebration, silly."

So that's why she insisted I wear her black cocktail dress tonight.

"This is Baritone," she explains. "It's a jazz bar in the building, a few doors down from the coffee shop. Killian spoke with the owner, and we got permission to use it. They're normally closed tonight anyway."

I stare at her in disbelief. "You did all this... for me?"

"Of course we did. You deserve it."

Emotion swells in my chest, and I turn to her, pulling her into a tight embrace.

"Thank you," I whisper, my voice catching slightly.

She returns the hug, patting my back. "Don't thank me yet —we're just getting started." She turns toward Zach. "Hey, how about some music?"

He grins, producing a small remote from his pocket. "On it." He clicks a button, and the speakers hidden throughout the room come to life. The smooth sounds of a saxophone fill the air, accompanied by gentle piano and soft percussion—the kind of music that makes you want to sway with a drink in hand.

Connor approaches, his hands in his pockets and a warm smile on his face. He stops beside me, leaning in slightly.

"What can I get the birthday girl from the bar?"

I raise an eyebrow at him. "Do you even have to ask?"

He leans in, his lips brushing softly against my cheek. The gentle pressure sends a flutter through my stomach.

"Be right back," he whispers, pulling away with a playful wink before heading toward the bar.

I watch him go, my fingertips unconsciously touching the spot where his lips were. When I turn back, I catch Cassie standing by the edge of the dance floor, talking to Drake, her eyes darting between me and Connor's retreating figure. She has a self-satisfied smirk on her face. *Huh? What is she up to?*

The saxophone solo transitions into a slower melody, something sultry and inviting. I feel a light tap on my shoulder and turn to find Zach standing there.

"Care to dance?" he asks.

"I'd love to." I smile, placing my hand in his outstretched one.

His is warm as he guides me to the polished wooden floor. We begin to sway.

"You clean up nice," I tease, nodding at his button-down shirt—different from his usual ripped jeans and T-shirt attire.

They must have changed when I went to Cassie's penthouse to get ready. They told me they had more work to do, and I'd see them later. *Liars.* I laugh inwardly.

He laughs, spinning me gently. "Don't sound so shocked."

As we move across the floor, I catch sight of Connor at the bar, his eyes following our movements. Something flickers over his face. I don't know what it is, but it's not jealousy or anger.

"So," Zach says, pulling my attention back. "Twenty-seven. How does it feel to be officially old?"

I'm about to deliver a witty comeback when Connor and Cassie approach, balancing drinks between them. Connor holds two whiskey glasses, amber liquid catching the light, while she carries my red wine and what appears to be plain water for herself.

"Mind if I dance too?" Connor asks, extending one of the whiskey glasses to Zach.

Zach steps back with a good-natured nod.

They are being too nice to each other.

I reach for the wine glass Cassie offers, my fingers wrapping around the delicate stem.

"To my new friend on her twenty-seventh," Cassie says. "May all your wildest dreams and secret wishes find their way to you this year." Her eyes dart between Connor, Zach, and me before she adds, "Every single one of them."

We clink our glasses together, and I take a sip of the rich wine, feeling its warmth spread through me.

She suddenly stretches her arms overhead with an exaggerated yawn. "Oh, wow, would you look at the time?" She glances at her bare wrist where a watch would be. "It's getting so late, and I have a thing in the morning." I nearly choke on my wine. "You three should stay and enjoy yourselves, though. Drake will escort me back to the penthouse." She looks pointedly at Zach. "Don't forget to lock up when you all leave, okay? Killian will have our heads if anything happens."

I stand in place, stunned, staring at her. Is she serious right now? This couldn't be more obvious if she'd written "SET UP" across her forehead in black marker.

She grabs her small purse from the nearest table and pulls Drake toward the door. "Happy birthday! Make it count!" She gives me a not-so-subtle wink before disappearing with Drake into the back door that leads to a hallway.

It clicks shut behind them, leaving the three of us standing in awkward silence as the saxophone continues its sultry melody in the background.

I look between them, my wine glass still in hand. "What just happened?"

Zach bursts into laughter. "I think your new friend is quite the manipulator."

Connor shakes his head. "Subtle as a freight train, that one."

"She made it pretty obvious," I admit.

"Cassie went through a lot of trouble to arrange this," Connor says. "Let's make the most of it."

"I—I can't believe she did this," I stammer, still processing her not-so-subtle exit strategy.

Zach chuckles, his eyes crinkling at the corners. "Just enjoy your birthday." He taps on the remote, and the music shifts to something smoother, richer. The sultry notes of a piano fill the room.

Connor swirls his whiskey. "The birthday girl deserves a proper dance," he says. His voice has a slight rasp with his accent, and it makes my stomach flutter.

"Well, then we shouldn't disappoint her," Zach says, taking another sip.

With our drinks in hand, the three of us smoothly dance to the jazz mix. We're dancing close, our bodies inches apart—me, sandwiched between them.

I feel a hand on my hip and look to see tattooed fingers splayed over my stomach. Another hand goes to the small of my back—Connor's.

The music pulses through me like a second heartbeat, and I surrender to the sensation of being held between them. Zach's chest presses against my back, his breath warm on my neck, while Connor's eyes lock with mine, dark and intent. The space between us seems charged with electricity.

"Happy birthday, Merlot," Connor whispers, his lips

brushing my ear as he guides me into a slow sway. His hand slides up my arm, leaving a trail of goosebumps in its wake.

Zach's fingers tighten slightly on my hip, possessive yet gentle. "Is this okay?" he asks, his voice a low rumble I feel more than hear.

I nod, not trusting my voice. I take another sip of wine, letting the rich flavor linger on my tongue as the alcohol works its magic, melting away my inhibitions. Not enough to blur my senses, but just enough to quiet the voices of doubt. Enough to let me feel, both men working together to make me happy on my birthday.

"Close your eyes," Connor whispers, gently taking my wine glass and setting it aside.

I do as he says, surrendering to the sensations washing over me. The saxophone crescendos as Zach's hands slide up my sides, his touch feather-light yet unmistakably present. Connor's fingers trace circles on my hips, guiding my movements to match the rhythm.

I feel myself melting between them, all thoughts evaporating. The music wraps around us, a fourth presence in our dance, binding us together. Connor's hand travels up my arm until his fingers find my chin. With gentle pressure, he tilts my face toward his.

"Kim." He breathes my name like a prayer.

His lips touch mine, tentative at first, then with growing confidence. The kiss deepens, his mouth warm and tasting faintly of whiskey. My heart hammers against my ribs as Zach's hands steady me from behind.

When Connor pulls away, his hand, massive and strong, spins me around to face Zach.

Zach's hand slides up to cradle the back of my neck, his

thumb gently stroking my jawline. With my eyes still closed, I feel him lean in, his breath mingling with my own, also scented with whiskey and something distinctly him. His lips brush against mine as if asking permission. They are still warm and moist from Connor's kiss. But when I sigh against his mouth and our lips connect, he takes my mouth with savage intensity, his fingers threading through my hair.

I feel caught in a dream, suspended between reality and fantasy. *Please fucking tell me this is real...*

"I want you," I blurt out softly. When I open my eyes, both men are looking between themselves, probably trying to figure out who I was talking to. "Both of you," I add.

Will they agree to this? For me? The silence in the room stretches on, not uncomfortable but somehow endless. I can't help but imagine what it would be like to be with both men at once, to surrender to my desires and indulge fully. Yet there's a part of me that worries about the consequences, the potential to ruin everything.

Connor is the first to break the silence, his eyes never leaving mine. "Kim," he says, his voice husky with desire but tinged with caution, perhaps. "Are you sure about this? The wine, the moment...we don't want you to regret anything tomorrow."

Zach nods in agreement, his fingers still resting lightly on my hip, the touch both grounding and electrifying. "Babygirl, this isn't something we can take back," he adds, his expression serious despite the flush on his cheeks.

The jazz continues to play softly in the background, a saxophone's mournful wail providing the soundtrack to the pivotal moment.

"I'm sure," I whisper, suddenly afraid they'll pull away,

that this magical bubble will burst. "I've thought about this—about both of you—more than I should admit."

The two men exchange another look, unspoken communication passing between them. What they are saying, I don't know yet.

Chapter Twenty

KIMBERLY

THE ELEVATOR RIDE to Connor's apartment is silent, the three of us together in the small space. The air is charged with tension—all sexual. And the walk down the hallway feels like miles.

Once inside, Connor clears his throat. "I'll fix us drinks," he says, heading for the kitchen.

Me—I go straight to the bedroom and begin to undress. I don't need to make a show of undressing myself for them.

I slip off my shoes first, then my jacket. I don't bother with slow teasing movements or coy glances over my shoulder. This isn't a striptease. It's just me, removing layers and becoming vulnerable—taking what I want.

By the time my dress is discarded on the floor, I hear footsteps approaching. I don't cover myself or rush to finish. Instead, I slide my thong down my legs with deliberate movements, stepping out of them just as the bedroom door opens.

Connor enters first, a glass of wine in one hand, whiskey in the other. He stops mid-step when he sees me. Zach follows, with his own glass of whiskey, nearly bumping into Connor's back.

"Jesus," Zach whispers, his eyes traveling the length of my body.

I meet their stares without flinching, owning the moment. The power of being the only naked person in a room is something I've always underestimated. Their open appreciative stares feel like physical touches—Connor's lingering on my breasts, Zach's drifting lower.

I cross the room toward Connor, my hips swaying naturally with each step. His Adam's apple bobs as I approach. I reach for the wine, my fingers brushing his as I take it.

The wine is a deep red, almost black in the dim light. I take a long swallow, feeling it warm my throat, then reach past him to place the glass on top of the dresser.

"So," I say, standing close enough to feel the heat from Connor's body, "are you both just going to look, or are you going to catch up?" I gesture at their clothing. "You seem a little overdressed."

Connor's eyes darken. He lifts the glass to his lips, taking a slow, deliberate sip of whiskey, his eyes never leaving mine. When he's done, he places it on the dresser next to my wine.

"You're right," he says, voice lower than usual. His fingers move to his tie, loosening it. "We are."

Zach still hasn't moved from the doorway, his whiskey clutched in a white-knuckled grip. His chest rises and falls rapidly beneath his polo.

"Zach?" I ask, turning to face him fully. "Are you still with me?"

He hesitates for a moment, his eyes darting between Connor and me. I can see the internal struggle—desire battling uncertainty.

"Yes," he says, voice hoarse. "Definitely, yes."

He drains his whiskey in one swallow, wincing slightly at the burn, then sets his glass next to ours on the dresser with a thud.

Connor's hands are already at his shirt buttons. He removes the shirt and tosses it on the floor.

I step toward Zach, closing the distance between us. My nakedness emboldens me as I reach for the hem of his polo. "Let me help you," I whisper, pulling the fabric upward.

The cotton slides over his sculpted torso, revealing tanned skin, tattoo upon tattoo and defined muscles. His breath catches as my fingertips graze his abs. Connor moves behind me, his lips finding the sensitive spot where my neck meets my shoulder. A small moan escapes me.

"God, that sound," Connor murmurs against my skin.

Zach watches, transfixed, as Connor's hands slide around to cup my breasts, squeezing lightly. He tosses his shirt aside and reaches for his belt.

"That's it," I encourage.

His hand finds the small of my back, pulling me toward him. His lips crash against mine, demanding. I still feel Connor behind me, his breath on my neck before lips follow, trailing kisses on my shoulder.

Zach's hands slide around my waist, his chest pressing possessively onto me. I'm sandwiched between them again, just like in the jazz bar. The heat of their bodies is overwhelming, like being caught between two flames that somehow don't burn.

Time seems to slow, but every nerve ending is alive with sensation. Connor's hands slide down my sides. Zach's mouth explores mine, his tongue teasing and tasting. He breaks our kiss, his eyes dark with desire. I reach behind me, finding Connor's hardness through his pants, and he groans against my ear.

"Bed," I whisper, my voice barely audible over the sound of our breathing. "Now."

They guide me backward until my legs hit the mattress. I sink down, looking up at them both—two different types of masculine beauty standing before me. Connor, with his lean swimmer's build and charming smile; Zach, broader and more rugged, tattooed, wearing his jeans that hang tantalizingly low on his hips.

Connor kneels before me, his hands parting my thighs with gentle insistence. "Let me taste you," he says, his voice a low growl that sends shivers up my spine. His mouth finds my pussy, hot and demanding, and I fall back onto my elbows with a gasp as he eats me out.

Zach watches for a moment, then he finishes undressing and joins us on the bed, positioning himself behind me. His strong arms wrap around me, and move magically over my breasts, kneading them, tweaking my nipples as I arch my back.

Connor's tongue slides between my pussy lips, finding a perfect spot that makes my thighs tremble. The sensation is incredible—insistent.

I've had men go down on me before, but Connor's technique is something else entirely. When he sucks on my clit while sliding two fingers inside me, I nearly come undone.

"Oh god," I moan, my hips rising to meet his mouth.

Zach's hands tighten on my breasts in response, his thumbs circling my nipples as he watches me.

"You like that?" Zach whispers in my ear, his voice rough with desire. "You like his mouth on you?"

I can only nod. My fingers find their way into Connor's hair, gripping the soft strands, guiding him exactly where I need him.

"I want to watch you come," Zach whispers roughly in my ear. "Let go for him."

I lock eyes with Zach. "I'm close."

When the orgasm hits, it's like electricity coursing through my body. My thighs clamp around Connor's head, but I force my eyes to stay open, to keep watching Zach. I want him to see everything—the moment of ecstasy crossing my face. Connor moans against my pussy, his tongue relentless as my essence coats his lips and chin.

"Fuck," he breathes, mesmerized by the sight of my orgasm. His pupils are blown wide, his breathing ragged as he witnesses my most intimate moment.

Connor eases back, wiping his mouth with the back of his hand as he looks up at me with a satisfied smirk. He suddenly grabs my waist and flips me over. My face is now perfectly eye level with Zach's cock.

"Suck his cock, baby."

My mouth waters at the sight of his cock, thick and veined, straining toward me. I wrap my fingers around his shaft, feeling it pulse beneath my touch. His skin is hot velvet over steel. I look up, meeting Zach's eyes as I part my lips and take him into my mouth.

"Fuck," Zach hisses as I swirl my tongue around the tip, tasting the salt of his precum. His hand moves to cradle the back of my head, not pushing, just holding, the gentleness surprising me.

Behind me, Connor's hands gripping my hips, positioning me. His cock teases my entrance, already slick from his earlier attention. He pushes in slowly, stretching me, filling me inch by delicious inch.

"You're fucking drenched," Connor groans.

A moan vibrates around Zach's cock, and his fingers tighten in my hair. "That's it," Zach says, his voice strained with pleasure. "Take us both."

I'm suspended between them, caught in a perfect rhythm. Each time Connor thrusts forward, I take Zach deeper into my throat.

"God, Connor," I gasp, pulling off Zach for a moment. "You fuck me so good."

Zach's eyes darken as he watches my face, transfixed by my pleasure. "Tell me," he says, his voice husky. "Tell me how good he fucks you."

"He's so deep," I pant, my words punctuated by Connor's thrusts. "The way he moves—fuck—."

Connor's hands tighten on my hips, his rhythm intensifying at my words. He slides one hand around to circle my clit, and I cry out.

"She's dripping down my cock," Connor tells him, his voice strained.

I push back against Connor, taking him impossibly deeper.

"Been thinking about this, haven't you?" Connor asks. "Us fucking you."

I can only make a muffled sound of agreement as I take Zach deeper, hollowing my cheeks around him. The dual sensations—the fullness in my mouth and my pussy—have me trembling.

"Yeah, she has," Zach says. "Dirty girl."

Fuck yes, this—this is exactly what I want. To get lost in between the two men I can't stop thinking about.

"Zach, switch with me," Connor says as he slows.

I let off Zach's cock with an audible wet pop.

Zach moves behind me, his large hands gripping my waist where Connor's had just been. I feel the loss of Connor for only a moment before he's in front of me, his smooth cock glistening with my arousal. He traces my lips with his tip, and the taste of myself on him is intoxicating.

"Open," he commands, and I open my mouth eagerly.

As I take Connor, Zach positions himself at my pussy. I feel the blunt head of his cock and the delicious stretch as he pushes inside me with agonizing slowness. I gasp at the sensation, my body adjusting to his girth.

"Jesus Christ," Zach mutters, his fingers digging into my hips. "You feel fucking incredible."

"She's got the tightest pussy," Connor adds. "And perfect lips for sucking cock."

I whimper around Connor's steely cock, and he thrusts himself deeper. I love how he throws his head back when I hollow my cheeks. My hands grip the sheets, anchoring myself as I take both of them into my body.

Connor's hand tangles in my hair, guiding my movements. "That's it, baby," he says, his voice strained.

The room fills with the sounds of our pleasure—skin against skin, breathless moans, and the wet sounds of sex.

"You should see how fucking sexy you look like this," Zach says.

His words ignite something in me. Being watched, being desired by both of them—I'm in fucking heaven.

I reach back, my hand finding Zach's thigh, urging him deeper. He responds with a particularly powerful thrust that makes me cry out around Connor's full cock. The vibrations of my moan send Connor over the edge, his fingers tightening in my hair as he holds me in place. His cock pulses against my tongue as his hot release floods my mouth. The taste is salt and musk. I swallow eagerly, greedily taking everything he gives me, my eyes locked with his as pleasure contorts his features.

"Fuck," Connor groans, his voice ragged. "Your mouth is fucking perfect. Swallow my cum, baby."

His grip on my hair loosens as the final tremors of his orgasm subside. I release him slowly, giving one last gentle lick to his sensitive tip that makes him shudder. A thin strand of saliva connects my lips to his cock for a moment before breaking.

Behind me, Zach's rhythm falters briefly as he watches us. "That was the hottest thing I've ever seen." His hands grip my hips tighter, pulling me back onto him with renewed vigor.

Connor drops to his knees beside the bed, bringing his face level with mine. His eyes are dark and satisfied, but there's still hunger there. He brushes a strand of hair from my cheek, then leans in for an open-mouthed kiss, tasting both of us on my lips.

"I'm so close," I gasp, breaking the kiss.

"Come for us," Connor whispers in my ear.

My body responds with a tightening around Zach's cock that makes him curse under his breath. My orgasm crashes through me like a tidal wave, my inner walls clenching and pulsing. A string of breathless profanities spill from my lips.

I'm dimly aware of Connor watching us, his eyes dark with renewed desire despite having just come. Oh yeah, he can go multiple rounds—I almost forgot.

"Fuck!" Zach curses.

I look back at him through heavy-lidded eyes, admiring the way his muscles flex with each thrust. Zach's body is a work of art in motion—his abs tightening, biceps bulging as he grips my hips, sweat glistening on his chest in the dim light. The veins in his forearms stand out as he holds me firmly in place, controlling the pace.

I breathe, watching the way his shoulders bunch and release with each powerful movement.

"Fuck—I'm gonna—" His words dissolve, and I witness the exact moment his control shatters as he drives into me one final time, burying himself to the hilt. His cock pulses inside me. The sensation of his hot cum filling me triggers another wave of pleasure, a smaller aftershock that has me whimpering.

For a moment, time stands still. The three of us are suspended in this perfect bubble of satisfaction, our ragged breathing the only sound in the room.

Zach slowly withdraws from me, and I feel suddenly empty. My limbs turn to jelly as I roll onto my back, sprawling across the sheets. My chest heaves with each breath, my skin flushed and glistening with sweat. He leans over me, his eyes intense. There's something possessive in his gaze that makes my heart race all over again.

"You know what this means, don't you?" he asks. "You're ours now." His hand slides up my thigh, where I can feel his cum beginning to leak from me. With deliberate slowness, his fingers gather our mixed cum and push it back inside me. The gesture is so primal, so claiming, that I gasp. "Nobody else's."

Connor moves to the other side of the bed as he watches Zach's possessive gesture. "Say it," he commands softly, his fingers tracing my jawline. "I want to hear you say it."

I look between them. "Yes," I whisper, my voice hoarse. "I'm yours. Both of yours." I swallow, about to say something that will shock me. "And you're mine." I add.

The words hang in the air, a promise, a surrender, a claim all at once. Connor's eyes flash with satisfaction, while Zach's expression softens into something almost vulnerable.

Zach bends, his lips capturing mine in a kiss that's surprisingly gentle after the raw intensity of what we just did. We're both still catching our breath, our chests rising and falling in tandem. His tongue teases mine, tasting of whiskey. When he pulls back, his eyes search mine, as if looking for any hint of regret or uncertainty.

He finds none.

Connor stretches out beside me, his hand tracing lazy patterns on my stomach.

"You good, babygirl?" Zach asks.

"Better than good," I reply, my voice a satisfied purr. "I'm fucking amazing."

Zach collapses on the other side of me, one muscular arm draped across my waist. I'm nestled between them again, but this time in a tangle of limbs and shared warmth.

Connor watches us, his cock already hardening again. He leans down, his lips capturing my nipple, sucking hard enough to make me gasp.

"Round two already?" I ask, my voice hoarse from moaning.

"We're just getting started," Connor speaks against my breast. "I have plans for you tonight."

Zach's hand finds my thigh. "Give me five minutes," he says with a lazy grin. "Then I'm ready for whatever you have in mind."

Connor's fingers dip between my thighs to feel the mess they've made of me. "So slick and swollen still," he growls lowly. "Does your pussy want more?"

"Yes," I admit, my cheeks flushing with heat despite everything we've already done.

"I want to watch you ride him," Connor says, nodding toward Zach.

Connor's words send a thrill through me. The idea of riding Zach while Connor watches—or joins—makes my pulse quicken.

The realization of what's happening hits me fully. I'm in bed with two gorgeous men who want me—who claim me as theirs. These two incredible men, so different yet complementary, both focused entirely on me. And it isn't just amazing sex—this is something more.

I can't help it—I smile the biggest smile I've felt in my life, a grin that stretches across my face and makes my cheeks ache.

"This is the best fucking birthday ever!" The words burst from me in an excited squeal that makes both men laugh.

Chapter Twenty-One

CONNOR

MY FEET MAKE contact with the cool floor as I scan the dim room. My boxers are crumpled near the foot of the bed where I'd hastily discarded them last night. I pull them on, then a pair of gray sweatpants from the dresser, wincing as it squeaks slightly. I'm trying not to disturb Kim and Zach, who are still sleeping.

I can't sleep, my mind fucking wired from recent events—all of them, good and bad.

After dressing, I pause to look back at the bed. Kim has shifted closer to him in her sleep, her arm resting on his chest, her dark hair splayed across the pillow. An exhausted little bird after being thoroughly fucked for hours. The sight of her peaceful face sends a warm current through my chest. Even in sleep, she has a pull on me I can't explain.

I make my way through the apartment. I grab my cigar box from the cabinet—I've been saving the Cubans for a special occasion. Is this a special occasion? Maybe not by normal standards, but I got the girl, so yeah, it is.

Grabbing my lighter from the kitchen, I throw on a coat and slide the glass door open to step onto the patio. The crisp, cool air startles my skin at first. Stars are splashed across the sky like someone flicked a paintbrush of silver over a black canvas. It's rare to see the stars in the city skyline—it must be my lucky night.

I settle into the wicker chair and clip the end of the cigar. As I rotate the cigar, the flame from my lighter dances, toasting it evenly before the first draw. That first draw is always the best—earthy, rich, with a hint of sweetness that makes Cubans worth the trouble of acquiring. Smoke curls upward, disappearing into the air.

Christ, what a fucking journey it's been with her. From that night in Boston, to finding her in the trunk of the car I was about to have destroyed, to finding out she was in a complicated relationship with her former stepbrother, someone I could tell she would not let go of. And I wouldn't ask her to. If she or Zach would have flat out told me to back the fuck off, then I would have. But neither did.

I take another slow draw, savoring the complex flavors as I watch the smoke disappear into the night. The ember glows bright orange in the night, a tiny sun burning between my fingers. I think about my life before Kim stumbled into it— organized, controlled, predictable. Now it's a beautiful fucking mess, and I wouldn't trade it for anything.

I chuckle to myself as I take another drag. If Kim and Zach could see how different my life is back home, they'd probably look at me differently, Zach more than he does now. In Ireland, the O'Brady name opens doors. Walking down the streets of Dublin, shopkeepers bow their heads slightly, politicians make time in their schedules, and even the fucking police look the other way when needed.

"Prince Connor O'Brady," they call me there—not officially, of course. Ireland hasn't had a monarchy in centuries, but my family might as well wear crowns for all the influence we wield. My father built an empire that touches everything from shipping to technology. Old money mixed with new keeps the O'Brady name relevant and powerful.

It's not that I don't want the empire—fuck, I've been groomed for it since birth. I've never had a problem with the idea of stepping into that role someday. The problem isn't the crown; it's who's currently wearing it.

My father. Declan-fucking-O'Brady. The man's a tyrant in a tailored suit, someone who commands respect with fear rather than loyalty. A man who sees people as chess pieces, not humans. He rules through fear disguised as respect, and he expects me to stand at his right hand, nodding along like a good little puppet prince. Working alongside him means becoming him, and that's something I refuse to do any longer.

I tap the ash from my cigar, watching the gray flakes scatter with the slight breeze.

Behind me, the glass door slides open softly. I don't turn around immediately, but I know it's Zach by the way the air shifts. His presence has weight to it, since we've both been after the same woman.

"Couldn't sleep either?" I ask, tapping ash into the small ceramic tray beside me.

He moves into my peripheral vision, hair mussed, wearing only sweatpants that hang low on his hips. The moonlight catches the defined lines of his torso, casting shallow shadows across his tattoos.

His eyes flick to the cigar, then back to my face. "She's out cold," he says, voice rough with sleep.

I offer him the cigar, holding it out for him to take. He hesitates before stepping fully onto the patio and sitting down. He takes the cigar from me, then takes a long drag, the embers glowing red-orange in the darkness, letting the smoke fill his mouth before releasing it slowly.

I drink some of my whiskey, then offer him that, too. Fuck, we've just shared Kim. We can share a cigar and whiskey, too.

He throws back the whiskey, finishing the glass.

"Damn," I say, reaching for the bottle I brought out to pour another glass. "I wasn't expecting you to channel your inner frat boy with that one."

The corner of his mouth quirks up. "The Fitzpatricks got me hooked on it. Irish whiskey is the only thing I'll drink."

"So," he says. "Are we going to talk about this thing with Kim, or just keep dancing around it until one of us fucks up?"

There it is. The elephant on the patio.

To buy myself time, I take a long drag from my cigar. "I'm betting you fuck up first," I say and smirk at him, obviously joking, but he remains serious. "What exactly is there to talk about? Seems like we've got a good thing going. Let's just try not to fuck it up."

He laughs, but it's hollow. "Right. Because three people sharing the same bed with no clear boundaries or expectations always works out perfectly."

"You think we need rules?" I ask, observing his face.

"I think we need honesty, boundaries."

"I don't know what to tell you. We can make them up as we go..."

"But—you've done this before, haven't you?"

"No," I answer quickly. "I've never shared a woman—not in bed or in a relationship."

"Huh," he says as he sits back in his chair. "Wouldn't have thought. You seemed very confident, like you knew what you were doing."

I shrug. "I was just giving her what she wanted. What about you? Have you ever shared before?" I ask. I'd be shocked if he said yes.

"No. In the military, some of my buddies did that, and I've watched them. Afterward, they'd toss the woman to the side and have a new one to fuck the next day. I thought that was all you could really do with a threesome. Just casual fun."

I take a deep breath, sighing, "Yeah, that's what I kinda thought, too. But then Ryan showed up with his girlfriend, who was engaged to Killian." I let out a low laugh.

"That caught me by surprise, too. But they seem to make it work."

"With the right people—for the right person—it could, I guess."

"She's something else, isn't she?" he says, his voice soft.

I nod, taking the cigar back when he offers it. "Never met anyone like her."

He runs a hand through his hair, a gesture I've noticed he does when he's trying to organize his thoughts. "You know, I've loved her since we were teenagers."

"I figured as much," I reply, watching the smoke dissipate

above us. "The way you look at her... it's not something new. Are you pissed that I stepped into your territory?" I ask, genuinely curious.

He shakes his head, a small smile on his lips. "Man, if there's one thing I learned in the military, it's that territory is an illusion. You can't own people." He reaches for the whiskey bottle and pours himself another finger in my now-empty glass. "Besides, I've seen the way she is with you."

"And that doesn't bother you?"

He swirls the amber liquid in his glass. "It did at first. Fuck, of course it did. I mean, what man wants to share the woman he loves?" He takes a slow sip. "But I noticed things," he continues, his voice low but steady. "Like, she drew a sketch of you and her at a bar. I didn't know it was you until after you came to New York, but she looked at it and smiled. And it was the same smile she gave me."

I'm quiet for a moment, letting his words settle between us. It makes me happy that she thought about me after she left.

"She loves you, Zach." The words come out simpler than I expected. "That's not something that changes because I showed up. I'm not here to take her from you."

His eyes connect with mine, searching for something—truth, maybe, or reassurance. Looking for any trace of bullshit or manipulation.

"From the moment I realized what was between you two, I knew I was stepping into something... sacred, for lack of a better fucking word," I say before taking another draw from the cigar, holding the smoke in my mouth before releasing it in a slow stream toward the stars. "You two have history—deep, complicated history. I'm here... for as long as she wants me. For as long as it works. Which I hope is forever."

He studies me for a long moment. I can almost see the gears turning in his head, weighing my words against whatever history and feelings he's carrying. Then something shifts in his expression—a subtle relaxing around the eyes, a softening of his jaw.

"You know," he says finally, "when I first met you, I had respect for you—I still do. Ryan and Killian are like family, but when she first told me about you, I was ready to hate you. Had this whole fucking image in my head of some suit-wearing mafia prince asshole trying to add her to his collection." He lets out a quiet chuckle. "Now, I can't even have the satisfaction of hating you properly."

I smirk at that. "Disappointed?"

"Fucking devastated," he replies, but there's no seriousness in it.

I chuckle, tapping the ash from the cigar. "Believe me, I felt the same when I figured out who you were to her."

"I saw how she lit up around you," he continues, his fingers drumming lightly against the glass. "And fuck, man... how do you fight against something that makes her that happy?"

The weight of his admission hangs between us. I watch as he drains the last of his whiskey, his Adam's apple bobbing as he swallows. When he sets the glass down, there's a noticeable change in his posture—a decision made, a tension released.

"You're good for her," he says quietly. "And I'm man enough to admit that maybe—we're both better for her together than either of us would be alone."

"She deserves the fucking world," I reply, my voice unexpectedly rough. "Between the two of us, we might actually give it to her."

The tension between us, coiled since the beginning—that electric current of competition and wariness—doesn't disappear completely, but it transforms into something else. Something more like mutual respect, maybe even the start of a friendship.

"Truce?" he says, a hint of a smile playing on his lips.

"Truce. Though I think we're past that point since we both had our faces buried between Kim's thighs tonight."

He laughs at that—and I chuckle with him.

The sliding glass door opens, and there she is—Kim, wrapped in nothing but my discarded dress shirt from earlier. For a moment, she just stands there, framed in the doorway. Goosebumps rise on her bare thighs as the night air cools her skin.

"What's going on out here?" she asks. There's caution in her tone, as if she's stumbled upon something delicate that might shatter if she steps too close. Her eyes dart between us, taking in the cigar, the whiskey, our postures. Something in her expression shifts—surprise, then a cautious sort of wonder.

"Just enjoying the night," I say, lifting my cigar slightly.

"And each other's company, apparently," she adds, stepping onto the patio, the breeze catching the hem of the shirt, making it lift slightly above her thighs. "I woke up, and you were both gone. Thought maybe one of you killed the other and was hiding the body."

Zach pats his knee. "Come here, you're going to freeze." She moves to sit on Zach's lap, and he wraps his arms and his body around her, keeping her warm. The smile on her face is priceless right now. She's happy.

And me—I'm finally happy, too. I recall my brother recently encouraging me to find my happiness, and I've found it unexpectedly with another man involved, but I'll take it.

Chapter Twenty-Two

CONNOR

I'D LOVE to spend days—or better yet, weeks—locked up in bed with Kim, but now is the time to see if O'Malley takes the bait. It's also the day that Deveraux expects her to be delivered on his doorstep, so everyone is on high alert.

I check my watch—almost noon. I chose a little Italian restaurant with an outdoor seating area in Manhattan to meet at. The sidewalks are starting to fill in already, mostly locals on their way to work, some tourists and the occasional annoying pigeon looking for food or warmth under the heat towers surrounding the patio.

"All units in position?" I murmur into my earpiece.

Zach and his team are in a van parked down the street, ready to jump in, in case this meeting doesn't go as planned.

"Alpha team in place," Zach's voice comes through, crackled by the comm. "Visual on the south sidewalk."

I sit up straighter in the patio chair, mentally preparing.

"Target approaching," I whisper, glimpsing O'Malley's pudgy frame walking toward me.

My phone vibrates, it's a text from Kim.

> Have classes today, but I'll be thinking of you. 😊

I can't help but smile even as O'Malley approaches the table.

"I know that kind of smile. That is a man in love," O'Malley says with a thick Irish accent.

"Guilty as charged," I reply with a simple grin, pocketing my phone.

I stand up and move around to shake his hand.

"Michael O'Malley," I say, gripping firmly. "Thank you for meeting me on such short notice. Please, have a seat."

His palm is calloused, his grip strong but not challenging. His eyes, a startling shade of blue-gray, scan the patio with practiced nonchalance. I recognize the look—he's checking for tails, potential threats, escape routes.

"Well, your proposition was intriguing, Connor," he says, settling into the chair across from me. "And I've always been a man who appreciates intrigue."

I signal the waiter, who brings over two espressos and a plate of biscotti along with some menus. O'Malley raises an eyebrow but accepts the coffee with a nod of thanks.

"I have a weakness for Italian food," he says, unbuttoning his suit jacket. "Though nothing compares to my Moira's cooking."

"How is Moira?" I ask about his wife, keeping my tone conversational.

"She's grand. But I'm meeting up with a tight piece of ass

in an hour, so I better not eat too much," O'Malley jokes with a laugh, a genuine sound that crinkles the corners of his eyes. He's disgusting, but I still fake a laugh with him. Even though he's been a friend of the O'Brady family for years, he's never seen a genuine one from me.

"I'll be direct," I say, leaning forward. "My old man is a fucking hard-ass—stuck in his ways. I am the heir—the prince. I envision operations a lot different than he does. With Matteo Valentino out of the way, thanks to Fitzpatrick, Valentino has no heir—their position is crippled." With a forced sly smile, I say, "I think New York City has potential for new management."

I feel like shit for saying all this, but Killian and Ryan came up with the lines, and we rehearsed it.

O'Malley sips his espresso, his expression revealing nothing. "And what would you want from me?"

"Investment."

According to Victor's uncovered texts from Matteo, that was the same deal he was working with him on.

He sits quietly, as if contemplating.

Come on, you piece of shit. Take the bait.

"And what about your brother? Aren't you worried he won't like what you're up to?"

"Fuck him." I shrug my shoulders. "He hates our father as much as I do. That's why he left Ireland. We're not close. He resents me for being the oldest—legitimate heir."

"I see," O'Malley says, dipping biscotti in his espresso.

I have to sell it more, to make it easy for him. "I have loyal men in Ireland and weapons. I can facilitate the takedown. I just need some funding and expertise after Valentino is overthrown."

O'Malley smiles. *Yes!* It had to be asking for his expertise that piqued his interest. For years, he's been trying to get in business with my father, learn the ropes, and gain some responsibility. O'Malley is a businessman wanting to get into organized crime. To him, it's some sort of luxury or power. "I know nothing about running it, but I want some say as I learn."

"Deal."

O'Malley's large hand pats my back roughly in celebration. "We have a deal, son."

The rough action dislodges my earpiece, and I hear feedback, so I do a stealthy move to take it out—keeping it in my closed fist. Hopefully, Zach got all of that.

"So tell me, son. How is your wife? Camille, right?" O'Malley asks.

"Yeah, she's great."

"I bet she's excited to move to the States. You've been married for five years now—isn't time for some little Connors or Camilles running around?"

"Yeah, maybe," I say forcibly, really wanting to move on from this subject.

O'Malley reclines in his chair, his eyes narrowing as he studies me. Then his face transforms, lips curling upward into an ugly, piggish grin that makes my stomach turn.

"Tell you what, Connor," he says. "I've got a place not far from here. Very exclusive. Beautiful girls—even better than those places back in Dublin you frequented. Since you'll be living here, you might as well see what pussy New York has to offer." He winks, that grotesque smile stretching wider. "My treat. To celebrate our new arrangement." I keep my face neutral, though inside I'm cringing, thinking of a polite way to turn him down. "Your wife will never know," he adds, trying to convince me.

A sudden commotion erupts behind us, causing heads to swivel in curiosity. We spin around to witness a scene unfolding—a waiter, arms flailing, has collided with someone.

That someone is Kim.

Her eyes lock with mine for a fleeting moment, a mix of surprise and urgency flashing across her face. Without a second thought, she pivots on her heel and bolts away, blending into the bustling crowd.

Fuck! How much of that did she hear?

I shoot to my feet so quickly my chair topples backward.

O'Malley's eyebrows rise in surprise. "Something wrong, son?"

My mind races, calculating. She shouldn't be here. She's supposed to be in class. *Where the fuck is Drake?!*

"I'm sorry. I need to handle this," I say. His expression darkens. But I don't have time to worry about that now.

I rush between a couple of people, nearly knocking over a busboy. I scan the crowded sidewalk frantically and spot her dark hair about half a block away, moving fast.

"Kim!" I call out, pushing past pedestrians. "Kim, wait!"

She glances back, then actually starts running. *Fuck, she definitely heard.* My heart pounds as I chase after her, ignoring the curious stares from passersby.

I catch up to her at the corner where she's waiting for the light to change. When I touch her shoulder, she whirls around, her eyes blazing with hurt and fury.

Zach approaches from the other side. She rushes to him, burying her face into his chest, seeking solace. "Fuck, Connor. I warned you she was coming—didn't you hear me?" *The earpiece. You took out the fucking earpiece.* "Go back to O'Malley. You can talk to her when you're done."

Drake appears, doubled over and out of breath.

"Where the fuck were you?" I push him into the brick building beside us.

"She spotted you from across the street and ran off to say hi. I got caught up in the crowd, a bunch of fucking nuns. What was I supposed to do? I can't push around some nuns," he admits between breaths.

My jaw drops with the bullshit Drake just spewed.

"Her class was cancelled, and they were on their way back home. Connor, go back to O'Malley," Zach says sternly.

I run a hand through my hair, heart pounding in my chest as I watch Zach lead her away, and Drake follows. Every instinct screams to go after her, to explain, but there's too much at stake.

"Fuck," I mutter under my breath, turning back toward the restaurant. This operation is too important to blow now. I'll have to fix it later.

I compose myself, straightening my jacket and setting my face into a neutral expression as I approach the patio again. O'Malley is still sitting at our table, tapping his finger impatiently against the ivory tablecloth. His demeanor has hardened, the earlier camaraderie replaced with suspicion.

"Sorry about that," I say, sliding back into my seat. "Small personal matter."

O'Malley's tapping pauses. "Seemed more than small to me. That a piece you have on the side?"

"Yeah, just a recent fuck," I say, pulling out cash from my wallet and tossing it on the table. "Friends with benefits situation. I need to take care of this. We'll continue later."

"Ah," he says, a slow, knowing smile spreading across his weathered face. "The lass didn't know about Camille. Messy business, that."

"It's not what you think," I say automatically, then curse myself for the defensive response. He doesn't need to know Kim is someone I care about.

He leans back, clearly enjoying my discomfort. "Never is, lad. Never is."

—————

O'Malley is suspicious, but I manage to smooth things over with promises of another meeting soon to finalize details. All I can think about is getting back to the apartment, hoping against hope that Kim will be there.

I unlock the door and step inside, immediately spotting her in the living room. Her eyes are red-rimmed, her posture rigid as she stands by the window.

"Kim—" I begin, but she cuts me off.

"Get out," she says, her voice low and trembling with anger.

I close the door behind me. "Let me explain—"

"I said, get the fuck out!" Her voice rises.

"I fucking live here!" My voice rises, too.

"I don't care." Her eyes flash dangerously. "Zach told me everything—that you were meeting O'Malley, that this whole thing is some kind of operation. He said you were pretending to be friends with that guy."

"Yes, I was," I confirm.

"But he couldn't tell me if the wife part was pretend, too."

She swallows hard, crossing her arms over her chest. "Tell me, Connor—tell me you're not married."

I notice Zach sitting on the couch, looking uncomfortable, as though he's a child caught between two parents fighting.

I take a deep breath, feeling like I'm standing on the edge of a cliff. "Yes, technically, I am married."

Her face crumples. "You son of a—"

"Kim, please, you've got it all wrong. The marriage is—"

"Kiss my ass, Connor!" she shouts, cutting me off. Her hands ball into fists at her sides.

"I'll fucking eat it," I shoot back, my voice rough with frustration. "If you'd just shut up for two seconds and let me explain—"

I take a step toward her, close enough to catch her scent, but not daring to touch her. "My marriage to Camille is over. I'm just waiting on the paperwork."

Her eyes narrow, her expression shifting from rage to something—a mix of hurt and calculation.

"The paperwork?" she asks, her voice suddenly quiet. "When exactly did you file this paperwork? Before or after Boston?"

I can feel Zach's eyes on me, waiting for my answer just as intently as Kim is.

"After," I admit, holding her gaze. "It was after Boston."

She lets out a strangled laugh, turning away from me to stare out the window. "So, you weren't even in the process when we—" She can't finish the sentence.

"Our families arranged the marriage," I say, my voice low and urgent. "We've been living separate lives. It was never real."

"Never real?" She spins back to face me. "But real enough that you didn't bother to mention it until I caught you talking about her with some Irish mobster!"

"I didn't tell you because I didn't want to complicate things between us more than they already were." I step closer.

Zach clears his throat. "I'll just... go to the other room," he mutters, backing toward the hallway.

"No," she says sharply. "Stay. I want a witness to whatever bullshit he's about to feed me."

"You had a boyfriend," I snap back, instantly regretting it after seeing the rage on her face.

I glance over at Zach. With a subtle shake of his head and a slight roll of his eyes, he conveys that I have just put my foot in my mouth.

Kim laughs, but it's a horrible sound, brittle and wounded. "A fake boyfriend—Connor. Fake. Do you understand the difference?"

"Kim, it's complicated—"

"Complicated?" she explodes, grabbing a throw pillow from the couch and hurling it at me, which I dodge, and it falls to the floor. "You're married. You have a wife! Oh! And you fuck whores!"

"No!" I immediately say with a raised and firm voice. "You don't understand the expectations of me living under my father's rule as heir. He was a complete womanizer and expected me to be the same. I let him and our business associates *think* I had women all over town and frequented brothels. But I used that as a fucking excuse to escape that suffocating house and my asshole father." My eyes connect with hers, pleading. "I married Camille as a business arrangement. We are not in love. We consummated the marriage once, Kim—just once—the night of our wedding because of the pressure of our families. We haven't touched each other since. We've never slept in the same bedroom. I—I haven't been with anyone else in five years—five long fucking years—until you."

"Why's that?" she asks, almost sarcastically.

"We both loved other people."

She gasps sharply.

Zach turns to look at me once more, his eyes conveying a silent message that screams, "Dude, you're making it worse."

And I might be. But if I'm going to lay everything on the line, I might as well go all the way.

"There's someone else," she whispers, looking heartbroken all over again.

"Was," I breathe. "She's dead."

Zach steps over to her, giving her arm a comforting squeeze. "I'll be in the bedroom."

She doesn't stop him this time. After he's gone, providing us some privacy, I continue.

"I met Isabelle when I was seventeen," I say, sinking onto the couch, my eyes fixed somewhere beyond the room. "She was the daughter of one of my father's business associates. Red hair—wild curls she could never tame and these incredible green eyes."

She doesn't move, but I can feel her listening.

"The first time I saw her, she was arguing with her father in the garden at some boring function. He wanted her to meet some politician's son, and she was having none of it. She told him in perfect, proper English, exactly where he could shove his matchmaking attempts." I can't help the small smile that forms. "I fell in love with her right there."

"What happened?" she asks, her voice softer now, curious.

"We were young. Stupid. Sneaking around for years, meeting in libraries, abandoned buildings. We'd talk for hours about everything and nothing. We made plans. She was brilliant—aspired to study medicine—heal people. She'd go to medical school in America, I'd break free from my obligations, and we'd build something real together." I swallow and take a deep breath. "My father found out about Isabelle and forbade me to see her. He had already made a deal with a Frenchman to marry off his daughter, Camille, and he could see my attachment to Isabelle. I refused—continued to sneak away and see her. When my father found out, he—he—" I reach for the whiskey on the coffee table. It must have been Zach's, but fuck it. I need this right now. "He raped her," I say, then quickly chase my words with the whiskey, feeling the burn down my throat. She gasps, then comes to sit next to me on the couch. "A few weeks later, she killed herself—cut her wrists in the bathtub. I've lived with that guilt for so long. I should have ended it with her when he told me to. She would have been heartbroken but still alive."

The room fills with a heavy silence, broken only by my ragged breathing. Kim shifts closer, her warmth seeping into my side as she leans her head against my shoulder.

"Connor," she whispers, her voice thick with emotion. "That wasn't your fault. None of it was."

I stare straight ahead, the familiar weight of guilt pressing on my chest. "I knew what my father was capable of. I should have protected her."

She reaches up, her fingers tracing the hard line of my jaw, turning my face toward hers. "Your father is a monster. What he did—" Her voice breaks. "—that's on him. Not you."

I close my eyes, feeling something crack inside me. How many nights had I lain awake, replaying every moment, searching for the decision that could have changed everything?

"After she died," I say, "I decided I would never love anyone else again."

I stand and walk to the window, looking out at the city below. She remains silent, giving me the space to find my words.

"I became a machine," I continue, my voice rough with emotion. "My father arranged the marriage to Camille to take place six months later. She was grieving, too—her boyfriend had been killed in a car accident. We both knew what it was—a business arrangement, nothing more. Two broken people going through the motions. We had an agreement. Both of us wanting to be depressed and grieve in our own ways. It would buy us some time. I locked away my heart. I became exactly what was expected of me—cold, calculating, the perfect heir my father wanted. I thought part of me was dead."

I turn back to face Kim, who's watching me with those eyes that somehow see everything I try to hide.

"Then I bumped into you on that ridiculous sidewalk in Boston," I say, my voice softening, and go back to sit next to her on the sofa. "Looking annoyed, cursing me out and fucking beautiful doing it."

A small smile tugs at her lips, despite the tears still clinging to her lashes.

"I didn't expect to feel anything that day," I continue, moving back toward her. "I certainly didn't expect you. I spent five years pretending to be someone's husband while feeling nothing. I convinced myself that was all I deserved after

Isabelle. That emptiness was my penance." I pause, struggling to find the right words. "But you... you wrecked everything."

She looks at me, her eyes questioning.

"You made me laugh—really laugh—for the first time in years. You challenged me, frustrated me. And I started feeling again."

A single tear escapes down her cheek. I reach out, brushing it away with my thumb. "I'm sorry, Kim. I should have told you about Camille from the beginning." My voice cracks with sincerity. "I was terrified of losing you before I ever really had you."

"You lied to me," she says, but there's less fire in her voice now.

"Not about how I feel about you," I answer, taking her hands in mine. "Never about that. I filed for divorce as soon as I got back from Boston. Camille and I both agreed even before then it was time to end the charade."

"I need to know everything, Connor. No more secrets."

"No more secrets," I agree, taking a deep breath. "But there's one more thing I need to tell you."

She nods and seems to prepare herself mentally for my next confession.

I know this is probably the worst possible timing. She's still reeling from finding out about Camille, still hurt and angry. But I can't hold it in anymore—not with the way she's looking at me, not with everything laid bare between us.

"Kim," I say, my voice suddenly hoarse. "I love you."

Her eyes widen, lips parting in surprise.

"Fuck, I know it's too soon and probably the last thing you want to hear right now," I continue, the words tumbling out before I can stop them. "But I need you to know. I love you in a way I never thought I'd love anyone again. I'm in love with you, Kimberly *Merlot* Stanton. Completely, utterly in love with you."

She bursts into laughter. "Quit being so cheesy," she teases, punching my arm playfully.

"Cheesy can be good," I state quietly, repeating what I told her at the pizza place in Boston.

Her expression shifts serious, holding our gaze. "I fucking love you, too," she murmurs, her words barely above a whisper, but carrying sincerity and spoken in true Kim fashion.

The four words echo in my head—well, five, if you include "fucking." After years of emptiness, of going through the motions, something warm and bright unfurls in my chest.

She's looking at me, those beautiful eyes searching mine, waiting for a response. But all I can think is: *She loves me back*. After Isabelle, I never thought I'd hear those words again. Never thought I'd feel this way.

The door creaks open, and Zach pops his head out from the hallway. "I thought I heard laughing. Is it safe to come out?"

"Yes, Zach," she responds with a soft smile.

"Good, now you can fuck and make up," he says, a teasing suggestion wrapped in humor.

Kim looks at me and bites her lip before speaking. "You did mention something about my ass." Her eyes twinkle with mischief.

A sinister grin splays across my lips. "I did, didn't I?"

With a swift, effortless motion, I lift her up, her petite body easily hoisted over my shoulder in true caveman style.

Her squeal of surprise turns into laughter as I take her to the bedroom.

Chapter Twenty-Three

KIMBERLY

I MAY HAVE BEEN a little dramatic about Connor, but fuck, it hurt to find out that he was—is—married. I appreciated how he opened up to me about his past. It showed me a side of him that I didn't know was there, and it only makes me love him more. Love—he told me he loves me.

I love him, too. When I say it in my head, it feels right, as scary as that is. But then there's Zach. God, Zach—I fucking love him, too.

How is this my life now? I never even had a real boyfriend before, and suddenly, I have two. Two people who actually see me—the real me—and somehow think I'm worth loving.

My phone buzzes inside my pocket. This professor has a strict no-phone policy, so I ignore it. It's probably Connor or Zach. I resist the urge to check it. Professor Wright is busy droning on about macroeconomic theory. His monotone voice washes over the lecture hall like audible Ambien.

I stifle a yawn and glance at the clock. Twenty-three more

minutes of this torture. My phone vibrates again. Probably a voicemail.

My pencil taps against my notebook where I've doodled more than I have actual written notes. Little hearts with "C+K" inside them along with "Z+K". God, I'm pathetic. A geriatric college student drawing doodles like a middle schooler. The phone buzzes once more. *Damn, get a clue, I'm busy...* I move to reach in my pocket, but then the door creaks open, and heads turn. Professor Wright pauses mid-sentence, his bushy eyebrows furrowing in annoyance at the interruption.

Two uniformed police officers step inside, followed by a man and woman in plain clothes with badges clipped to their belts. What the hell?

"We apologize for the disruption," the man in plain clothes says to Professor Wright.

My first thought is that someone's parent died, or there was a car accident. It happens sometimes—that terrible moment when someone's normal day shatters with news delivered by solemn-faced officers. I've been in this moment before with my mother.

The officers scan the room methodically, their eyes moving over each tier of students until they find what they're looking for. My row. My seat. *Me.*

I feel the weight of everyone's eyes as they all shift toward me. The room goes so quiet that the hum of the projector now sounds like a jet engine.

"Kimberly Stanton?" the female detective asks, her voice cutting through the stunned silence, though it's clear she already knows who I am.

"Yes?" My question comes out as a croak as my throat constricts.

The uniformed officers position themselves on either side of my row. She approaches, her face professionally blank, but I detect something in her eyes—pity, maybe.

"I am Detective Reyes, Ms. Stanton, we need you to come with us."

My classmates shift in their seats, the rustle of clothing and notebooks suddenly deafening. Someone whispers something I can't make out. A phone camera clicks with a flash.

"What's this about?" I ask.

"You're under arrest for the murder of Matteo Valentino."

My eyes bug out of my head. *WHAT THE FUCK?!*

The two uniformed officers each grab an arm and guide me out of my seat and down the small steps of the stadium seating. Students are in a tizzy with all kinds of loud but hushed whispers. I can feel them staring.

My heart is pounding out of my chest. When we get outside, another officer is holding Drake back. He looks furiously at officers, trying to reach me.

"Don't say anything!" he shouts, his voice cracking with desperation as he struggles against the officer restraining him. "Not a single word! I'll call Connor and Zach!"

The officers tighten their grip on my arms as I try to process what's happening. Matteo Valentino—the man is still haunting me. We anticipated questions regarding Matteo's disappearance, but we hadn't considered that they would arrest me for his murder.

Detective Reyes shoots Drake a look before turning back to me. "You have the right to remain silent. Anything you say can and will be used against you in a court of law." Her voice sounds distant, like I'm underwater, while cold metal handcuffs click around my wrists. "You have the right to an attorney," she continues. "If you cannot afford an attorney, one will be provided for you."

Drake is still yelling at me, his voice growing more distant, too.

My legs feel like they're made of jelly as the officers guide me down the hallway. Students line the corridor, phones out, recording every humiliating second. Tomorrow, I'll be a viral sensation—the college girl arrested during Macroeconomics 301 for murdering a crime lord.

Zach and Connor will get me out of this, right?

The interrogation room is as minimalist as you would think: four walls painted a shade of gray, so bland it feels deliberately designed to break the human spirit. A metal table is bolted to the floor, two chairs on one side, one on the other. Mine. The fluorescent lights above emit a persistent hum, making it hard to think clearly. Sitting here in silence is torture in itself.

I've been waiting here for two hours and forty-three minutes. I know, because there's a clock on the wall, its second hand ticking maddening loud. Tick. Tick. Tick. Each sound is a reminder that I'm trapped here. Waiting.

The door finally opens. Detective Reyes enters, followed by an older man with salt-and-pepper hair.

"Ms. Stanton," she says, placing a manila folder on the table. "You're in a lot of trouble. Do you understand that?"

I sit up straight, hands folded in my lap, trying to look calmer than I feel.

Drake told me not to talk. And I've seen enough crime shows to know not to.

"I'm not talking to you. I want a lawyer," I state firmly.

"That's fine. You can listen," the salt-and-pepper haired man says.

Detective Reyes slides a photograph across the metal table. The image is grainy—security camera footage of Matteo and me leaving the venue for the underground boxing match. I know that it's me, but the quality is so poor I can barely make out any distinguishing features. *Really, this is what they have?*

"What's interesting," he says, "is the murder weapon. A tire wrench. Sterling silver. Belonged to the victim—his car." *Oh, you mean the one I was in the trunk of?* He pulls out another photo—a bloodied tire wrench. "And guess what we found on it?"

My heart hammers against my ribs. This is all an obvious setup. This is not how Matteo died. But I hold my tongue.

"Your fingerprints, Ms. Stanton." Reyes leans forward. "Clear as day. After the boxing event, you two had a heated argument. And you killed him. Tell us where the body is, and we'll tell the judge you cooperated."

My mouth goes dry. But I continue to keep it shut even though the stubborn bitch in me wants to scream and fucking curse these assholes out.

There's a knock on the door, and Detective Reyes walks to it, cracking it to whisper to the person. She closes the door and turns to look at me with a devilish grin.

"Your attorney is here."

I sigh. *Thank God!* They sent someone here for me.

The door swings open, and my relief evaporates instantly. Something about him seems familiar. I've seen this man before. The scar. It's Deveraux.

"Detectives," he says, his voice smooth.

As the detectives file out, he takes the seat across from me.

"Kimberly, wonderful to see you again."

Those eyes, slate gray and calculating, scan me from head to toe as if he's assessing merchandise or livestock.

He unbuttons his suit jacket before sitting, revealing a silk lining the color of dried blood.

He smiles, showing teeth too perfect to be natural. "The police believe I'm your attorney because that's what I told them." He leans forward, and his cologne—something expensive and suffocating—invades my space. "And they're quite happy to leave us alone for a while."

Chapter Twenty-Four

CONNOR

I PACE the halls of the police station, waiting for someone to tell Zach and me what the fuck is going on.

I check my watch for the hundredth time. Six and a half hours she's been here. God knows what they've been saying to her. But she's smart—she'll know not to talk.

Whenever the door at the end of the hall opens, my heart stops for a second, only to sink when it's just another officer or some random person I don't recognize.

"She'll be okay," I mumble.

The linoleum floor squeaks under my shoes as I continue my pacing. Seven steps one way, turn, seven steps back. Posters about community policing and crime prevention are posted on the main wall, their cheerful graphics a mocking contrast to the situation we're in.

"You need to sit," Zach says from where he's sitting on the bench, his hands holding his head. "You're making me more anxious."

I ignore him and keep moving. Sitting still feels impossible. My mind races through every possible scenario, every question they might ask her. They can't think that a petite woman could kill a two-hundred-plus-pound boxer, do they? And hide the body?

I stop mid-pace, running my hand through my hair for what must be the hundredth time.

"They don't have any actual evidence. She's being set up," I say out loud.

The door to the hallway opens again. We both look over and freeze, watching as Kim appears, followed by Lincoln, Killian's lawyer, and a woman in a charcoal pantsuit, her light-brown hair pulled back in a bun.

Her face is unreadable, but her eyes tell everything—exhaustion and that she's been crying. The woman extends her hand toward Kim, passing her a small white card.

"Remember what we discussed, Ms. Stanton," she says, her voice carrying that practiced professional tone.

Kim nods, taking the card.

The woman turns to Zach and me. "She's free to go." She gives us a quick, calculating glance before turning on her heel as she walks back through the door.

I don't wait another second. My feet carry me across the worn linoleum, and I pull Kim into a fierce embrace. She feels smaller somehow, fragile in a way she never has before.

"You okay?" I whisper against her ear, not trusting my voice at full volume.

Zach rises from the bench, joining us, wrapping his arms around both of us. "Let's get out of this hellhole," he says.

On the ride back to the Fitzpatrick building, Kim is quiet. She just stares out the window, occasionally closing her eyes as if she's reliving a moment and hates it. But that is to be expected after something traumatic, I suppose. Being accused and arrested for murder is a serious thing.

When we get to the door of my apartment, we open it to find Killian and Ryan standing inside. I forget this used to be Ryan's place, and he still has access.

She sinks onto the couch, her fingers working at the buttons of her coat. The fabric rustles as she shrugs it off, revealing a wrinkled blouse underneath.

Ryan approaches with a glass of water, placing it on the coffee table in front of her. "Drink something," he says softly.

She moves to pick up the glass but hesitates. "Fuck that. Give me something stronger," she says.

"I'm on it!" Zach shouts, bolting toward the kitchen. He emerges in seconds with a bottle of Cabernet Kim hoards—one that's 14.5% alcohol.

The dark liquid swirls against the crystal as Zach carries it carefully across the room. She takes the glass from him, her fingers still trembling slightly. "Thanks," she murmurs before taking a long, deep gulp. Some color returns to her cheeks as she closes her eyes, savoring it.

"So," Killian says, sitting opposite her on the coffee table. "What happened there?"

She drinks another sip, longer this time. When she lowers the glass, there's a dark stain on her upper lip that she wipes away with her thumb.

"They had photos," she says. "Me and Matteo at the boxing event. Us leaving. I was the last one he was seen with, so I guess they're trying to pin it on me."

Zach hands her a blanket from the back of the couch. She wraps it around her shoulders. The gesture makes her seem even smaller, more vulnerable than before.

"Um, they have a fingerprint of mine on a tire wrench— the murder weapon," she continues. "But lucky for me, Lincoln found a clerical error on some of the evidence paperwork, so they had to let me go." She shrugs, almost as if now, the entire ordeal was just a minor inconvenience. But her body language still says otherwise.

I lean against the wall, arms crossed, watching her face carefully. There's something she's holding back—something she's not saying.

"What did you discuss?" I ask, suddenly remembering the woman at the police station. "The detective—she wanted you to remember what you discussed. What was that?"

She swallows hard. "Detective Reyes," she acknowledges. "That I still have time to come forward. Save myself—tell my side of the story and set the record straight."

"Which means they have nothing at all," Ryan states. "They're fishing—using her to get to us. They know we're involved somehow."

I would agree with my brother. Out of all of us, they probably think Kim is our weakest link. But they don't know how tough she really is.

Killian shifts from where he's seated. His jaw works as if he's chewing on words he's not sure he should spit out. I recognize that look—the one that precedes a question I don't want to hear.

"Kim," he says finally, his voice low and careful. "Did you..." He clears his throat, eyes darting briefly to Zach and me before returning to her face. "Did you say anything to them? About Cassie?"

I exchange a glance with Zach, whose face has gone completely rigid. He agrees. The audacity...

"Okay, everyone out." I say at the same time Kim says, "No, I didn't."

They're only thinking about Cassie right now. I mean—I don't blame them, but Kim would never say anything, and don't you think if Kim told them that Cassie killed Matteo, the police would have taken her into custody by now?

Killian and Ryan filter out at my command—Killian with reluctance, Ryan with understanding.

As the door closes behind them, I slump into the armchair across from Kim, my body suddenly heavy with exhaustion. The adrenaline that's been keeping me going is fading fast.

She takes another long sip of her wine, her gaze fixed on some invisible point beyond the far wall. The wall clock ticks loudly in the quiet room.

Zach shifts uncomfortably on the edge of the couch, glancing at me with raised eyebrows. I give a small shrug in response.

The red liquid catches the light as she tilts the glass, studying it with an intensity that feels deliberate. She's avoiding our eyes, creating a barrier between us with her silence.

Minutes pass. Zach clears his throat, but she doesn't react. She simply raises the glass to her lips again, nursing her wine.

"You want something to eat?" I finally ask, unable to bear the tension any longer.

"Babygirl, you're eerily quiet. Please, what can we do?" he asks.

As if snapping out of whatever trance she was in, Kim looks up at us both. "Can we order pizza, make popcorn, and watch movies with some wine?"

"Yeah, anything you want," he agrees and pulls out his phone to scroll through delivery options.

"God, I feel disgusting," she says suddenly, setting the wineglass down. Her fingers run through her tangled hair, grimacing when they catch on a knot. "I need to wash the police station off me. I'm going to grab a shower before the food gets here."

She rises from the couch, the blanket falling away from her shoulders. For a moment she stands there, looking at us with an expression I can't quite read.

"Thank you both," she whispers. She leans down, pressing a soft kiss to my cheek, then moves to Zach and does the same.

Without another word, she walks toward the bedroom, her footsteps fading down the hallway.

As soon as I hear the bathroom door close and the shower run, I turn to Zach.

"She's hiding something," I whisper.

He sets his phone down, his forehead creased with concern. "She's definitely off," he admits in a hushed tone. "But hiding something?"

I slide closer to him on the couch, making sure my voice doesn't carry down the hallway. "She's deliberately keeping something from us. Did you see how she avoided eye contact?"

"I noticed." He sighs, running a hand over his stubbled jaw. "But maybe she just needs time. Think about it—she's been accused of murder and had evidence presented against her, however flimsy. But she spent half the day at a police station. She's probably trying to process everything herself before she dumps it all on us. Or better yet—knowing Kim— she doesn't want to bother us with it at all."

The shower continues running in the background, a steady white noise that makes our whispered conversation feel even more conspiratorial.

"We should give her space," he adds, picking up his phone again to complete the pizza order. "She'll tell us when she's ready."

I want to argue, but what he's saying makes sense.

A few minutes later, she steps out into the living room. Her face is freshly washed, and she's wearing one of Zach's military hoodies that's oversized for her.

"What are we going to watch?" she asks, her voice lighter than it has been all day, though the dark circles haven't completely left her eyes.

"You pick," I say.

Two hours later, the coffee table is littered with empty pizza boxes, along with three half-empty glasses of wine and a large bowl of popcorn.

We nestled her between us on the couch, and her body finally relaxed. Her hair is pulled up in a messy bun, a few stray strands framing her face.

On the screen, an action movie plays out—something mindless with explosions and car chases, the kind where you don't have to think too hard about plots or character motivations. It's exactly what she needs.

The final explosion fades to black, and music plays as the credits scroll.

She stretches her arms above her head, the sleeve of Zach's hoodie sliding down to reveal the delicate bones of her wrist. She sighs, a sound of contentment.

"Thank you," she murmurs, her voice husky from disuse. "For getting me out of there. For not asking too many questions. For this." She gestures vaguely at the remnants of our impromptu movie night.

Zach's hand finds hers in the semi-darkness, his thumb tracing slow circles on her palm. "Always," he says.

I watch them from the corner of my eye, the way they lean into each other.

The room feels different somehow, charged with an electricity that wasn't there a minute ago. Maybe it's the wine, or the relief of having Kim back safe, or simply the closeness of our bodies on the couch.

Her eyes meet mine, something vulnerable and hungry in her look. The day's trauma has left her raw, and I can see a need there—not just for comfort, but for connection.

The wine has softened the edges of everything, giving the room a dreamlike quality. Outside, rain has fallen, droplets pattering against the windows. The city lights filter through the blinds, painting her skin in alternating stripes of shadow.

She turns to Zach, her fingers trailing up his arm with deliberate slowness. When she reaches his face, she traces the line of his jaw. His breath catches as she leans in, pressing her lips against his with a tenderness that quickly escalates into something more urgent.

I should look away. I should give them privacy. But I can't. I watch, mesmerized—the subtle movements of their mouths, the slight tilt of her head, the way his hand cradles the back of her neck.

When they part, she turns to me, the whites of her eyes looking dark in the low light. Her lips are slightly parted, a question in her eyes that I answer by leaning forward. Our lips meet.

Hers are soft against mine, tasting faintly of wine and salt. The kiss deepens, and I feel her hands on my shoulder, then wrapping around my neck.

He reaches for the hem of her borrowed hoodie. She raises her arms obediently, allowing him to pull it over her head in one fluid motion. Beneath the hoodie, she wears only a simple black thong.

"Beautiful," I say.

I lower my head to her chest, taking one nipple into my mouth. She gasps, arching her back as my tongue circles the sensitive peak, my teeth grazing lightly against her skin.

He moves behind her, his hands sliding around her waist, dipping beneath the waistband of her thong. Her breath hitches as his fingers slip between her thighs. Her hips roll instinctively against his hand, seeking more friction.

I move to her other breast, giving it the same attention while my hand trails down her stomach, joining Zach's beneath her shorts.

She widens her thighs, allowing us better access as our hands work in tandem. Her wetness coats my fingers as I circle her clit, teasing her sensitive bundle of nerves, while his long fingers thrust in and out of her, hopefully curling upward to find that spot that makes her weak with need. We establish a rhythm without needing to speak.

"Oh god," she moans, her head falling back against his shoulder. He presses kisses along the column of her neck, then leaves to nibble at her earlobe. Her thighs tremble as we increase our pace.

I lean forward, capturing her mouth with mine as we

continue fingering her. Her breathing becomes erratic, little whimpers escaping between her lips. I can feel her getting closer, her muscles tensing beneath our touch.

Zach adds another finger, stretching her further while I press harder against her clit, tight, focused circles that have her bucking against our hands.

"I'm going to—" She gasps, unable to finish her sentence as her orgasm crashes through her.

Her body trembles against our hands, her mouth opening in a silent cry as she comes undone. I watch, transfixed, as her face transforms—eyes fluttering closed, lips parted, cheeks flushed. A dirty little angel.

I've seen many women come before, but none like her. She glows from within, radiating something both pure and filthy at once. The contradiction of her fascinates me—how she can look so innocent while doing such wicked things, how her face can hold such sweetness even as obscenities spill from her lips.

A sense of satisfaction warms my chest, knowing I'm one of only two men who get to witness her like this, who gets to reduce this fierce, complicated woman to shuddering bliss.

As she comes down, her breathing gradually slows, and she opens her eyes. They're hazy with bliss, pupils still dilated. She gives me a lazy, contented smile that makes my heart twist with love. That smile—it's a weapon she doesn't even know she wields.

She reaches for me, her fingers curling around my neck to pull me in for another kiss. Against my lips, she whispers, "I need you both."

Tonight is about making her forget everything else but us.

Chapter Twenty-Five

ZACH

Kim's small hands work to unbutton my jeans. I lift my hips and help her pull them down so that she can gain access to my bulging cock. She tugs at my boxers, and my erection springs free.

"You're so hard," she whispers.

I take her hands and guide them to my shaft, encouraging her to explore.

Her eyes, still heavy-lidded with her own satisfaction, lock with mine as she slowly strokes me.

"I need to taste you," she says, sliding off the couch cushion. She positions herself between my legs and kneels, looking up at me through her lashes.

"Babygirl," I groan, unable to form more coherent thoughts as she leans forward, her tongue darting out to trace the underside. The wet heat of her mouth sends a jolt through my body, and my fingers instinctively thread through her hair.

She takes me deeper, her lips stretching around my girth.

The sight of her like this, on her knees, taking me with such eager devotion, nearly undoes me.

"God, Babygirl," I whisper, watching her head bob rhythmically. "That feels amazing."

Unlike other women I've been with who treated this as some obligatory chore, Kim genuinely enjoys this—revels in it. I can see it in the way her own breathing quickens, in the little hums that vibrate around me. That's what makes this so mind-blowing. Not just her skill—though God knows she's talented—but her enthusiasm.

Behind her, Connor positions himself on his knees, his large hands spreading her thighs wider. His fingers trace the thin fabric between her legs. Without warning, he grips the material and tears it away with one forceful motion. The sound of ripping lace fills the room as she gasps around my cock.

"Fuck," I hiss. The sight of his dominance combined with her mouth on me brings me dangerously close to the edge. I have to clench my jaw and grip the couch cushion to keep from losing control completely.

Kim moans as he exposes her. He slides beneath her, positioning himself on his back, his broad shoulders settling against the hardwood floor. His hands grip her thighs, pulling her down until she's hovering just above his face, her knees on either side of his head.

Her mouth slides off me with a wet pop, her eyes widening. "Oh!" she gasps, her warm breath puffing against my slick shaft.

I can tell the moment his tongue makes contact. Her body jerks slightly; her hands grip my thighs for support. She takes me back into her mouth, deeper this time, and I fight the urge to thrust upward.

"That's it," I encourage, my voice rough with need. I cup her cheek with one hand, thumb tracing her stretched lips where they meet my cock. "You take it so well."

The three of us find a rhythm that's both chaotic and perfect—Kim pleasuring me while Connor pleasures her, each of us feeding off the others' reactions.

Her technique is exquisite—alternating between taking me deep and pulling back to focus on the tip, her hand working what her mouth can't reach. Her eyes flutter closed as she works me, her rhythm faltering momentarily whenever he licks a sensitive spot.

His hands slide up to caress her ass, spreading her wider as he devours her. The sight of her caught between us, lost in ecstasy, is almost as arousing as her mouth on me.

"God," I say between ragged breaths.

Her eyes flick up to meet mine, and the sight nearly undoes me.

"You taste amazing," Connor murmurs against her pussy, his voice muffled. His hands grip her hips, steadying her as she trembles.

She pulls back. "I need more," she says, her voice raspy and desperate.

The raw need in her voice makes my cock twitch. He pulls back from between her legs, his chin glistening with her arousal. His eyes are dark, pupils blown wide with lust.

He rises to his feet, his own erection straining against his pants. Without hesitation, he unbuttons his jeans, pushing them down along with his boxer briefs in one fluid motion.

His cock springs free, thick and ready, and he strokes himself in anticipation.

Kim rises too, her flawless naked body flushed and perfect in the dim light. I grip her hips as she positions herself above me. She's so wet that when she sinks down, I slide in with almost no resistance. We both gasp at the sensation. She's tight and hot around me, her inner walls clenching as she adjusts to my size.

"Fuck," I groan.

She leans forward, pressing her luscious breasts against my chest, her lips brushing mine.

"God, Zach," she moans as she takes me completely inside her. "You feel so good."

I grip her hips, guiding her movements as she rides me, rotating them. The couch cushions compress beneath us with each thrust, the leather sticking slightly to my bare skin. Her breasts bounce enticingly with each movement, and I can't resist leaning forward to take one perfect nipple into my mouth, flicking it with my tongue in short strokes. She gasps at the contact, her inner muscles clenching around me.

Connor moves beside us, his cock standing proudly at attention. She turns her head toward him without breaking her rhythm on me. Her mouth opens eagerly to welcome him, creating a triangle of pleasure between the three of us again.

"That's it, baby," he encourages as her lips close around him. His hand gently cups the back of her neck, his expression one of pure bliss I'm familiar with—I'm sure I have the same look.

I thrust upward to meet her downward movements, causing her to moan around him. The rhythm between us grows more frantic as we find our stride.

The sensation of Kim around me is unlike anything I've experienced before. She's impossibly tight, almost velvety, gripping me perfectly with each slide of her hips. Most partners I've had felt good, sure, but this—she's different. There's a difference between someone who's just physically compatible and someone whose body seems designed specifically to complement yours—taking you to new heights of pleasure you've never experienced before.

I feel her thighs trembling against mine, her body tightening around my rock-hard cock with each downward plunge. Her movements become more desperate. Connor's breathing grows heavier as he watches her face, his hand now tangled in her hair, falling out of its messy bun.

"Fuck," I groan. "Babygirl, you're going to make me come."

She releases him momentarily, her head falling back as she focuses on the sensation of me inside her. "Me too," she pants, her voice barely above a whisper. "I'm so close."

I slide my hand between us, finding her clit with my thumb. The moment I make contact, she cries out, her body arching beautifully.

Connor steps back, stroking himself slowly, watching us, allowing her to focus fully on her building orgasm.

Kim leans forward, changing the angle of each thrust.

"Right there," she whispers against my ear, her breath hot and ragged. "Oh, god, right there."

"That's it," he murmurs in her ear. "Let go, beautiful."

I feel her body beginning to tense, those telltale flutters around my cock signaling her approaching climax. My hands grip her hips tighter, guiding her movements with increasing urgency as my orgasm builds. The pressure at the base of my spine intensifies with each thrust.

She gasps, her nails digging into my shoulders. "Zach, I'm—"

Her words dissolve into a cry of pleasure as her orgasm crashes through her. My vision blurs as I thrust upward one final time, burying myself to the hilt. My muscles contract, and my cum spurts deep inside her.

For a moment, we remain frozen in a perfect tableau of pleasure—her body trembling on top of mine, our breathing ragged and uneven, hearts pounding against each other's chests. Her forehead drops to my shoulder.

As the final tremors of our shared climax subside, Connor moves forward. Without warning, he hooks his arms under her armpits and lifts her effortlessly off my still-sensitive cock. She gasps at the sudden movement, her body still quivering as he carries her across the room.

"My turn," he growls against her neck, his muscles flexing as he holds her weight with ease.

Kim's legs wrap instinctively around his waist, her arms clinging to his neck for support. Her back meets the wall with a soft thud, causing her to inhale sharply.

I watch from the couch, mesmerized by the sight of them —her slender form pinned between Connor's larger body and the wall, her skin flushed and eyes half-lidded.

He positions himself, the head of his cock nudging at her entrance. Despite her recent climax, Kim's body responds eagerly, her hips tilting to meet him.

"Please," she whimpers, her fingers tangling in his dark hair. "I need you inside me."

With one powerful thrust, he pushes his cock inside until

it disappears. Her body bows from the wall, mouth falling open. Her fingers dig into his shoulders, no doubt leaving crescent-shaped marks on his tanned skin. I can see every detail from my position on the couch. The way her thighs quiver around his waist, the perfect arch of her spine, the flush that spreads from her cheeks down to her heaving breasts.

His muscles flex as he holds her up. The veins in his forearms stand out as he grips her thighs.

"Fuck, you feel incredible," he growls, his voice deeper than usual, strained with restraint as he moves. "So tight."

He moves, each thrust deliberate and powerful. The muscles in his back ripple with the effort. Her head falls back against the wall, her eyes closed in concentration as she surrenders to the sensation.

There's something profoundly intimate about watching them this way—seeing Kim's expressions of pleasure from a distance, noticing details I might miss when I'm lost in my own sensations with her.

His thrusts slow, each one drawing a breathless gasp from her parted lips. Her head falls back against the wall again, and he takes advantage, leaning forward to trail kisses down her neck, occasionally nipping at her skin.

"Harder, please," she begs.

Connor responds with a primal growl, his hands gripping her thighs tighter as he increases his pace with renewed vigor.

The room fills with the wet slap of skin as he pounds into her. Each powerful thrust forces a high-pitched gasp from her throat that mingles with his deeper grunts. I find myself hardening again at the sheer eroticism of their sounds.

"You take me so fucking good," he says between thrusts.

I shift on the couch, unable to tear my eyes away from

them. The leather creaks beneath me as I adjust, my hand unconsciously moving to stroke myself. My spent cock twitches with renewed interest as I watch and listen to them lose themselves in each other. This is like my own personal porno, where my girlfriend is the star.

The wall provides the perfect leverage as his large hands grip her thighs tighter, fingers digging into the soft flesh as he lifts her slightly higher, changing the angle of his thrusts. Kim's body responds to his—her heavy breasts bounce with each thrust.

Connor's rhythm becomes more urgent, more desperate. His body tenses with each thrust, the cords in his neck standing out.

Her slender fingers tangle in his hair, pulling him closer as she crashes her lips against his. Their kiss is hungry, desperate, all clashing teeth and dueling tongues as he continues to thrust.

He shifts his grip, supporting her with one arm while his other hand slides between their bodies. His fingers find her clit, circling the sensitive bud.

The effect is immediate—Kim's body jerks against him, a strangled cry escapes her lips. Her nails rake across his back, leaving red trails across his skin.

"Oh god, oh god, oh god," she chants, her voice rising with each repetition as Connor works her toward a third orgasm. Her legs tighten around his waist, heels digging into the small of his back as she pulls him deeper. The wall creaks slightly under their combined weight and the force of his increasingly frantic thrusts.

I can see the precise moment she falls apart. Her eyes

widen before squeezing shut, her mouth forms a perfect "O." The sight is magnificent.

With a final, powerful thrust, he gives in to his own orgasm, his body tensing as he erupts inside her. His groan is primal, and he buries his face in the crook of her neck. His arms tremble with exertion as he holds her against the wall, their bodies locked together as they ride out the waves.

"Merlot," he breathes against her skin. "Fucking incredible."

For several moments, they remain frozen in that position —Kim pinned between Connor's muscular frame and the wall, both of them panting, their skin slick with sweat. I watch as he presses gentle kisses along her collarbone, on the pulsing hollow at the base of her throat, a stark contrast to the roughness just moments before.

Slowly, carefully, he withdraws from her body, eliciting a small whimper from her as he slips free. Her legs are unsteady as he lowers her to the ground, his hands remaining on her waist to keep her upright. Her knees buckle slightly, and a soft laugh escapes her lips.

"I don't think I can walk," she giggles.

"I've got you, Merlot," he murmurs against her temple.

"That was..." Kim says, then her eyelids snap shut. "Breathtaking..." she manages to say, her voice catching. Suddenly, her eyes fill with tears, the droplets clinging to her lashes before spilling down her flushed cheeks. Her shoulders begin to tremble, not with pleasure now, but with emotion.

Connor's expression shifts immediately from satisfaction to concern. "What's wrong?" His thumb gently brushes away a tear from her cheek, his other arm wrapping protectively around her waist.

I'm off the couch in an instant, crossing the room to her. The three of us stand there naked, but there's nothing sexual about this moment—just raw vulnerability.

"I'm sorry," she says, her voice breaking as she tries to keep her tears in check. The way her body shakes suggests there's something profound happening within her.

I reach for her hand, interlacing our fingers. "It's okay," I whisper, moving closer so that she's cradled between him and me. "You're safe."

We guide her to the couch, sitting her between us. Her naked body seems suddenly vulnerable, and I pull the throw blanket from the back of the couch to drape around her shoulders.

"It's just..." Her voice quivers as she leans into my shoulder, the blanket clutched tightly around her.

I exchange a worried glance with Connor over her head. He shifts closer, his thigh pressing against hers as he rubs gentle circles on her back.

"Hey," he murmurs, tucking a strand of damp hair behind her ear. "Talk to us."

She draws in a shaky breath. "It's overwhelming. Being with both of you like this..." She gestures vaguely at the space between us. "It's like every part of me is seen and wanted and... loved."

"You are loved," he says, his voice low and certain.

A fresh wave of tears spills down her cheeks. "I never thought I could have this. I'm glad I got to experience it," she continues, her voice growing steadier as she tries to articulate her feelings. "It was... being with both of you. Feeling so..." She swallows. "I love both of you so much. I want you to know that. Remember this, please—I want to always remember this."

Her words hit me like a punch to the gut. Something about the way she says it—with such uncertainty, like she's going to lose this feeling, like she's afraid Connor or I might not love her—makes my chest tighten.

Maybe Connor was right earlier. Maybe there is something she's not telling us, whether it's something that happened at the police station, or a thought or feeling she has.

I gently tilt her chin up, forcing her to look at me. The shimmering tears make her dark eyes look like polished obsidian, beautiful even in sadness.

"We love you, Babygirl," I say, trying to ignore the growing unease in my stomach. "That's not going to change."

She nods but doesn't meet my eyes. Her fingers fidget with the edge of the blanket, twisting the fabric into small knots before smoothing it out again. Connor's eyes meet with mine and his brow furrows slightly. He notices it too—something's wrong.

Chapter Twenty-Six

KIMBERLY

HERE I AM AGAIN, tiptoeing through the apartment, getting dressed while trying not to awaken someone. But this time, it's Zach and Connor. I couldn't sleep, knowing I'd have to leave them in the morning—I have to. This is the best thing to do.

My heart feels as though it's being torn in two as I quietly gather the few items I need. Deveraux made it clear that if I come with him willingly, he won't retaliate. So, as long as I'm here, everyone I love and care about is living with a target on their back.

I pull out my phone and scroll to the text Deveraux sent last night.

> Break up with them. Be ready at 4 AM.
> Pack light.

The clock on the microwave reads 3:20. Forty minutes until I walk away from everything.

My duffel bag feels impossibly heavy when I pick it up and sling it over my shoulder.

Earlier, I wrote them a note—a goodbye letter.

I poured my heart into these words, trying to explain—to make them understand—why I have to leave. My hands trembled as I wrote it. Tears blurred my vision and fell onto the paper, making tiny wrinkles that I smoothed with my fingertips.

The letter:

My dearest Zach and Connor,

By the time you read this, I'll be gone. Please know that leaving you and my mom is the hardest thing I've ever done, but I'm doing it because I love you all more than my own life.

Deveraux won't stop until he has me and won't hesitate to hurt those I care about. He's giving me the chance to go with him willingly and avoid a war with the Fitzpatricks and Valentinos.

I truly wanted to build something beautiful with you, and for a while, I believed I could. These past few mornings waking up between you two were the happiest moments of my life, and I thank you for it.

I'm doing this to protect you, and that means cutting all ties. Please don't look for me. Don't put yourselves in danger. Live your lives fully and find happiness. And please, please forgive me someday for loving you enough to leave.

All my love, always and forever,
Kim

I fold it carefully along crisp lines, my fingers smoothing each crease with finality. I slip it into the envelope, seal it with a kiss that leaves the faintest imprint of my signature red lipstick, and write their names on the front in my neatest handwriting.

I place it on the kitchen table, propping it against a bottle of whiskey.

My fingers hesitate to leave the envelope, questioning if this is the right decision. But yes—it is. I have to believe that. The alternative is watching everyone I love die because of me.

The hardwood floor creaks behind me, and my heart stops.

"Kim?" Zach's voice is thick with sleep.

I freeze, caught in the act of my betrayal, unable to turn around and face him. The duffel bag now feels like I'm carrying cinder blocks.

"What are you doing?" His bare feet pad across the floor.

I force myself to pivot, my pre-rehearsed excuses failing me at the sight of him.

"What are you doing?" he asks again with confusion on his face as he notices my packed bag and the coat draped over my arm. The envelope on the table catches his eye, too, and I see the exact moment understanding dawns on him. His face, half-illuminated by the dim glow of recess lighting under the kitchen cabinets, transforms into disbelief, hurt, and then a flare of anger.

"You're leaving." It's not a question, and his voice cracks on the second word.

"Zach, I—" My throat closes around the words. What do I even say? "Don't," I whisper, but he's already moving, his eyes locked on the envelope.

I lunge forward, my fingertips grazing the paper as he snags before me. "Please, just let me—"

We collide as I reach desperately for the letter, but he easily holds it above my head, using his height against me. I jump once, twice, my hand batting uselessly at his wrist as he backs away.

"I need to know why," he states. "I deserve that much."

"My dearest Zach and Connor," he reads aloud. "By the time you read this, I'll be gone..."

His eyes darken as they dart across the page, his expression crumbling with each line. I watch helplessly as the blood drains from his face, his jaw clenching.

"What the fuck is this? Deveraux? Were you really going to just disappear in the middle of the night? After everything?"

I reach for him instinctively. "Please, let me explain—"

He steps back, avoiding my touch as if it'll burn. "Explain? What's there to explain?"

Before I can respond, the hallway light flickers on. Connor appears in the doorway, hair mussed from sleep, wearing only boxer briefs.

"What's going on?" he asks. His eyes dart between us, taking in the scene—Zach's rigid posture, the letter clutched in his hand, my bag packed and ready.

Zach turns to him, waving my letter. "She's leaving,

Connor. To go to Deveraux. She was going to sneak out while we slept."

His eyes widen. "Give me that," he says. He crosses the kitchen in three long strides.

Zach releases it without protest. And now I watch Connor as his eyes move across the page. His face changes—subtle shifts in expression, just like Zach's did.

"What makes you think this is a good idea?" he says.

I hesitate to speak, but I'm caught, so I may as well tell them. I slip the duffel bag off my shoulder. It hits the floor with a loud thud that seems to release something inside me—the floodgates open, and suddenly I find myself talking faster than I can think.

"Deveraux came to see me yesterday at the police station. He fabricated the evidence that led to my arrest and also the clerical error that got me released. He threatened everyone's lives again—if not dead, then to destroy them completely. I'm supposed to meet Detective Reyes downstairs at four am."

We all look at the clock. 3:31.

"Detective Reyes?" Connor asks.

"Yeah," I shrug. "She's in on it with him."

Zach's anger seems to dissipate slightly. "Why didn't you tell us yesterday?"

"Because he threatened me—threatened all of you," I say, my voice breaking.

Connor slams his palm against the counter, the impact sending the salt shaker toppling. Grains scatter across the surface. "And you believe that after giving yourself over, that it'll end? Easy. Just like that? You'll take the word of a human trafficking criminal? But you won't take the word of the men you claim to love when we say that we'll protect you?"

"Do you trust him?" Zach asks with disbelief.

Their words hit me like a physical blow.

"It's not about trust," I whisper, the statement feeling inadequate. "I trust you both more than anyone."

Connor's eyes, usually so warm, are hard with frustration. "Then why, Kim? Why choose this?"

When he puts it like that—framing it as a choice between trusting them or trusting Deveraux—it does sound terrible. Foolish, even. But they don't understand the stakes.

"What happens when Deveraux sends his people after you?" I ask, my voice stronger now. "What happens when they come for my mother? For Cassie? For Ryan and Killian?" I look between them, these men I love so desperately. "Who has to die so I can stay? Which one of you takes the bullet for me? Which friend do I bury because I was selfish enough to want this life with you? Whose blood would be on my hands?"

Connor steps forward. "We're not helpless."

"Neither am I," I counter. "I'm standing here, making what feels like an impossible choice, and all I can hold on to is the belief that Deveraux will honor our agreement. That if I choose to go with him, he'll leave all of you alone. That's the only thing keeping me upright right now—faith in a devil's promise."

Zach's laugh is harsh, humorless. "A man like that doesn't keep promises, Kim. He manipulates. He lies."

"You don't think I know that?" I snap, then immediately regret my tone. "But what choice do I have? If there's even a chance he'll leave you all alone, I have to take it."

Zach moves closer. "There's always another way."

"Not this time," I say, shaking my head. "Not when he's already shown what he's capable of. The evidence against me appeared out of nowhere. He got me arrested with a snap of his fingers. What else can he do? Who else's lives can he ruin?"

Zach runs his hands through his hair, frustration clear in every line of his body. "And what about you? Who keeps you safe from him?"

The question hangs in the air between us. I have no answer that won't break their hearts further.

"You think I could live with myself, knowing you sacrificed yourself for me?" Connor's voice cracks. "That any of us could?"

"I'd rather have you alive and hating me than dead because of me," I whisper.

"We fight. Together," Zach states.

I sink into one of the kitchen chairs. The microwave's digital display reads 3:47. Thirteen minutes until Deveraux expects me downstairs.

"You should have told us. Now we've wasted a day. We could have been planning—preparing," Zach says.

I shake my head, tears welling in my eyes. "No, Zach, it wasn't a waste. Not at all." My voice cracks with emotion. "Last night with you two... it was... perfect. Even with this hanging over me, those hours with you both were everything."

The kitchen falls silent except for our breathing. The digital clock changes: 3:51.

Connor's stare narrows. "It doesn't make sense," he says finally, moving to the table and pulling out a chair to sit. He crosses his arms over his chest as he sits, fixing me with an intense gaze. "Why would Deveraux give you a day? Why the delay? Why not just have you go with him then and there?"

"Because," I say slowly, the realization dawning on me as I

speak, "he wanted me to leave without you following me, a clean break up."

Zach leans forward, his elbows on the table. "But if you vanished in the night, leaving only a goodbye letter..."

"We would have been hurt and confused," Connor finishes, "but we still would have searched for you. He thought that if you left willingly, we would just let you walk away?" He huffs.

Zach frowns, leaning back in his chair as he processes this. His eyes lock with mine, suddenly alert and suspicious. "He already threatened us before. We ignored him—didn't deliver you. Why would he go through all this trouble—setting you up for arrest, getting you released, and then giving you time to say goodbye?"

"What do you mean?" I ask.

"I mean," Zach says, pacing the kitchen, "there's something else going on here. He's avoiding starting the war he declared would happen. But why?"

"So, what do we do?" I ask.

"Oh, it's 'we' now?" Connor says, and I immediately shrink in my seat.

Zach looks at Connor, a sly grin forming on his lips. "We call his bluff."

Chapter Twenty-Seven

CONNOR

"Fuck!" Zach yells as soon as the metal door closes on the elevator. "She was going to fucking leave us and give herself to that human trafficker."

I understand his frustration, but I wouldn't expect anything else from Kim. She's not selfish. Deveraux was threatening everyone she loves and cares about. I would have done the same in her position.

I say nothing, just press the lobby button.

We both threw on some clothes before going downstairs to confront whomever was supposed to pick her up at four a.m. It's a little after four now, but my guess is that someone will still be there waiting for her.

My mind is racing, piecing together what we know about his operation. She isn't safe while that monster is still out there, and neither are we—even if his threats appear to be empty.

The elevator descends with agonizing slowness. Zach paces the small space, his fists clenching and unclenching.

It dings as we reach the lobby. We burst through the large doors of Fitzpatrick Enterprises and step out onto the sidewalk with our eyes peeled.

There she is—Detective Reyes, leaning against her unmarked car half a block down, checking her watch.

"That's her," I say, grabbing Zach's arm to slow his charge forward. "Let's be smart about this."

His jaw tightens. Without hesitation, he strides across the street, and I hurry to keep up. Reyes doesn't notice us until we're almost upon her. When she finally looks up, there is no surprise on her face.

Zach pulls away, storming toward her. "Hey, Detective!"

"Deveraux had a feeling this would happen." Reyes shakes her head in disappointment. "By her not coming willingly, you've just declared war."

"You want a war?" I step forward, placing myself between Zach and Reyes. "Then you'll get one."

"You think we're afraid of that monster?" he adds.

"You should be. You clearly don't understand who you're dealing with," she says.

"You're just another corrupt cop," Zach spits. "How much is he paying you to betray your badge?"

A flash of genuine anger crosses her face, but she doesn't answer the question.

"Tell him something for me," I say, my voice steady despite the rage building inside me. "This ends now. Tonight."

"You're making a mistake," Reyes warns, but her confidence is cracking. She opens her car door. "I strongly advise you to deliver Ms. Stanton. I assure you she will be safe —if that's your concern."

"Fuck off," he says.

She gets in the car and speeds off.

Zach turns to me. "We need to call Killian and Ryan. Tonight, Connor—really? You didn't give us much time, did you?"

"I was angry."

"So was I," he mutters, running a hand through his hair. "Let's go upstairs."

Twenty minutes later, we're in the Fitzpatrick boardroom, and you could cut the tension with a knife. Kim sits at the far end of the table, arms crossed, refusing to look at either of us. Her jaw is set stubbornly, an expression I recognize—she's furious that we intercepted her self-sacrificial plan.

Zach isn't much better. He keeps shooting daggers at her with his eyes, then at me.

I sit in the middle, feeling the crossfire of their anger from both sides. I drum my fingers on the polished mahogany. Kim believes she was doing the right thing, protecting us all by giving herself up. He's having a hard time forgiving her for being willing to leave.

Zach's frustration at me, I deserve. I made a rushed decision that we weren't prepared for. But I stand by what I said. This needs to end before anyone else gets hurt.

The door to the boardroom opens, and Cassie comes in, running to Kim to give her a hug.

She pulls away from her, her hands gripping Kim's shoulders. "I heard what you were going to do," she says. "Giving yourself up to that monster? Are you insane?"

Kim can't look at her. "I was trying to protect everyone."

"By what? Becoming some trafficker's property?" Cassie's voice rises.

"I didn't have a choice—"

"There's always a choice," she interrupts calmly. "And yours sucked. Big time." She takes a deep breath, her expression softening. "But I get why you did it. Doesn't make it less stupid, but... don't be a self-sacrificing idiot."

Kim's eyes fill with tears, and she lets out a small laugh that sounds more like a sob.

"We fight together or not at all," Cassie states.

Ryan and Killian enter the room with game faces on.

Zach clears his throat. "Now that we've established Kim's plan was terrible, we need a new one—a good one, and quick," he says as he eyes me.

Killian steps forward. "What resources do we have for an attack? If we're doing this tonight, we have to know what we're working with."

Zach, clearly frustrated, shifts into tactical mode. "Not enough. We've got three handguns with limited ammo, my hunting knife, and whatever we can cobble together from the Fitzpatrick security office. We also have a few handguns between us and Connor and Ryan's sniper rifles."

"That's it?" Ryan asks, leaning against the wall. "We're going up against a human trafficking kingpin with a few guns and a knife?"

"You used it all to save me, didn't you?" Cassie asks.

I nod. "We depleted it, but not entirely. We had to destroy the evidence in the cleanup."

"The shipment with more weapons and ammo is due next week. But if someone hadn't put a timer on this—" Zach begins.

"Then what?" I interrupt, tired of hearing this. "Everyone would be on high alert, anticipating an attack. Excuse me for wanting to end this as soon as possible."

"Connor." Killian's voice cuts through. He places a hand on my shoulder, squeezing gently. "Take a breath. You did the right thing by forcing our hand. Sometimes we need a deadline to make things happen."

The unexpected support catches me off guard. I expected more pushback.

The tension in my shoulders eases slightly. "So, what do we do with limited resources?"

Ryan glances at me. "Connor, remember that job in Prague? The one with the hedge fund manager?"

A slow smile spreads across my face as I catch his drift. "Minimal resources, maximum impact."

"Exactly." He turns to the others. "We don't go after Deveraux directly. We go after his operation." Ryan's eyes light up. "He might be bulletproof, but his infrastructure isn't."

"In Prague, we had to take down a hedge fund manager with ties to the Russian mob. We couldn't touch him directly —too well-protected—so we went after what he cared about most."

"His money," Ryan adds. "More specifically, we created the illusion of his operation being compromised, someone— his closest allies—stealing his money."

"We need to do something similar for Deveraux." Zach says, understanding dawning on his face. "An attack on the tech side."

"Exactly," I say.

"So, we don't need manpower or weapons for a direct assault?" Cassie asks.

"Nope," Ryan replies, pulling up a map on his phone and placing it on the table. "His entire operation hinges on moving people. What if that was compromised?"

"Get law enforcement involved," Killian says, leaning forward with growing interest.

"Exactly." I point to the map where Ryan has highlighted the port. "We create chaos. Make enough noise that authorities can't ignore it."

"The shipping manifests," Ryan says suddenly. "Every ship that docks has to file paperwork. Deveraux may have corrupted officials, but federal agencies have overlapping jurisdictions."

I catch on immediately. "If we can access his shipping manifests and alter them..."

"We could flag his containers for inspection," Killian finishes. "Not just any inspection—homeland security, DEA, FBI, everyone."

"It'll become a raid," I state.

"What about Reyes?" Kim asks. "Won't she warn or cover for him?"

"What we're planning will go beyond a crooked New York City detective," I say, pacing now as the plan takes shape in my mind. "She can relay all she wants to him, but it's way beyond her jurisdiction."

Zach points to a spot on the map. "There's a harbormaster's office here. They maintain digital copies of all manifests. With the right access, I can alter the documentation to show suspicious materials."

"And I can plant a trail connecting those shipments directly to Deveraux's other businesses," Ryan adds. "Nothing obvious—just enough breadcrumbs for investigators to follow."

"That's the core of it," I say, standing up. "But we need to draw this out. Killian, grab that whiteboard."

Killian wheels the large whiteboard from the corner while I uncap a black marker.

"All right, we've got four primary objectives," I start, writing them down in bold letters. "Access the harbor master's system, plant false flags in the manifest, create a trail connecting to Deveraux, and ensure multiple agencies respond."

Ryan takes a blue marker from me. "I'll handle the digital trail." He sketches a quick network diagram, arrows pointing between databases. "If we can link his legitimate businesses to these shipments, even tangentially, federal agencies will freeze everything while they investigate."

"Perfect." I add notes beside his diagram.

Zach grabs a red marker. "The harbormaster's office has security, but nothing special. Standard alarm system, maybe a guard." He draws a rough layout of the building. "I can get us in here," he says as he circles a back entrance, "and we'll need about fifteen minutes in their server room."

"What about cameras—" I begin, but I notice the others have stopped listening and are looking toward the far corner of the room behind me.

I turn around to follow their gaze. Kim has crumpled into a chair, her face buried in her hands, shoulders shaking with silent sobs. Cassie is kneeling beside her.

"Hey, hey," Cassie whispers, her voice gentle. "It's okay, let it out."

She's breaking down, and it feels raw—the culmination of everything she's been holding back.

"Watching you all—your planning—it's good, it's a good plan." Kim's voice breaks, muffled by her hands. "I almost—I was going to just give myself to him. The things he does to women... What was I thinking?"

Cassie strokes her hair. "You were thinking about protecting the people you love."

She looks up at Cassie, her face blotchy and tear-stained. "I thought I was being brave, but I was giving up, wasn't I?"

Zach crosses the room, pulling up a chair beside Kim.

"You weren't giving up," he says, his voice low and certain. "You were facing something terrifying head-on to protect others. That's the definition of courage." He takes her hand. "But you don't have to face him alone. We're all here—not just because we want to stop him, but because we want to protect you."

Kim looks up at him, tears still streaming down her face. "I didn't want anyone else to get hurt because of me."

"That's not how family works," Zach says. "And like it or not, that's what we've become. A weird, dysfunctional family of broken people who somehow fit together."

A small laugh escapes her lips, surprising even her.

"We've all got our demons," Zach continues. "But we fight them together. That's the deal."

"He's right," I say.

"I'm not used to having people I can depend on," she admits quietly.

"Well, get used to it," Ryan says from across the room.

"You're part of the Fitzpatrick clan now," Killian adds. "Connor, too."

I give a nod of appreciation to Killian and look to my brother, who's smiling with pride.

"We're your family now. And family doesn't let family face monsters alone." Zach's voice cracks slightly on the last word. "You don't have to carry this weight by yourself. That's what we're here for—to share the load."

A fresh tear slides down her cheek, but something shifts in her eyes—a spark of determination.

Chapter Twenty-Eight

ZACH

EVERYTHING IS IN PLACE. We planted the seeds—the false evidence that will flag Deveraux's shipments. Now comes the fun part. Killian, Ryan, Connor and I are staking out the docks where his yacht sits. We're watching and waiting for the feds to bust him while Cassie and Kim stay at the penthouse until we get back.

We're huddled in my SUV, parked strategically behind an abandoned warehouse that gives us a perfect view of the marina.

Connor shifts in his seat, binoculars still trained on the yacht's deck. "How long before they show?"

"Could be an hour, could be by dawn," I say, checking my watch.

Killian leans back against the van's interior wall, a smile crossing his face as he looks between Connor and me. "Speaking of not seeing things coming, I still can't believe you two are in a relationship."

Ryan chuckles beside him.

Connor leans forward. "We—" He motions at me. "—are not in a relationship. We are just dating the same woman."

Killian smirks. "What are the odds of that? Ryan and I end up with Cassie, and now you two end up with the same woman? Well, if you need relationship advice...don't ask me."

"I'm pretty sure the girls already do that?" Ryan adds.

"What?" I ask.

"Cassie and Kim are probably talking about us—you know, girl talk." Ryan says.

I look at Connor, and he shrugs.

"I don't even want to know what they're saying," I mutter, turning my attention back to the yacht.

"Whoa." Ryan suddenly leans forward, his body tensing. "Movement."

My eyes snap to the marina entrance where a convoy of black sedans and SUVs—at least twenty vehicles—race toward the yacht. They move with synchronized precision, no sirens but unmistakable urgency.

"Shit, that's them," I mutter, adrenaline instantly flooding my system. "Feds don't mess around."

Connor drops the binoculars to his lap. "They're not trying to be subtle."

The unmarked vehicles fan out. They screech to a halt near the gangway, blocking all exit routes from the dock. Men and women in tactical gear pour out, weapons drawn, moving toward Deveraux's yacht.

I grab my own binoculars. Through the lenses, I can see Deveraux on the upper deck, drink in hand, completely oblivious to the storm rushing his way. Two of his security guards notice the commotion and reach for their weapons, but they're already too late.

"This is better than I thought it would be," Connor says.

"Front row seats to the take-down of the century," I murmur, unable to tear my eyes away.

The feds swarm the yacht like ants on sugar. Deveraux's face transforms from confusion to shock to rage as agents flood his deck. They move with the efficiency of people who've done this a hundred times before. His security team makes a half-hearted attempt at resistance before wisely dropping their weapons when confronted with the overwhelming federal presence.

"Look at that asshole's face," Connor says, a hint of satisfaction in his voice. "He really thought he was untouchable."

Deveraux himself looks utterly bewildered, his drink falling from his hand as agents rush him. He tries to back away, but there's nowhere to go. Two agents grab his arms, spinning him around and shoving him against the railing. Even from this distance, I can see his mouth moving rapidly, likely threatening lawyers and retribution.

"Ten million says he's trying to bribe them right now," Ryan says with a snort.

Killian leans forward, elbows on his knees. "Think they found everything we planted?"

"They will," I say confidently. "The evidence trail is solid. By the time his—"

"What the fuck!" Ryan yells.

I follow Ryan's gaze, expecting to see something like Deveraux attempting to flee, or perhaps one of his men making a desperate move beginning a shootout. Instead, what I see makes no sense at all.

One agent, a tall man with a crew cut, is speaking into Deveraux's ear. The agent's posture has completely changed, almost apologetic. Then, inexplicably, he reaches for Deveraux's handcuffs and removes them.

"What the hell is happening?" Connor breathes.

We watch in stunned silence as he rubs his wrists, nodding at whatever the agent is saying. The other feds are backing away, their weapons lowered. Some are even holstering them.

"Are they letting him go?" Killian asks, with disbelief in his voice.

"This isn't right," Connor says. "We planted enough evidence to put him away for decades."

The agents who moments ago stormed the yacht with weapons drawn are now standing down, some even shaking Deveraux's hand. It's as though they've switched from a raid to a friendly visit in seconds.

Faster than the convoy of unmarked cars came in, they leave the dock, one by one

Killian's phone rings, and he removes it from his pocket, staring at the screen. "It's him," he says to us before answering. He puts the call on speakerphone.

"Mr. Fitzpatrick." Deveraux's voice fills the vehicle, dripping with smug satisfaction. "I must admit, you and your friends set up quite the show. But I too can be quite the showman. The offshore accounts linked to the shipping container were a nice touch. Very elaborate."

My stomach drops as I exchange glances with Connor.

"What do you want, Deveraux?"

A low chuckle comes through the speaker. "Just to

congratulate you on your creativity. The evidence was quite convincingly planted. Masterful work, really. Unfortunately for you, I've had federal contacts on my payroll for years. The moment they saw your little breadcrumb trail, they called me directly. I told them to proceed with the raid—that I had a failsafe plan just for this situation. I was prepared for it." Deveraux sounds amused. "You should know that I've already redirected the investigation. Your evidence now points squarely at O'Malley and a person who's been in contact with him quite recently...Connor O'Brady."

We all look to Connor, whose jaw is tense.

"And the rest of you are wanted for questioning about your involvement with Mr. O'Brady," Deveraux continues. "But perhaps they'll officially arrest you. I have friends at the DA's office who are quite motivated."

Ryan mouths *What the fuck?* silently.

Connor's face goes white as marble. He looks like he might throw up right here in my SUV.

"You know," Deveraux continues, "I've been far too nice in our little chess match, Killian. That ends now." There's a pause, and then the sound of ice clinking in a glass. He's making himself a drink. "It's my turn to show you what retaliation truly looks like. You should have handed Kimberly over when I asked. She should have come freely, as I asked. And when I'm done with you, you'll be begging me to take her."

Killian's knuckles turn white around the phone. "I'm going to—"

"You'll do what?" Deveraux interrupts with a laugh, the sound chilling. "You're in no position to make threats. You had your chance for a clean exchange—twice now. Now the price will be much higher. I want your little wife, too."

"We're coming for you," I growl, unable to contain myself.

"You can try, but should you? Authorities are already on their way to the penthouse as we speak. Quite convenient that you left the women there alone, isn't it?"

"Cassie," Ryan whispers, reaching for his phone.

"Oh, and don't bother with phone calls," Deveraux continues, as if reading our minds. "Cell service to that area has been... temporarily disrupted. Jammers are set up in the area. A necessary precaution."

Connor starts the SUV's engine.

"How unfortunate that in a few hours, every federal agency will hunt the four of you. I wonder how Cassie and Kimberly will feel, being in love with America's most wanted?"

The line goes dead.

For several seconds, nobody speaks. We have to race to get to the girls.

Chapter Twenty-Nine

KIMBERLY

CASSIE COMES BACK to the patio with another glass of wine for me. I don't know yet if drinking is helping or not. But we sit on the penthouse rooftop around the fire pit, waiting for the men to return after confirming Deveraux's arrest.

"Have you thought about what you're going to do after the baby comes?" I ask, trying to distract myself from the gnawing anxiety. "I mean, with everything going on..."

She rubs her barely visible bump, a small smile forming on her lips. "We've been talking about moving somewhere quieter. Maybe near the coast. Somewhere the baby can grow up away from the city, at least."

"That sounds perfect," I say, swirling the wine in my glass. "I can visit on weekends, be the cool aunt who spoils—"

The loud wail of sirens cuts through the air, sudden and jarring.

"What the hell?" She stands, moving toward the edge of the rooftop, looking through the plexiglass wall.

I follow her, setting my drink down so quickly the liquid sloshes over the rim. Below us, the street has transformed into a sea of flashing red and blue lights. Police cruisers, at least ten, have surrounded the building's entrance. Officers pour out, weapons drawn.

"Something is wrong," she says.

The sound of the stairwell door slamming open makes us both jump. Drake bursts onto the rooftop, his chest heaving, sweat glistening on his forehead.

"We need to move," he gasps, doubling over to catch his breath. "Police... coming up the stairs now. They've got the elevators locked down."

"What about—" Cassie starts.

"They're looking for all of you," he cuts in, straightening up. "The guys can't get in here with all the police presence. They're going to a safe house."

"We planted evidence against them. Why are they coming for us?" I ask.

"No time," he says, already moving toward the service exit. "Cassie, you have the code to the panic room?"

I grab Cassie's arm, feeling the tremor that runs through her body. "The what?"

She yanks my arm as Drake moves to usher us back into the stairwell and to the penthouse. "We need to move fast."

She drags me down the stairs, her grip surprisingly strong for someone so petite. We go past the kitchen and through a hallway I haven't seen before.

"Where are we—" I start, but she presses a finger to her lips.

We stop at what appears to be a regular wall at the end of the hall. She runs her hand along the edge of a bookshelf, pressing something I can't see. A soft click, and the wall slides inward, revealing a narrow passage.

We race through the dimly lit corridor. My heart threatens to pound right out of my chest as we reach a door with a keypad to the left.

Her fingers work quickly, punching in a code. A soft beep, then the door slides open.

"Get in," she orders, her voice barely above a whisper.

I step through the doorway, finding myself in a room about the size of a large bedroom, with steel walls, two rows of black monitors, a small bathroom, and enough supplies to last weeks.

Cassie punches in a code on the keypad inside the room, and the door seals with a pneumatic hiss.

"Security system engaged," announces a computerized voice from somewhere overhead.

"Jesus Christ," I mutter, dropping into a leather computer chair positioned in front of the wall of monitors. "What the hell is happening?"

She doesn't answer immediately. She's busy checking the equipment, her fingers flying across a control panel. The screens flicker to life one by one, showing different areas of the penthouse. My eyes dart between them, taking in the chaos we fled.

"There," I gasp, pointing at the center screen.

Drake stands in the middle of the living room, his hands raised above his head. At least six agents in tactical gear surround him, their weapons trained on his chest. The letters *FBI* on their jackets are clearly visible even through the grainy footage.

"On your knees! Now!" Their commands come through the audio feed, tinny but clear enough.

Drake complies, his face a mask of calm resignation as they force him down. One agent steps forward, spinning him around and forcing him against the wall while another secures his wrists with zip ties.

"He let them catch him," Cassie says, her voice hollow. "He made himself a distraction. They had to find someone in the penthouse."

I can't tear my eyes from the screen as they read him his rights. Drake's face remains impassive, but I notice the slight tilt of his head toward one of the hidden cameras. He knows we're watching.

"Can they hear us here?" I ask, suddenly paranoid.

"No. It's completely soundproof and signal-blocked. Even if they found the room, it's designed to keep people out." She sinks into a chair. "Killian and Ryan built this room right after my rescue. It was already mostly built, just needed the supplies and equipment."

I watch the screens in horror as they lead Drake away. The other monitors show officers methodically searching the apartment, opening closets and looking under furniture. One of them pauses near the bookshelf we'd used to access this hidden room, and my breath catches. He runs his hand along the spines of the books before moving on.

"What about the others?" I ask, my voice barely audible even to myself. "Where are they?"

She switches to an exterior view, showing the street below. More police cars have arrived, their lights painting the night in alternating red and blue strokes. I can make out figures being escorted into vehicles, but the angle makes it impossible to identify them.

"What do we do now?" I turn to her, panic rising in my throat. "We can't just sit here while they take everyone."

Cassie's expression shifts from fear to something harder, more resolute. She straightens in her chair, one hand still resting on her belly.

"We wait. That's the protocol. No matter what we see on these screens, we stay put until the guys come for us. They will come back," she says calmly while picking up the landline and dialing. "Dad, it's me."

While she's talking to Victor Valentino, I'm gradually tuning her out, wondering where it all went wrong. They had a plan—a brilliant plan. This is exactly what I didn't want to happen.

The room feels like it's closing in on me. Cassie's voice fades to background noise as she speaks with her father.

I curl up on one of the small cots in the corner, pulling my knees to my chest. The tears come without warning, hot and fast, streaming down my face. I try to muffle my sobs with my sleeve, not wanting to distract her from her call.

"We'll be okay," she whispers, reaching over to squeeze my shoulder before returning to her conversation.

But I'm not convinced. The images of Drake being arrested play on a loop in my mind. My fault. It's all my fault. And it's just a matter of time before the guys are arrested, too.

I don't remember falling asleep, but suddenly I'm no longer in the panic room. I'm running through tall grass, laughing as the summer sun warms my skin. I'm small— maybe five years old—and someone is chasing me.

"Can't catch me!" I giggle, looking over my shoulder.

A man's face comes into view, smiling, but most of it is blocked by the sun. His eyes crinkle at the corners, kind and warm. "I'm going to get you!" his voice yells playfully behind me.

I dart between trees now, the landscape shifting as dreams do. The grass becomes taller, the trees closer together. I'm still running, but now there's a sense of urgency, of actual fear.

"Kimberly!" he calls, his voice different now. Not playful. Desperate.

I turn, and there he stands in a shaft of sunlight filtering through a canopy of leaves. My father. His face is clearer than I've seen it in years—the strong jaw, the kind eyes. But what catches my attention is the jagged scar running from his left temple down to his cheekbone, It's raised and pink, still relatively fresh.

"Daddy?" I whisper, reaching toward him.

I step closer, drawn to the scar. My fingers hover inches from his face. "What happened to you?"

He catches my wrist gently. "You know what happened. You were there."

The surrounding forest darkens.

The scene changes again. I'm no longer standing with him in the forest. Instead, I'm crouched in the darkness of the coat closet in my childhood home, peering through the slats of the door.

Three men storm in. I can't see their faces—just dark silhouettes against the hallway light. My father rushes in from the kitchen, still holding a dish towel.

"Where is it?" the tallest one demands, his voice like gravel.

"I don't know what you're talking about," my father says, backing up slowly.

"You took something that doesn't belong to you." Another man circles behind my father. "Tell us where it is."

"I don't know what you're talking about," my father insists.

The tall one nods to the third man, who pulls out a knife. The blade catches the light from the table lamp.

"Last chance."

My father's eyes dart toward the closet where I'm hiding. He sees me peeking through.

The third man lunges forward. I clamp my hand over my mouth to stifle a scream as the blade connects with my father's face, slicing a deep gash from temple to cheekbone. Blood immediately wells up, streaming down his face and dripping onto the collar of his shirt.

"Jesus!" my father yells, clutching his face. "Stop! I'll tell you!"

The man with the knife steps back, blood coating the blade. "That's better. Where is it?"

My father's shoulders slump in defeat, his hand still pressed against his bleeding face. "It's in the crawlspace. Behind the water heater. There's a loose board."

The tall man nods to his companion. "Check it."

As the third man disappears down the hallway toward our utility room, my father's eyes find mine again through the closet slats. He looks at me with shame and resignation. A single tear mixes with the blood on his cheek.

"You'll find everything there," my father says quietly. "The ledger—"

I jolt awake with a gasp, my heart hammering against my ribs.

It was a memory—one I'd buried so deep I'd convinced myself it never happened.

The scar. Now I remember that scar.

I sit up slowly, my mind racing as puzzle pieces click into place. My father's disappearance. Deveraux's obsession with me.

"Oh my God," I whisper, pressing my palm against my mouth.

Deveraux is my father.

The same eyes that had stared coldly at dinner with Matteo while drugging a woman—that had manipulated me at the police station—belonged to the man who had once pushed me on swings and taught me to ride a bike.

I look over at Cassie, curled up on the other cot. She's fallen asleep, one hand still protectively resting on her belly.

My father became someone else. Or maybe he was always someone else, and the loving dad I remembered was the disguise. Either way, he's bad now.

I slip quietly from the cot, careful not to wake her. Fuck, I need to stop sneaking away from people—fucking old habits die hard.

The security footage shows the penthouse is empty now.

I move toward the control panel, my fingers hovering over the keypad. The realization pounds in my head like a physical force. All of this—Drake's arrest, the others being hunted—it's because of me. Because of who my father is. Not because he wants to traffick me.

An inner torment began to gnaw at me. *You can end this. Right now.*

With trembling hands, I locate the emergency release for the panic room door: a small red button protected by a plastic cover. I flip it open, hesitating for only a moment before pressing it.

"Emergency override initiated," the computerized voice announces, a little louder than I'd hoped.

Cassie stirs on the cot. "Kim?" she mumbles sleepily. "What are you doing?"

The steel door slides open with a soft hiss. I take one last look at Cassie, who's now sitting up, confused.

"Stop! You can't go out there!"

"I have to," I say, "I figured out who Deveraux is. I can stop this—I'm certain this time."

I step through quickly, pressing the close button on the keypad to lock her back inside.

Chapter Thirty

CONNOR

We stayed the night in a safe house outside the city. From what we can tell, the authorities arrested only a couple of men from Fitzpatrick Enterprises, including Drake. Interpol arrested Victor and Seamus, Killian's father, who were out of the country separately. But before his arrest, Victor confirmed he spoke with Cassie, and both women are secure inside the panic room in the penthouse.

We've been up all night talking out scenarios, trying to figure out what our next move is, how we get out of this.

"So, we wait for this to blow over, get the girls, and then what? We can't exactly go back to our normal lives," Zach says, running a hand through his already disheveled hair.

Killian huffs. "We have contacts in South America. We could—"

The sharp ring of Killian's phone pauses him. He pulls it from his pocket, glances at the screen, and his expression shifts. "It's him," he says before answering and stepping toward the window.

His shoulders tense with each passing second as he listens, but nothing that gives us any clue about what's being said.

When he finally lowers the phone, he turns back to us. The harsh morning light streaming through the dusty blinds casts shadows across his face, highlighting the grim set of his jaw as his eyes move from Zach to me.

"It's Kim," he says, his voice low and controlled.

He offers his cell phone.

Why the fuck is she calling from Deveraux's number?

Zach strides toward Killian, taking it. Killian nods toward Ryan, and they walk out of the room, giving us privacy.

He puts it on speakerphone.

"Kim." My voice croaks.

"I'm sorry," she cries into the phone. "I did what I had to do, what I should have done. And I'm glad I did, because you're all safe now. Deveraux fixed everything. You're safe to go home. Drake and the others are being released right now."

"Bullshit," he says. "He's just saying that to get us out of hiding."

"No, he's doing it for me," she states.

"Why would he do that?" he asks.

"He's my father."

Zach and I stare at each other in confusion.

"What makes you think that?" I ask. "Did he tell you that?"

"No. I remembered it."

"You just remembered it?" I ask. "So what if he's your fucking father, Kim—he makes money selling people."

"I know!" But right now, all I am thinking about is you.

He's keeping it pinned solely on O'Malley, taking out another potential enemy of Fitzpatrick's. As long as you don't go after him, he won't go after you."

"And what happens to you?" I ask.

"I don't know. He wants to... reconnect." Even as she says the words, it sounds like she doesn't believe it.

"And you want that too?" Zach asks.

"I want what's going to keep you safe."

There's a long pause on the other end of the line. I can hear her breathing, waiting.

"She's leaving us willingly—like he's wanted all along," he says, looking at the phone with a mixture of anger and disbelief.

I sink onto the worn sofa, the springs creaking beneath me. My hands are trembling. The weight of everything—the running, the betrayal—suddenly feels too heavy.

"I love you both," she says, her voice barely above a whisper. "I don't know what's going to happen next, but I need you to know that."

Zach is watching me, his eyes searching my face for a reaction, a plan, something to change what's happening. At this moment, I realize what I have to do.

"Kim, can I speak to your... to Deveraux?" I ask, my voice steadier than I feel.

"Connor, no—" he starts.

I hold up my hand, silencing him. "Please."

There's rustling on the other end, murmured voices, then a deep, smooth voice comes through the speaker. "Gentlemen?"

"I need your word that we'll all be safe. Me, Zach, Killian,

Ryan, Cassie, Drake, Seamus, and Victor. No retaliation, no surveillance, nothing."

"You have it," Deveraux says without hesitation. "Just stay away from my business. And my daughter."

"Okay. We'll let her go." I say, and Zach stares at me like I'm crazy.

I swallow hard and hang up the phone.

The moment I toss the phone to the couch, he lunges at me, his face contorted with rage, his fist connecting with my jaw before I even have time to react. The impact sends me stumbling backward, knocking over an end table.

"What the fuck is wrong with you?" he roars, advancing on me again. "You're giving her up? Just like that?"

I taste blood in my mouth as I steady myself. "It was her choice, Zach. Her choice! We can't force her—"

He swings again, this time catching me in the ribs. The pain radiates through my torso, but adrenaline pushes me forward. I tackle him, both of us crashing into the wall, picture frames clattering to the floor.

"You fucking coward! You didn't even fight for her!" he shouts, struggling against my grip, but somehow he grabs the front of my shirt and shoves me against the wall. "After everything we've been through!"

I turn him and slam him against the wall, our faces inches apart. "What was I supposed to do? Force her to come back? She made her decision!"

He breaks free, shoving me hard. I stumble, then charge at him. We collide in the middle of the room, trading wild punches. One catches me above the eye, instantly splitting the skin. Blood drips in my vision as I drive my fist into his stomach.

"Enough!" Killian's voice thunders through the room as firm hands suddenly grip my shoulders, yanking me backward. Ryan simultaneously wraps his arms around Zach's torso, lifting him off his feet as he struggles.

"Let me go!" Zach snarls, thrashing against Ryan's grip.

Killian shoves me down onto the couch, standing between us like a barrier. "This isn't helping anyone," he says, his voice lower but no less commanding. "You think beating each other senselessly is going to bring her back?"

Ryan maneuvers Zach to the opposite side of the room, still restraining him as he tries to break free. "Cool it, man. Breathe."

"He just gave up on her," Zach spits, blood trickling from his split lip. "Like she means nothing."

"I was trying to keep us all alive!" I shout back, wiping blood from my eye with the back of my hand. "What was your plan? Storm his yacht? Get us all killed? He thinks we're done. We've bought ourselves the goddamned time you wanted so fucking much, Zach."

"She's in the hands of a monster," Zach says through his teeth.

"If he's her father like he says he is—he won't hurt her."

Killian stands between us, his gaze shifting from me to Zach and back again.

"Connor's right," Killian says, his voice quiet but firm. "If she is his daughter, she's safer there than anywhere else right now. And so are we. We need to regroup, figure out our next move."

Zach's face contorts with disbelief. "Are you fucking kidding me? You're siding with him again?" He wrenches himself free from Ryan's grip, stepping back. "So that's it? We abandon her?"

"No one's abandoning anyone," Ryan responds. "We're being strategic. There's a difference."

"Strategic?" He spits the word out like it's poison. "She's the only family I have left, and you want me to be strategic?" His eyes dart around the room, taking in our faces, his breathing ragged. "Fuck this. Fuck all of you."

He storms across the room, snatching his jacket from the back of a chair and shoving his arms through the sleeves.

Ryan steps in front of the door, arms spread wide. "Come on, man. You're not thinking straight."

"Get out of my way," Zach growls.

"Where are you even going to go?" he asks, not budging.

Zach's laugh is bitter, hollow. "I'll hitchhike back to the city if I have to. Find her myself, since none of you seem to give a shit."

I press the heel of my hand against my bleeding eyebrow, the pain throbbing in time with my heartbeat. Part of me wants to stop him, to try one more time to make him understand, but I know that look in his eyes. There's no reasoning with him right now.

Maybe someday, when we've figured out a way to get her back safely—because I have no intention of abandoning her forever—he'll understand why I did what I did. Maybe by then, he'll forgive me for letting her go now so we can save her later.

Ryan looks over at Killian, silently asking what to do.

"Let him go."

Chapter Thirty-One

KIMBERLY

THAT WAS the right thing to do. You did the right thing. You did the right thing, I repeat to myself like a mantra.

My cell phone rings. Briefly, I hope it's Zach and Connor, although Deveraux took my phone earlier to have Reyes install some sort of spyware on it to monitor my calls. I don't know if I want him listening in on my calls with them, or if a desperate moment will have them spoil a plan to try and get me back. But it's not them. It's a number I don't recognize.

I stare at the phone for a few seconds, then swipe to answer.

"Hello?" I try to sound normal. Not like someone who just had their heart torn in two fucking different directions, meanwhile taking residence with a father who is a human trafficker. *What would that even sound like?*

"Kim? This is Rebecca Sloan from The Vanguard Gallery."

My breath catches. Rebecca Sloan—the owner of the

gallery where I applied for the curator internship. The one that could have changed everything. I grip the phone tighter.

"Yes, hi, Ms. Sloan," I say, trying to keep my voice steady.

"I'm calling with good news," she says. "We found your application and essay very impressive. I'd like to offer you the curator internship position."

"I... wow. Thank you," I stammer, a surreal feeling washing over me.

"I'll email you the details tomorrow. It's a four-month position initially, with the potential for extension. We're excited to have you join us."

I hang up the phone, then reality hits me. I can't take it. I've agreed to go to Europe with Deveraux. We'll be setting sail tomorrow.

I'm truly sacrificing everything. It was nice to know that I could have had all my wishes fulfilled, though. Men that love me, my mother living close by, and an entrance position to the career I want after graduation.

I hear the clacking of heels on the yacht's floor and turn around and find Reyes. "Your father is upstairs. We're waiting for you for dinner."

I swallow hard and follow her up the narrow staircase.

The sunset paints the sky in shades of orange and pink, a beautiful backdrop to this surreal scenario. Deveraux sits at an elegantly set table with fine china and crystal glasses. A big bodyguard stands beside him, his posture relaxed but his eyes alert.

"Kimberly," Deveraux says, standing to pull out a chair for me. "Join us."

I slide into the seat. A server appears with plates of seafood

—lobster, scallops, things that would normally make my mouth water. Tonight, my appetite is nonexistent.

"Wine?" he offers, already pouring a Pinot into my glass without waiting for my answer. Detective Reyes bends and gives Deveraux a loving kiss on his scarred cheek, which he gladly accepts from her. *So, they're an item, huh?*

"You look troubled," he observes. "Second thoughts?"

I stare at the wineglass, watching the liquid catch the fading light. "Not only am I leaving the loves of my life behind, but I was just offered a position at a gallery that I applied to. But I won't be here to take it."

"There should be plenty of opportunities for you in Europe—better art, too," Reyes says before taking a bite of her salad.

Deveraux sets down his glass. "We depart at dawn," he announces, his eyes locking with mine. "The tide will be favorable." He gestures around us. "We'll sail to Key West first, where my larger vessel awaits. From there, it's a straight shot across the Atlantic." His expression softens slightly. "You'll have your own suite, of course. I've taken the liberty of having some art supplies brought aboard. I thought you might find comfort in your work."

Oh, how nice of him—not. I stare at him. "How long will the journey take?"

"Ten days, perhaps twelve if the weather turns," he replies. "We'll dock in Marseille initially. From there..." He waves his hand. "We have options. I have properties in several countries."

The lobster suddenly tastes like sand in my mouth. Dawn. Hours from now. This isn't just some abstract future plan anymore—it's happening. Now.

"I've created your new identity," Reyes adds casually, as if mentioning the weather while reaching for the bread basket.

"New identity?" I echo.

"You'll need to leave Kimberly behind," Deveraux says, his eyes cold. "As I have left Kenneth."

"Kenneth." My father's name. The father who disappeared from my life so completely I barely remember his face.

"Why did you leave us?" The question bursts from me. "Why did you abandon Mom and me?"

My father—Kenneth—sets down his fork slowly. "It's complicated," he finally says.

"No," I shake my head. "That's not good enough. You're asking me to give up everything, to vanish from my life. I deserve to know why you did the same thing to us."

"I made powerful enemies. People who would have hurt you and your mother to get to me."

"In Oklahoma? The bumfuck of nowhere?" My voice cracks.

"Watch your mouth." He points his fork at me. "Yes, in Oklahoma. Believe it or not, small towns make their livelihood in not-so-small ways. It's not just farmers out there."

My father's expression shifts, a complex mixture of pain and resignation crossing his face. "The past is the past, Kimberly," he says, his voice softening as he reaches across the table, not quite touching my hand but close enough that I can see the scars across his knuckles. "Why I left doesn't matter anymore. What matters is now—this opportunity we have."

His eyes, so much like mine, hold an intensity that makes me want to look away.

"I've missed years of your life. But now we have time. All the time in the world to build something new. Better."

"You think I'm going to just forget?" I ask, my voice barely above a whisper.

"No," he says, refilling his wine glass. "But someday you'll understand. Someday you'll look at me and see your father again, not some stranger." He smiles, and for a second, I catch a glimpse of something genuine beneath the calculated charm. "I know it. I can be patient."

Wow. He's crazy. Delusional if he thinks I will ever forgive him.

"I didn't know about your connection to Matteo Valentino," Deveraux continues. "What a coincidence that turned out to be." He laughs humorlessly. "When you walked into that business dinner with him..." He pauses, swallowing hard. "I nearly knocked over my drink. You looked so much like your mother, but I saw myself in you, too. You didn't recognize me. I knew then that fate had given me a second chance. I had to find a way to connect with you again."

"So you orchestrated all of this?" I gesture around us and the yacht.

"The Fitzpatricks have been trying to nail me down for years. I risked everything to come here and get you. I never thought I'd find you mixed in with the mafia. After the dinner meeting with Matteo, I called him to ask about you. Acted like I had customers who would be interested."

I shoot him a dirty look. *Disgusting pig.*

"He hinted that he'd be killing you once his use for you ran out. So, I made a deal, set it up like I wanted you as payment for our failed trafficking ring if he wanted continue doing business with me. He promised to bring you to me after his fight. He would have killed you, but I saved you."

"You did not save me," I state matter-of-factly. "Zach and Connor did."

My father looks at Reyes, then back at me, seemingly choosing his words carefully. "Kimberly—I really didn't want to start a war. I just wanted my daughter back and out of this life."

"But you're in it," I state.

"Not for long." He lays his hand out on the table open-palmed next to Reyes. She brings her hand up and places hers in his. "Shelly and I want to settle down, enjoy each other's company. I want to retire. We have many houses to choose from, and one of them can be yours. You can do your art sitting by the beautiful European countryside. I'll have your mom transported when you're settled, if you like."

"And not that I care, but what about your business? You're done, right? Going to let anyone you've kidnapped go?"

He sighs. "Not that simple."

I shake my head in disbelief.

"There's a crime family from Eastern Europe that wants to buy him out," Reyes states.

Un-fucking-believable. There is no remorse or redeeming this man.

"What happened to my father?"

His shoulders slump slightly, the confident businessman facade momentarily cracking.

"I lost myself," he says quietly, tracing the rim of his glass. "It happened so gradually I barely noticed. First, it was just bending the rules to make a living after the factory closed in

Oklahoma. Then it was crossing state lines with items that weren't exactly legal. Then betting...then..." He trails off, looking out at the darkening horizon.

"Then what?" I press.

"Then I met people who saw my potential. The money was..." He whistles softly. "... beyond anything I'd imagined." Deveraux shifts uncomfortably in his seat, clearly not enjoying this heart-to-heart. "But there was never enough," he continues. "And the deeper I got, the more dangerous it became to contact you. Your mother remarried. You were growing up without me. It seemed kinder to stay away."

"Kinder?" My voice cracks.

"I made a choice I've regretted every day since. But I want to make it right. This move to Europe—it's not just about escaping Fitzpatrick. It's about starting over. Clean."

Clean.

The word ricochets through my mind like a bullet. I stare at my father as the truth crystallizes inside me. This isn't about me at all. This has never been about me.

This is about him. *His* guilt. *His* redemption story. *His* second chance.

He's dragging me across oceans, tearing me away, all so he can sleep better at night. So he can look in the mirror and tell himself he fixed things.

My dreams mean nothing to him. My art, my relationships, everything I worked hard for—they're all just collateral damage in his quest for absolution.

Chapter Thirty-Two

ZACH

I RETURNED TO MY APARTMENT. I haven't been here since I moved Kim in over at Connor's. Since she's gone, there's no point in going back there.

All that talk about buying more time for us to get Kim—I know I said I wanted more time, but now I'm the fucking anxious one. Yes, I want to go over to that yacht and open fire on every motherfucker. But I know that will only get me killed.

I pour myself a glass of whiskey from the kitchen. *Fuck it.* Instead of drinking from the glass, I drink from the bottle.

A knock sounds on my door. My breath catches. Is it the police? Or Kim?

I take a deep breath and walk to the door, the whiskey bottle still clutched in my hand. I steel myself for whoever might be on the other side—Kim, the cops, Deveraux—anyone.

When I swing it open, Connor's face greets me, and my shoulders slump.

"Oh," I manage, the anticipation draining from my body. "It's just you." I step back, gesturing him in with a half-hearted wave. "Come on in. Party for one just became a party for two."

He walks in and looks around my apartment. "Nice place. Very... Americana bachelor pad."

"What do you want, Connor?" I ask, closing the door behind him.

"Just checking in," he says, but his tone suggests otherwise.

"Don't you worry about me," I say before taking another swig.

He sighs, taking the bottle from my hand. "I'm not worried about you. I'm worried about what you might do."

"Like what?" I sneer. "Storm a yacht single-handedly? I'm not that fucking stupid."

He grabs the full glass I poured previously sitting on my counter. "Grief makes people do surprising things," he says before downing it in one shot.

"I'm not grieving," I snap. "She's not dead."

"I know." His voice softens. "I miss her, too."

I slump onto my couch. "What are we supposed to do next? Wait?"

Connor sits beside me, the leather creaking under his weight. "For now. Until we figure out a better plan."

"And if we never get her back?" The question I've been afraid to ask even myself slips out before I can stop it.

"We will," he says with certainty. "We have to."

We sit in silence for a moment, two grown men staring at our drinks like they hold answers.

My phone vibrates, and I pull it out to see a text alert.

Unknown: Heartfelt Living Facility. 10 p.m.

"What the fuck?"

"What is it?" he asks.

"I got a text from an unknown number wanting to meet at Heartfelt Living Facility."

Connor's phone buzzes.

"10 p.m.?" he asks. "I just got it too."

"It's the long-term care facility I put Kim's mom in," I say.

"You think it's Kim?"

"Could be," I say, staring at my phone. "Or it could be a trap."

"Only one way to find out." He looks at me with that determined look in his eye. "We're going." It's not a question.

Twenty minutes later, we're walking through the sterile hallway of Heartfelt Living Center. The place smells like disinfectant. It's quiet at this hour—visiting hours technically ended at eight.

We round the corner to Mrs. Stanton's room and stop dead in our tracks. Detective Reyes is leaning against the wall beside her door, arms crossed, looking like she's been waiting for us.

"Gentlemen," she says, pushing herself off the wall.

"What the hell are you doing here?" I demand, my hand instinctively moving toward my waistband for my gun but not drawing it.

"She's here—inside with her mom," Reyes says. "I don't

want you to give up hope. I also don't want you in my way. What you guys tried to do was good. But if I want to build a case and put away Deveraux for good, I need legit evidence, not the planted kind."

Connor and I look at each other, confused.

Reyes rolls her eyes, then turns to open the door and peeks her head in. "They're here."

The door opens slowly, and out comes Kim—seemingly unharmed. She seems shocked that we're here.

"You have five minutes. Deveraux is waiting for us," Reyes says before walking down the hall toward the cafeteria.

"You came," she whispers.

"Reyes' message was pretty vague, but yeah," I say.

"Are you okay? Are you hurt?" Connor asks.

"I'm okay," she says. "I thought for certain you'd both be mad at me and never want to see me again."

"What's going on?" I ask.

"Detective Reyes—Shelly—she's been undercover for years, playing Deveraux, getting him to open up to her. We were supposed to leave at dawn, but tonight he's making a deal —selling his trafficking network. Reyes wants to take down everyone."

"Everyone?" Connor asks.

"Except the Fitzpatricks and Valentinos. She knows well that the Fitzpatricks have been trying to take Deveraux down, too. Been close to sabotaging her case, apparently, just like we did yesterday. Deveraux wants to retire and sell it to another family. She's taking down both."

"And why did you need to get involved?" I ask.

"Reyes said that my father was insistent that he wouldn't sell and retire if he didn't have me away from all of it. That's why he made the deal with Matteo for me. His twisted way of saving me, along with some bullshit about wanting to be a family again."

"So, she arrested you and tried to get you to go quietly to help her case," Connor concludes.

"She used you as bait," I add.

"Yes." Kim shakes her head. "But it's helping. It's all for the greater good. We can take down a large human trafficking ring. Tonight, the deal is going down, and it means that this could all be over in a few hours."

As she says this, I should be happier, but I'm not. Maybe I still don't believe it. Or maybe I'm just unsure that she'll actually stick around. I look at Connor, but he's unreadable.

Her face falls as she studies our expressions. Hers shifts from relief to uncertainty. The silence stretches uncomfortably as neither he nor I rush to embrace her or express our overwhelming joy. "You don't seem happy," she says, her voice small. "I thought... I thought you'd be relieved."

I clear my throat. "Of course we're glad you're okay."

"But?" she presses, wrapping her arms around herself.

Connor shifts his weight. "It's a lot to process."

This moment should feel like victory—she's standing here, unharmed, telling us there's an end in sight. But instead, there's this hollow ache spreading through my chest that I can't seem to shake.

I reach for her, but she flinches away. "Kim—"

"No, I get it. I really do." She swipes angrily at her eyes. "You think I chose him over you. That I betrayed you both. Left you."

"Left us?" I can't hold back anymore, my voice rising.

"You didn't just leave us. You did the one fucking thing we asked you not to do."

Her face pales. "That's not fair—"

"Fair?" I step closer, the anger I've been drowning in whiskey finally finding its target. "We told you not to go to him. Not under any circumstances. And what did you do? You walked right to him at the first sign of trouble."

"I was trying to help!" Her voice rises, her composure cracking. "I was trying to end this!"

"By running straight to daddy?" Connor interjects, his calm facade finally breaking. "We had a plan, Kim. We were working together."

"That plan wasn't working!" she shouts.

"But you stick with it and come up with a new one— together!" I shout back.

Connor puts a hand on my shoulder, steadying me, but he keeps his eyes fixed on her. "You made a choice without us. That's what hurts."

Her tears spill over now, tracking down her cheeks. "I was protecting you."

Reyes walks back to us and stops short when she notices that the tension is pretty rough.

"I'll be in the car," Kim tells Reyes and walks away without another glance at us.

"I guess that didn't go well," Reyes states.

"You used her as bait," Connor angrily states.

"I did. But she would have been safe with me. I tried to tell you that before. Deveraux is cold and calculated, but I could see that he cared for his daughter. The question is, how much do you care for her? Enough to be there when this is all over?"

Chapter Thirty-Three

KIMBERLY

I HURT THEM, and this time there is no coming back. *Is there?*

The car ride back to the yacht is quiet until Reyes speaks. "Kim, let's go over this again. What do you do?"

"I remain in the cabin with the door locked until I hear three consecutive knocks."

"Right," she confirms. "That will be my team. You'll be safe with them. Deveraux will have a guy outside your door. When you hear the knocks, you'll know my team got him."

I nod, but my thoughts are elsewhere. Zach's face—the hurt. And Connor... the distance he stood away from me.

"You okay?" Reyes asks.

"Yeah," I lie. "Just ready for this to be over."

But what then? I'll be safe, but where will I go? Who do I go to?

Back in my cabin, I lock the door as instructed and sink onto the bed. My phone sits in my hand. No messages from either of them. Of course not. Why would there be? I threw away everything we built together.

I scroll through our old texts—the warmth in their words, the promises we made to each other. All gone now. Despite my attempts to explain, neither would listen. I wouldn't have left the panic room if I hadn't realized it was personal.

But here I am. I know Reyes used me, but now, I'm thinking of everyone else. All the men, women, and children I'll be helping by taking down both rings. I owe nothing to my father—Deveraux, Kenneth—whoever.

I toss my phone on the bed. It's not going to bring me comfort now.

A distant popping sound makes me freeze. Then another. And another in rapid succession.

Gunshots.

I jump to my feet, my heart hammering against my ribs as I glance at my watch. 11:03 p.m. The raid wasn't supposed to happen until after midnight.

More shots ring out, followed by shouts and what sounds like breaking glass. The yacht rocks slightly as heavy footsteps pound across the deck above me.

I move to the wall beside the door and press my ear against the solid surface, straining to hear what's happening. Someone screams. One of the staff?

My hand hovers over the doorknob. Reyes was clear—stay put until the three knocks. But if the raid is happening now, ahead of schedule, does the plan still stand? Ugh, I think I've proven I'm not fucking good with following directions.

The commotion grows louder. More gunfire, closer this time. I back away from the door, scanning the room for anything I could use as a weapon. *Think, Kim, think!*

A thud against my door makes me jump. Then another. Not knocks—someone's trying to break in.

"Someone's in here!" yells a voice I don't recognize.

I scan the room frantically. The bathroom—too small. Under the bed—too obvious. The closet—a trap. The window—fuck! *We're on water, you idiot.* My pulse thunders in my ears as I spin in circles, unsure what to do. The doorknob rattles violently.

"Break it down!" someone shouts.

My mind goes blank. I can't think. Can't breathe. The walls seem to close in as I panic. I stumble backward until I hit the wall, sliding down to the floor as my legs give out.

This is it. After everything—the lies, the sacrifices, the heartbreak—I'm going to die here, alone. No Zach. No Connor. Just me and whatever monster waits on the other side of that door.

A crash against the door splinters the frame.

"Please," I whisper to no one, "please..."

In desperation, I lunge for my phone, fingers fumbling as I try to dial. Who? Zach? Connor? The police? What could any of them do right now?

The next crash breaks the lock. As the door swings open, I lunge for the bedside lamp, yanking it from the socket. Two men burst in, guns drawn. I don't recognize them as Deveraux's men, and they definitely aren't the police. I hurl the lamp at the first man's head. It misses him and shatters against the wall. I scramble backward, my back hitting the edge of the bed as the men advance.

"Got you," the taller one snarls, raising his gun.

Four shots crack through the air in rapid succession. For a moment, I think I was hit, but I feel no pain. Instead, the men in front of me jerk violently, red blooming across their chests before they crumple to the floor.

I look up to see Zach in the doorway, gun still raised, Connor right beside him.

"Move!" Connor shouts, lunging forward to grab my arm. He pulls me off the floor with such force I nearly stumble.

Zach takes my other arm. "Stay between us."

They hustle me into the narrow hallway as another burst of gunfire erupts from somewhere above. The yacht rocks beneath our feet as we crouch low, pressing against the wall.

"How did you—" I start.

"Later," Connor hisses.

What the fuck is going on? The Fitzpatricks wouldn't have raided the boat, knowing it was supposed to end tonight. *Who are we fighting?*

We hurry down the corridor, staying low. Connor leads, checking corners before waving us forward. The yacht rocks with each explosion, making it hard to keep our balance.

"This way," he whispers, pulling me toward a service stairwell.

We descend rapidly, the metallic clanging of our footsteps drowned out by the chaos above. At the bottom, Connor pushes through a swinging door, and we stumble into the kitchen—sleek, industrial. Adjoining the kitchen is a small dining room.

Reyes crouches behind a stainless-steel island, cursing as she fumbles with her gun's magazine. Her hands are bloody, though I can't tell if it's her blood or someone else's. She looks up sharply, the gun aimed at us before recognition flashes across her face.

"Jesus Christ," she hisses, lowering her weapon slightly. "I almost shot you."

"What's going on?" I ask.

Reyes slams the magazine into the gun with the heel of her palm. "Deveraux's buyer decided he didn't want to buy anymore—he wanted to take instead. I called for backup. They'll be here in two minutes if we can hold them off a little longer."

Connor and Zach nod to each other, then Reyes.

A loud crash from above signals the arrival of more men. The double doors to the dining room doors burst open, and five armed men pile through. Behind them stands Deveraux, a cruel smile spreading on his lips.

"Kimberly. Shelly," he says, as if greeting us at a dinner party. "How disappointing. First my buyers, now you two." His eyes set on Zach and Connor.

Everything happens at once. Reyes, Connor, and Zach move like a synchronized unit, weapons raised in perfect unison. The air explodes with gunfire as they open fire on Deveraux and his men. I duck behind the island, hands over my ears, as bullets ricochet off stainless-steel surfaces and shatter glass cabinets.

The kitchen becomes a war zone. Zach takes down two men with shots to the head. Connor fires rapidly, forcing Deveraux's remaining guards to scatter for cover.

Deveraux dives behind a prep table, returning fire wildly. A bullet grazes Zach's arm, tearing his sleeve and drawing blood.

I gasp, watching helplessly as Zach clutches his arm but continues firing. Through the chaos, something catches my eye—a handgun that slides across the floor, knocked from the grip of one of Deveraux's men. It stops just feet from me, partially hidden beneath a fallen chair.

I lunge for it, my fingers closing around the cold metal. The weight of it feels foreign in my hand. I've never shot one before.

Reyes takes a hit to the shoulder and stumbles back against the refrigerator, cursing through gritted teeth. Connor's magazine clicks empty, and in that split second of vulnerability, Deveraux emerges from cover, gun trained on him.

"No!" I scream, raising the gun. The recoil surprises me as I pull the trigger, and my first shot goes wide, shattering a light fixture above Deveraux's head. The next bullet, though, finds his upper thigh.

Deveraux howls in pain, his leg buckling beneath him. His eyes find mine, filled with a mixture of shock and rage. He raises his gun again, aiming at me this time, his face contorted with fury. Before he can pull the trigger, the kitchen door explodes inward, and a flood of tactical officers in full gear pour through, weapons raised.

"FBI! Drop your weapons! Now!"

I immediately drop the gun. It falls to the floor with a thud, and I kick it away.

Reyes raises her uninjured arm, badge clutched in her bloody hand. "Agent Reyes, CIA! These three are with me!" She gestures toward Zach, Connor, and me with a jerk of her chin. "The target is Deveraux—man in the suit, wounded leg!"

The lead agent signals to his team, and they swarm Deveraux, kicking away his weapon and forcing him face-down on the floor. He struggles briefly before a knee is pressed on his back, and the click of handcuffs subdues him.

"Any other hostiles we should know about?" the agent says, his weapon still at the ready as his team secures the room.

"Upper deck," Reyes says through gritted teeth, her hand pressed to her bleeding shoulder. "Anyone who isn't you or the four of us."

The tactical team swarms the yacht, securing every deck. A medic rushes to Reyes, quickly working to stabilize her shoulder wound while another checks Zach's arm.

Two officers haul Deveraux to his feet. Blood stains his expensive pants where my bullet hit. His face is pale, either from blood loss or the realization that his empire is crumbling around him. As they drag him past me, his eyes lock with mine —cold, calculating, hateful.

"You'll always be my daughter," he hisses, a last attempt to wound me.

My voice doesn't waver when I speak. "No. I'm not. You made that decision when you left and chose this."

The agents push him toward the door, a limp becoming more pronounced as they move.

I follow them up to the deck, needing to see this—closure.

The night air hits me as I step onto the veranda, where red and blue lights cut through the darkness. A swarm of agents and officers zip-tie and line up Deveraux's men and the buyers who'd come to purchase human lives like commodities.

I stand at the railing. Guards escort Deveraux down the gangplank to a waiting vehicle, his shoulders slumped in defeat.

"It's really over," I whisper to no one, my voice breaking.

"Kim," Reyes calls. She stands a few feet away, her arm

now in a sling, a small amount of blood seeping through the bandage. "Need you over here for a minute." She gestures toward a makeshift command center where agents have set up laptops on folding tables. "We need your statement while it's fresh. Then you're free to go."

After a brief onsite interrogation, mainly agents asking about the history between me and my father, I look around, unsure of where to go now. I have no idea where Zach and Connor went—I haven't seen them in a while.

I pull my phone out of my back pocket and realize my hands are shaking. I take a deep breath, trying to calm myself enough to order a ride share.

I attempt to focus on the app. My thumb hovers shakily over the screen, missing the icon twice before I finally manage to tap it. I try to type in my destination—where am I even going? I terminated the lease on my shitty apartment to move in with Zach.

A nearby siren wails, drawing my attention up from the phone, and an ambulance pulls away from the dock, red lights flashing. As the vehicle disappears around the corner, my eyes drift past where it had been parked, and my breath catches in my throat.

Time seems to stretch and slow, just like in those dramatic movies in moments I always thought were so unrealistic. The chaos surrounding me fades to background noise as I see them standing there, illuminated by the harsh dock lights.

Zach and Connor lean against a black SUV. A bandage covers Zach's arm, and Connor's face is smudged with what looks like gunpowder or blood.

They didn't leave me here.

After everything I said. After breaking their trust—they're still here.

My phone slips from my hand. Then my knees buckle beneath me, and I crash down onto the black asphalt of the marina parking lot, my palms scraping against the rough surface while I struggle to catch myself. Every emotion I've been holding back—fear, exhaustion, relief, love—crashes through me in overwhelming waves.

I hear their footsteps running toward me, feel their hands on my shoulders before I can even look up.

"Kim!" Connor's voice is tight with concern as he kneels beside me.

Zach drops on my other side, his injured arm still bandaged but forgotten as he reaches for me. "Hey, hey, we've got you."

"I thought—" My voice breaks. "I thought you both hated me. I thought I'd never see you again."

Connor's hand cups my cheek, turning my face toward his. "We could never hate you."

"You did what you had to do," Zach says, his fingers gently brushing the hair from my face. "Fuck, babygirl, we're mad, but please, please, never do that to us again."

"After you left your mom's facility, we decided we weren't going home without you. So, we went to the marina to wait for you until after the raid," Connor says.

"But then we saw a lot of men with weapons, who were not the police, go onto the yacht, and we knew something was wrong," Zach adds. "Luckily, I had a few guns and some ammo in the car. We bumped into Reyes on the yacht, and she told us where to find you."

They both help me stand up.

"Let's go home," Connor says.

"Home." The word slips from my lips.

I'll go anywhere as long as it's where they are. I think about how I don't deserve them. Not after leaving. Yet here they are, solid and real.

"I'm sorry," I whisper as Connor opens the passenger door.

Zach's eyes meet mine, the hardness from before replaced with something warmer, though still cautious. "We know."

Connor helps me into the backseat, sliding in beside me while Zach takes the wheel. As the engine comes to life, I lean into his side, drawing strength from his warmth.

Chapter Thirty-Four

KIMBERLY

AFTER SHOWERING, the three of us get into bed.

I settle between them, my body finally registering just how exhausted I am. The soft mattress feels like it's pulling me down, and my eyelids grow impossibly heavy. I'm so tired inside, I could sleep through a landslide. The warmth of Zach's chest against my back and Connor's arm draped over my waist creates a cocoon of safety.

My mind, which has been racing for days, suddenly goes quiet. I don't even remember closing my eyes before darkness claims me completely. I sleep deeper than I have in months. No dreams, no tossing and turning—just oblivion.

When consciousness finally seeps back in, sunlight streams through the curtains, and for a moment, panic flutters in my chest before I remember where I am. The bed is empty, but I hear low voices from the living room.

I push myself up, wincing at the stiffness in my muscles.

According to the clock on the nightstand, I've slept for fifteen hours straight.

The bedroom door opens, and my breath catches. Zach steps in first, his broad shoulders filling the doorframe, followed by Connor, both of them wearing nothing but snug boxer briefs that cling to their muscular thighs. I'm a lucky fucking bitch to have two men who look like Calvin Klein underwear models. Morning light plays across their bodies, highlighting the defined planes of their chests and the subtle ridges of their abs. My mouth goes dry at the sight of them.

"Well, look who's finally rejoined the land of the living," Zach says. His dark hair is tousled, and this makes him appear younger and impossibly more handsome.

Connor's eyes, that striking green, light up when they meet mine. "We were wondering if we should check for a pulse," he teases.

The mattress dips as they climb in from either side. Before I can fully process what's happening, their strong hands are on me, gently tugging me back to the mattress, my head finding the pillow. I find myself once again nestled between them. Zach slides his arm beneath my head, while Connor's hand settles on my hip.

"How are you feeling, Merlot?" Connor asks, his thumb making small circles against my skin through the thin T-shirt I'd borrowed.

Instead of telling them how I feel, I decide to show them.

I turn to Zach and bring my face to his. His mouth brushes against mine, and I respond immediately. Our lips connect, my body remembering his touch. My hand slides up to cup his face as he continues to capture my mouth, more demanding with each pass, his tongue slipping between my lips.

Connor shifts behind me, his chest pressing against my back as his arm drapes over my waist. His breath is warm against my neck. His fingers trail along my hip, ghosting over the fabric of my T-shirt.

Zach pulls back slightly, his gaze flickering over my shoulder to Connor, a silent communication passing between them. Then his mouth is on mine again, more insistent this time, as Connor's fingers slip beneath the hem of my shirt, palming my breasts.

With a soft groan, Zach pulls away from my lips, his eyes dark with desire as they meet mine. I tilt my head back instinctively, seeking Connor's mouth and, lucky for me, his lips are there waiting. Connor's tongue slides against mine as his hands continue playing with my nipples, rolling the peaks between his fingertips.

Zach watches us for a moment, his breathing heavy, before he shifts downward. His fingers bunch the fabric of my shirt, pushing it up to expose my breasts and Connor's hand to the cool air. I gasp into Connor's mouth as Zach lowers his head, taking the nipple Connor isn't touching between his lips. His tongue circles the sensitive peak before sucking gently. It sends electricity coursing through me, and my back arches involuntarily. Connor's hardness presses against my ass.

"God, yes," I breathe against Connor's mouth, my mind swimming with sensation.

Connor's hand slides into my hair, holding me to him as his lips press against mine, then gently cover my mouth, swallowing my moans. His other hand trails down my side, fingers dipping beneath the waistband of my underwear, pulling them off.

Zach's mouth moves lower, trailing heated kisses along my stomach while his hand slides between my thighs. His fingers part my pussy lips, and he makes a low sound of appreciation in his throat before slipping his fingers inside me. First one, then two.

"Sopping wet," he murmurs, his voice husky with desire. "You really want us."

Zach withdraws his fingers, moves his boxer briefs down and off his body, then positions himself between my legs. His eyes lock with mine as he guides himself to my pussy. With a slow, deliberate thrust, he pushes inside, filling me completely. I cry out at the pressure of my body stretching for him.

Zach groans, his hands gripping my hips as he seats himself fully inside me. "You feel amazing, Babygirl."

Connor breaks our kiss, his breath hot against my ear. "I want in, too," he whispers, his hand sliding down to cup my ass.

Behind me, he shifts away momentarily, removing his own briefs, then the mattress dips as he reaches toward the nightstand. I hear the drawer slide open, followed by the distinctive sound of a cap being flipped—lube.

"We're going to take care of you," Connor promises, his voice a low rumble as he returns to press against my back. "Let me in, too, baby."

I nod, breathless with anticipation, as Connor positions himself behind me. I brace myself for the stretch I'm expecting, but then he shifts, nudging the head of his hard cock against my pussy, right where Zach is already buried inside me.

"Oh—" I gasp, as I realize what he's about to do.

"Trust us," Connor murmurs, his lips brushing my ear as he pushes forward. "We want to try something."

The pressure is intense, unlike anything I've ever felt before. I feel myself stretching impossibly as Connor works his way in alongside Zach, who has gone completely still inside me.

"Oh my god," I breathe, my fingers digging into Zach's shoulders as Connor continues his slow, relentless progress. The burn gives way to a fullness. "You're both—you're both in my—"

"Is it too much?" Zach asks, his voice strained with the effort of holding still, observing my reaction.

Connor's hips finally press flush against me, both men now fully seated inside my pussy. The sensation is indescribable—being completely filled, stretched to the max.

They begin to move in tandem, and I reach out, desperate to anchor myself. My right hand grips Zach's shoulder. My left hand seeks Connor, grabbing at his thigh, pulling him closer, keeping him with me.

"That's it," Connor breathes against my neck, his lips brushing my skin. "Hold on to us."

The connection grounds me as they move within me, their cocks sliding against each other inside my stretched pussy.

My grip tightens as they find a perfect rhythm, one pushing in as the other pulls back, never leaving me empty. My world narrows to just this—my hands on their bodies, their cocks inside me, the three of us connected in the most intimate way possible.

"You're taking us so well," Connor murmurs against my

neck, his teeth grazing my skin before he sucks gently, marking me.

I can barely think, barely breathe as they work my body between them. The friction, the fullness, the way they seem to know exactly what I need—it's too much and not enough all at once. My muscles tighten as heat builds low in my belly, spiraling.

"I'm close," I gasp, my head falling back against Connor's shoulder. My muscles begin to tighten. Their movements are synchronized in a way that suggests they've fantasized about this moment.

"We've got you," Zach states.

The tension inside me coils tight until it snaps. Waves of pleasure crash through me, and I cry out, my body convulsing between them as my orgasm hits with stunning intensity. My inner walls pulse violently around both of them, gripping and releasing in rhythmic contractions.

"Fuck, Kim," Zach groans, his rhythm faltering as my body squeezes him. His fingers dig into my hips, and his face contorts in pleasure. "I can't—I'm coming—"

Behind me, Connor curses, his breath hot against my neck. "Me, too," he pants, his thrusts becoming erratic. "God, this feels so good."

I feel them both pulse together inside me, filling me with their cum as they reach their peak almost simultaneously.

For a moment, we remain frozen, connected, our ragged breathing the only sound in the room. Then slowly, carefully, Connor eases out of me, pressing a gentle kiss to my shoulder blade as he does. Zach follows, his eyes never leaving mine as he withdraws.

I collapse onto my back on the bed, boneless and utterly spent.

"I feel completely wrecked," I mumble against the pillow, a lazy smile spreading across my face as they settle on either side of me.

Connor reaches over to brush a strand of hair from my face, his touch gentle. "Good wrecked or bad wrecked?"

"Definitely good," I whisper. "The best kind."

Zach's arm drapes across my waist, pulling me closer to him. "We aim to please."

"I never thought I could have this," I whisper into the comfortable silence, my voice thick with emotion. "Both of you, here with me, safe." I turn to look at Zach, then Connor, drinking in their faces in the dim light. "I'm so excited for whatever comes next—for us, together. I... I can't imagine my life without either of you in it anymore."

Zach's arm tightens around me. "You don't have to," he murmurs against my hair. "We're not going anywhere."

"He's right," Connor adds, propping himself up on one elbow to look at me. His eyes are soft, vulnerable in a way I rarely get to see. "After everything we've been through, you think we'd let you go now?"

I smile, my heart so full and bursting with an emotion I'm still learning to recognize—a sense of belonging that feels both terrifying and perfect.

"I love you both," I whisper, the words slipping out naturally. "So much."

Connor's lips press against my temple. "We love you, too."

Zach's fingers intertwine with mine, squeezing gently in silent agreement.

As my eyelids grow heavy and sexual exhaustion overtakes

me despite the fact that I already slept, I make a silent promise to myself. No more running, no more holding back. After coming so close to losing everything—to losing them—I won't waste a single moment we have together. Not one touch, not one smile, not one ordinary Tuesday morning. Each day is a gift.

The rhythmic sound of their breathing lulls me toward sleep, my body nestled securely between theirs. Tomorrow will bring new challenges, new adjustments as we figure out what this relationship means for all of us. But at this moment, everything is perfect.

Epilogue

CONNOR

AROUND THREE YEARS LATER...

"Weee!" Ryan says, holding Aiden while going down the slide. The smile on Aiden's face is pure joy. My nephew is a cheerful boy.

I stand, leaning against the playground fence, watching as he scoops Aiden up again. "One more time?" my brother asks, and Aiden enthusiastically nods, sending his red curls bouncing. They climb back up the ladder, Ryan's hands steady on the toddler's sides.

"Higher, Daddy!" Aiden demands as they position themselves at the top.

He laughs. "Any higher and we'd need a rocket ship, buddy."

The two of them push off, Ryan's arms wrapped protectively around my nephew as they spiral down the twisty slide. Aiden's giggles echo across the park, drawing smiles from other parents nearby.

"You should join them," Killian says, appearing beside me with two coffee cups. He hands me one. "You've been standing here like a statue for fifteen minutes."

"Just taking it all in," I reply, accepting the coffee. "It's nice seeing Ryan like this, you know?"

He follows my gaze to where Ryan is now helping Aiden across the monkey bars. "Fatherhood changes people."

"Some people," I correct him, thinking about my father.

"You're right. Not all are meant to be fathers," he concedes, then looks back at Ryan and Aiden. "They could do this all day," he says.

Ryan comes over to us with Aiden. "Thanks for coming today, Connor. I know you've been busy with the new job."

It's true. Both Killian and Ryan have embraced fatherhood and moved to the suburbs. Zach and I are working full-time at the office while they are part-time between the office and running Blaze Gym locations.

"Daddy, swing!" Aiden says, looking at Killian.

"Take this." Killian hands Ryan his cup and takes his son to the swings.

"I should get going. Drive back to the city. Are you all coming to Kim's art show tomorrow?"

"Yes, Cassie's excited. We got Victor and Seamus to babysit for us. We're making a big date night out of it."

"You three deserve a night out," I say, watching his eyes follow Killian and Aiden. "Must be hard balancing everything—the gym, office work, parenthood."

He shrugs. "It's all about priorities now. And we're happy doing it."

"We got your wedding save-the-date. Kim's never been out

of the country. I can't want to show her all my favorite places in Ireland."

I look at my brother for a moment, seeing him in a new light. The years have mellowed both of us, and somehow we've found our way to this place where conversations flow without the old tension.

"You know," I say, watching Aiden's delighted face as Killian pushes him on the swing, "I never thought we'd end up like this."

He raises an eyebrow. "Like what?"

"Like... brothers. Real ones." I shift my weight, uncomfortable with the vulnerability but pushing through it. "I'm sorry I wasn't there for you more. I was so wrapped up in my own stuff that I missed a lot."

Ryan's expression softens. "Con—"

"No, let me finish. When I see you with Aiden, how natural you are with him... I realize I missed so much by keeping my distance. Not just with you, but with everything."

"We're good now, though. That's what matters." He looks away, blinking rapidly. "Damn it, Connor. You're going to make me cry at the playground."

"Sorry," I say, not feeling sorry at all, and we laugh together.

I walk through the door of the penthouse, where Kim, Zach, and I now live. It's much bigger than living in Ryan's old apartment. Killian and Ryan still keep it for when they need to spend the night in the city, though.

"Anyone home?" I yell through the space.

"Hey, man," Zach says, coming from the hallway. He looks like he just got out of the shower. His hair is wet, and he's got on sweatpants. "How was your visit?"

"Good," I state, taking a seat with him on the sofa. "We took Aiden to the park. Ryan—he's a great father."

He claps me on the back. "You're proud of him," he says with a smile.

I nod. "Where's Kim?"

"She went to the store to get ingredients for dinner tonight." The elevator dings. "Speak of the devil."

She sees us in the living room and puts the purchases immediately behind her back—hiding what she bought from us.

I narrow my eyes suspiciously. "What's in the bags, Kimberly *Merlot*?"

"Just some groceries."

"Then why are you hiding them?" I stand up from the couch.

"I'm not hiding anything," she says, but her voice goes up at the end like a question.

"Ah-ha! Caught you," I say, pointing at her suspicious behavior. "What green-smoothie ingredients are you smuggling in today?"

She rolls her eyes but can't hide her guilty smile. "It's not what you think."

"Sure, it's not. Last week it was kale and spirulina. The week before that, it was wheat grass and those weird berries that cost more than my Rolex."

Zach groans. "Please tell me there's not more turmeric. My teeth were yellow for days."

"You guys are such... babies," she says, smiling. She moves

toward the kitchen. I follow her, curious despite my complaints. She's been on this health kick for a month now, turning our kitchen into some kind of laboratory for her increasingly bizarre concoctions. Zach and I are meat-and-potato types of men.

She sets the bags on the counter and turns her back so that I can't see.

"I'm just trying to take care of us," she says defensively. "Someone has to make sure you two don't survive only on takeout and whiskey."

"Hey, I had a salad yesterday," I protest.

"The lettuce, tomato, and onion on your burger does not qualify as a salad." She looks between us. "I love you both. Now, out of my kitchen," she says firmly.

"Speaking of whiskey, I'd like some," Zach says.

"I second that."

I head for the bar cart in the corner of the living room, but Kim holds out her hands to stop me. "You two relax. I'll get the drinks."

Something in her voice makes me question her. "What are you up to?" I ask, narrowing my eyes.

"Nothing," she says, the picture of innocence as she slides past me toward the bar cart. "Can't a girl make drinks for her two favorite guys?"

Zach drops onto the couch, oblivious to the danger signals. "Sounds good to me."

I watch her carefully as she pulls out glasses and the bottle of Jameson. Her movements are too deliberate, too casual. She's humming to herself—another warning sign.

"She better not have bought some kind of healthy whiskey," I hush-whisper to Zach, returning to the couch.

"They make that?" he asks, genuinely confused.

I shrug, still suspicious. "I wouldn't put it past her to find one."

Kim returns from the kitchen with a strange look on her face—part mischief, part something else. When she hands us our drinks, I nearly drop mine in surprise.

"What the hell?" I look down and nearly choke. In my hand is a baby bottle—an actual infant's bottle—filled with amber liquid.

Zach looks equally baffled, turning the bottle over in his hands. "Uh, Babygirl? I think you grabbed the wrong glassware."

I hold up the bottle, examining the rubber nipple on top. "Are we supposed to drink from these?"

She's practically bouncing with excitement. Then she reaches behind her and pulls two cigars from her back jeans pocket, handing one to each of us.

"Congratulations," she says, her voice suddenly thick with emotion. "You're going to be dads!"

The baby bottle nearly slips from my fingers. "You're—"

"Pregnant," she finishes, her hands going to her stomach. "Eight weeks."

Zach remains frozen, with the baby bottle halfway to his mouth and a cigar clutched in his other hand.

Was he actually going to drink from it?

"Say something," she pleads, her face still shining with excitement.

I stare at her, trying to process her words. Pregnant. Eight weeks. We're going to be dads.

My eyes meet Zach's. Time seems to stand still for a

heartbeat, then two. And then, as if by some unspoken signal, both our faces crack into identical grins.

"Holy shit!" I exclaim, leaping to my feet.

He jumps up too, and we slam our palms together in an exaggerated high five that echoes through the space.

"We're gonna be dads!" he shouts, and then we're both moving, practically tripping over each other to reach her.

We engulf her in a three-way embrace, my arms around her waist, Zach's around her shoulders. She's laughing and crying at the same time, her face pressed against my chest.

"Careful!" She laughs, her voice muffled against my chest. "You're squishing the baby."

"The baby," Zach repeats, pulling back just enough to place his hand gently on her stomach. His eyes are wet. "Our baby."

I rest my palm beside his, trying to wrap my mind around the fact that beneath our hands, beneath Kim's still-flat stomach, our child is growing.

My mind flashes back to the playground earlier today—Ryan and Aiden laughing on the slide, Killian watching his son with such pride, that moment of connection with my brother that had felt so important. And now this.

"You okay?" she asks, squeezing my hand where it rests on her belly.

"I'm..." Words fail me momentarily. "I'm better than okay. This morning, I was watching Ryan with Aiden, thinking about how much he's changed—how we've all changed. And now..." I swallow hard, emotion threatening to overtake me. "Now we're going to have our own little one."

Zach pats me on the shoulder. "We're gonna rock this parenting thing, man."

"When did you find out?" I ask, my voice hushed with wonder.

She wipes at her eyes. "Last week. I wanted to be sure before I told you both. I've been dying, keeping it a secret."

I pull her closer, pressing a kiss to her forehead. "You should have told us."

"I wanted this moment," she admits. "To see your faces. So go out on the patio, sip on your whiskey, and smoke your cigars. I'm going to make dinner—zucchini spaghetti.

"That sounds gross, but I'll eat anything you make," I say. "Especially today."

I take her face in my hands, lean down, and capture her lips with mine. The kiss deepens instantly, my arms wrapping around her, pulling her body flush against me. I pour everything I'm feeling into this kiss—love, excitement, promise. Her fingers tangle in my hair as she responds with equal passion, and I can taste the salt of her happy tears on her lips.

When we finally break apart, we're both breathless. I keep her close, my forehead pressed against hers.

"I love you so much," I whisper, my voice rough with emotion. "Thank you for this gift."

Kim's smile is radiant.

Zach steps forward, gently cupping her cheek with his palm. "We're having a baby," he whispers, his voice breaking on the last word. He pulls her into his arms. Their lips meet in a tender kiss, his thumb caressing her jawline as he holds her close. I watch them, the two people I love most in the world, sharing this moment of joy.

A strange warmth spreads through my chest. Gratitude. Pure, overwhelming gratitude for this unconventional, beautiful family we've built together. Three years ago, I couldn't have imagined this life. Now, I can't imagine any other.

As they part, her eyes find mine over his shoulder. She reaches out her hand, and I take it.

"Well," I say, holding up the baby bottle of whiskey with a sudden grin, "I guess this is what happens when you mix whiskey, wine, and lots of freaky sex."

Zach snorts with laughter.

Kim releases my hand. "Really? That's what you're going with at this momentous occasion?"

"Hey, it's factually accurate," I defend myself, gesturing between the three of us. "Think about it... it was roughly two months ago. Remember that weekend after Kim's gallery opening? We never left the penthouse. The expensive cabernet, the Jameson, and then ...and then that thing we did on the kitchen counter." I wiggle my eyebrows suggestively. "You know, when I lifted you up and—"

"Oh, god," she groans, her cheeks flushing to a dusky rose.

"Actually," Zach interrupts, "I think it was that night when we were in the shower. Remember? Kim had her leg wrapped around my waist, and you were behind her, holding her up—"

"That's it," she says, covering her ears. "I'm not listening to this."

"—and then we switched positions," he continues, undeterred, "and she did that thing where she arches her back—"

"The conception of our child is not a porno to be recounted!" she protests, but she's laughing despite herself.

I take a thoughtful sip from my ridiculous baby bottle.

"Could've been that morning on the balcony, too. When the sun was just coming up, and we thought none of the neighbors would see us."

"They definitely saw us," she mumbles.

"No, it was the next morning," Zach speculates. "When she woke us up with blow jobs. What we did after—that was some Olympic-level flexibility."

"The judges would have given you a perfect ten," I agree.

Kim drops her hands, giving us both an exasperated look. "Are you seriously trying to pinpoint the exact sexual position that led to conception?"

I laugh, wrapping an arm around her shoulders. "Just celebrating our virility, baby." I glance down at the baby bottle in my hand and experimentally squeeze the rubber nipple. A drop of whiskey lands on my palm.

"Her features soften, and she gets a mischievous twinkle in her eye. "You know…" She trails off. "We could always try to recreate each scenario," she suggests with a wink at us. "For science…"

"I'll get the whiskey and wine!" Zach shouts, already on his way to the kitchen.

Fuck, I love this woman.

The end.

Punches & Pirouettes

BONUS SCENE

Have you read the first book, ***Punches & Pirouettes***?
If not, go read it!
If yes, then enjoy the following bonus scene. You may
remember in the epilogue where Cassie mentions being
caught by Ryan and Killian watching their neighbors have sex
from a window. This is it...

Cassandra

Toys are everywhere, I realize as I'm picking Aiden's off
the playroom floor while he naps in his bedroom.

A faint noise coming from outside gets my attention. I
slide one of the window shutters up to find the source, and a
soft gasp escapes me. The neighbors, a newlywed couple with
no kids, are having sex in their bedroom. She's bent over doggy
style—she's cute for a brunette but has super big fake tits. The
guy is good-looking, but certainly not ripped like my guys.

I realize I'm staring and close the shutter with a sigh. I
begin to walk away, but something tells me to go back and
have another look. *Maybe they're putting on a show and they*

355

want someone to watch? Otherwise, they would make sure their blinds were closed for their intimate moments, right?

I walk back to the window and slowly open the shutter again. Now she's lying on her back and he's thrusting into her. The way she's grabbing her breasts looks a little pornstar-ish to me. *Huh, maybe they perform for one of those subscription websites.*

"What are you doing?"

I jump in place, startled, and turn around to find Ryan standing in the doorway, Killian beside him.

"Nothing," I squeak.

"Are they at it again?" Killian nods toward the window.

"Yep." I pick up a toy and throw it in a bin, trying to act casual.

This isn't the first time we've had to hear or witness our neighbors getting freaky. They have no shame in letting the whole cul-de-sac know, apparently...

Ryan gives me a knowing smirk. "You were watching, weren't you?"

"I heard a noise and peeked," I admit, picking up another toy.

Ryan walks over to me, takes the toy currently in my hand, and throws it back on the floor. "If I checked, would you be wet?"

I shrug and bite my lip, trying to hide a smile. He already knows the answer to that.

"Let's see if they're still there," Ryan says, leading me back to the window.

We have visual confirmation that, yes, the newlywed couple are still at it and he's giving it to her good.

Ryan positions himself behind me and reaches around to

lift my sundress—fingers teasing with the lining of my thong underwear, and I know I'm caught.

"You are wet, Princess." He moves the fabric to the side and dips a finger deep into my wet pussy, then moves it in a circular motion.

I look down to focus on his hand because it just feels so good.

"Keep watching them, Pet." Killian orders from the doorway.

My gaze goes back to the couple next door, and I watch them intently. Ryan adds another finger and continues his rhythm, moving in and out of me, while his thumb rubs my clit.

I'm four months pregnant with his child and in the part of pregnancy where I'm horny all the time. I'm watching this couple having sex, and it's intriguing and turning me on, yet I have no desire to be with them specifically. This is what Ryan must have felt when he used to watch strangers at Firefly.

My legs are getting weak, and I brace my hand on the wall on the side of the window, right next to a framed picture of a cartoon character from one of Aiden's favorite television shows.

I release a deep breath, really wanting something more than fingers inside me right now...

I'm watching them, but I'm also not—too focused on the pleasure I'm getting from Ryan; the neighbors are just there at this point. I'm so turned on, and it's almost like a "fuck you" to the newlyweds. We are adventurous too. Just because we have a toddler and another one on the way doesn't mean we have no sex life.

My vision is bright and blurry as I come—unleashing a

loud moan I'm sure the neighbors hear, and I quickly close the shutter.

Ryan's fingers stay as I ride the tremors of my orgasm and giggle because of what I just did.

When my body stops shaking, he withdraws his fingers and puts them in his mouth one at a time, enjoying my essence.

"Now it smells like sex in our son's playroom." Killian chuckles.

"Cassie might be a voyeur too," Ryan says, and I hit him playfully.

"Were you being a naughty girl, Sunshine? Watching our neighbors..." Killian asks in his dominant voice and wags his finger like what I did was a no-no.

"Yes, Sir," I admit proudly.

"Come on, Ry, it's time for her punishment."

I giggle as Ryan picks me up bridal style and carries me out of the room toward our bedroom, where I gladly take my punishment.

Acknowledgments

To my friends—Tiffany, Priscilla, Biz & Kellyn—you have been my cheerleaders from the beginning of my writing journey. Thank you!

A special thank you to my husband for being there when I needed to talk out a line or a scene.

To my editor, Sarah Hart, thank you for your feedback and edits. You have polished my book baby and made her publish-ready! I hope to work with you again in the future.

About the Author

Lulu Hart

Lulu Hart is a passionate storyteller who has been fascinated by the written word since childhood. From the whimsical worlds of Disney and Dr. Seuss to the thrilling adventures of Goosebumps and Sweet Valley High and the literary classics studied in high school. While in college, she dabbled in poetry, eventually publishing a collection that captured her creative spirit.

Lulu decided to bring her own love stories to life and share them with the world. Her debut novel, *Punches & Pirouettes*, marks the beginning of an exciting chapter in her writing journey. With its emotional depth, unforgettable characters, and engaging storytelling, this love story will keep lovers of contemporary romance captivated and yearning for more.

Lulu is a full-time professional in administrative healthcare and lives in Las Vegas, Nevada, with her loving husband and adorable daughter. In her free time, she finds fulfillment in watching horror movies, reading romance novels, and celebrating the joy of the holidays—Christmas being her favorite.

Also by Lulu Hart

The Fitzpatrick Clan

Punches & Pirouettes

Whiskey & Wine

<u>Coming Soon!</u>

Interludes with Insects

The Killer Bee

TBD Book 2

TBD Book 3